April 22, 2003

To Roddy.

With Best Wishes
and Many thanks.
May you find your own
Panacea.

Bob Turgeon

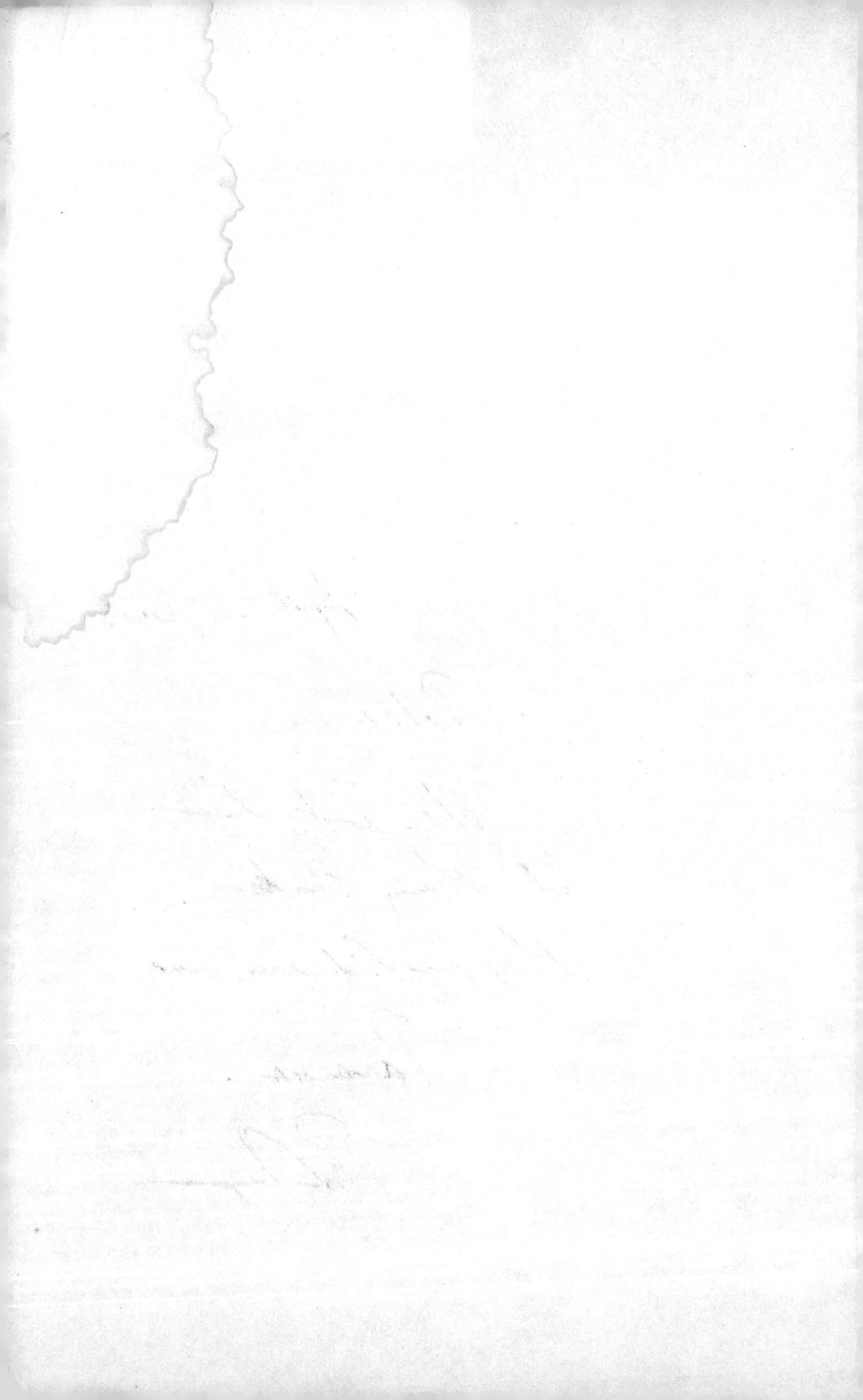

PANACEA

Printed in Victoria, Canada

National Library of Canada Cataloguing in Publication Data

Thompson, Bob, 1966-
Panacea/ Bob Thompson.
ISBN 1-55369-552-6
I. Title.
PS3620.H67P35 2002   813'.6   C2002-902379-3

TRAFFORD

This book was published *on-demand* in cooperation with Trafford Publishing.
On-demand publishing is a unique process and service of making a book available for retail sale to the public taking advantage of on-demand manufacturing and Internet marketing.
On-demand publishing includes promotions, retail sales, manufacturing, order fulfilment, accounting and collecting royalties on behalf of the author.

Suite 6E, 2333 Government St., Victoria, B.C. V8T 4P4, CANADA
Phone   250-383-6864   Toll-free   1-888-232-4444 (Canada & US)
Fax   250-383-6804   E-mail   sales@trafford.com
Web site   www.trafford.com   TRAFFORD PUBLISHING IS A DIVISION OF TRAFFORD HOLDINGS LTD.
Trafford Catalogue #02-0365   www.trafford.com/robots/02-0365.html

10   9   8   7   6   5   4   3

The Author gratefully acknowledges the following individuals
and organizations for their contribution to this book:

The Manuscript Readers: Angie U., Sharon U., Joyce U., Dad & June,
Cindy A., Kami B., Talarie B., Heather B., Noelle, Kim S., Wendell,
Lyndsey, Dar-Dar, Cathe D., Mary B., Tim O'Brien, Alison

The Inspirations: Florida State University, The Florida Epsilon Chapter
of Sigma Phi Epsilon, Northern Illinois University College of Law,
T.T., K.C., Charles P. Cook, Andy J., Jeff W., Dr. Ferrol Sams & his
kind sister, Jimmie, Stephanie S., Angie, mom & dad

The Places: Posey's Oyster Bar - Ms. Daphne Becham, proprietor,
Books on First - Larry Dunphy & Carolyn Chin, owners, Trafford
Publishing, The Florida State University, Sauk Valley Newspapers,
Creative Printing - Tracey & Toni Montgomery, owners

The Use of Copyrights: "Brown Eyed Girl" - Words and Music by Van
Morrison, © Copyright Universal Music Publishing International Ltd.
Administered by Universal-Songs of Polygram International, Inc (BMI)
International Copyright Secured. All Rights Reserved. "Don't Bury
Me" - by John Prine © 1973 (Renewed) Walden Music, Inc. All Rights
Reserved. Used by Permission. Warner Bros. Publications U.S. Inc.,
Miami, FL 33014.

The Boys: Scott, Michael, Bruce, Paul & Lee – for all the stories we
could tell.

Honorable Mention: Maker's Mark Bourbon

Very Special Thanks: to my Editor, Joyce U. Gibson

To Angie,
Mom & Dad

There's a divinity that shapes our ends,
rough hew them how we will.

— *William Shakespeare*

Pan-a-ce-a: (pan 'ə-sē' ə) n. -- a remedy for all diseases, evils, or difficulties; a cure-all.

PROLOGUE

To an outsider, images of the state of Florida include pictures of a tourism capital and visions of make-believe theme parks, rocket ships, and condominium-lined beaches. These visions fill the mind and entice the spirit to visit this former swampland covered with man-made cement and natural orange groves in a semi-tropical setting.

The Florida panhandle extending off the northwest end of the state's peninsula, however, holds no theme parks, launching pad or orange groves. When most beach-goers visit the state in late winter, the lonely panhandle plays hosts to temperatures that can range from twenty-five to seventy-five degrees Fahrenheit. Though the beaches here rival the most beautiful sands in the world, the land is hardly a paradise of winter warmth, yet its residents like it that way. Eschewing the world of make believe, large cities, and Caribbean aesthetics, the people of this area are happy with their panhandle hinterland.

Most of the panhandle is not a vacation attraction, as it reflects a wealth of both poverty and pine trees. It is bordered by what the locals have proudly coined the Emerald Coast, which is so named for its clear green and turquoise waters that are the northern Gulf of Mexico. The beaches themselves are so white that pouring a cannister of bleached sugar on top would not be noticed moments later. It is in these pristine waters of the Gulf that myriad species of marine life thrive, providing sustenance to their own way of life, and human beings as well.

Deep in this region, away from any metropolis, is a different side of Florida that a tourist rarely sees or ever hears about in travel commercials. It is the part of Florida that borders Georgia and Alabama and, perhaps most important to its inhabitants, the Gulf of Mexico. The geographic design and layout of the land would easily confuse one to think that it is really part of the Old South, with its flowing hills, pine, and

Spanish Moss tree lines. Tall palm trees in this region are visible only when shipped in from the southern part of the state to enhance the aesthetics of the more popular cities that want to look like a semi-tropical location, like Pensacola, Panama City Beach and Tallahassee.

This coastline region of the Florida panhandle hosts several small towns where the people who live there hope, and know, that they will never see a tourist. The Gulf waters flowing south of, and tracing, the panhandle coastline provide food and recreation for both man and animal alike.

Ensconced along the Gulf shoreline here, and bordering the Apalachicola Bay, is a small fishing community whose creation and existence has depended entirely upon the area's many mineral springs and the Gulf sound waters since it was founded over one hundred years ago. The village is nestled between the St. Mark's Wildlife Refuge to the East and the Apalachicola National Forest to the West.

In this community exists a people who aren't really Floridian, but more just plain Southern. Living here is simple, people are kind, and the world revolves around the people rather than the people around the world. The community in which they live was built upon the commercial fishing industry and many of its residents fish for the world outside and for their own family table as well. Life here is slow, peaceful and without consequence.

While the village boasts a modest variety of businesses, the small population lives in framed houses and trailer homes, except for the handful of wealthy individuals who own the fishing industry, or live there on old money. For the most part, the wealthy people here are benefactors to their fellow citizens and the rich are more admired than envied. With the exception of an occasional tragedy that affects one or two of the town's citizenry, life goes on here without incident. Occasionally, a hurricane will batter the area causing the town to rebuild and regroup according to mother nature's plan, but these episodes are not only accepted, they are embraced as part of the circle of life on the panhandle. The town is numb to the rest of the state and to the world for that matter. It is a small and run-down area that isn't ugly, yet it isn't beautiful, either. The town is called Panacea.

PART ONE
- Symptoms -

1

The grown man who felt, and behaved, like a boy, woke up to a frosty sunrise, nursing a hangover and a memory lapse as to who was the woman sleeping next to him in his bed. The Windy City, usually engulfed in traffic, was practically empty on this Sunday morning in late September. His twenty-seventh floor condominium in Lincoln Park was chilled because he had left the windows open on the crisp autumn night before. The translucent curtains of the bedroom were blowing lightly toward the plush bed, making the thick, feathered comforter more appreciated than usual for this time of year. The brightly painted walls and beach pictures hanging in the bedroom reflected the early morning sunlight and, also, an earlier period of the boy's life when he lived near the beaches of the Florida panhandle. The boy's room was bright as midday, but only he was awake. For the couple in bed, the night had just ended three hours ago, but the boy couldn't sleep in the new sun, as it seemed to penetrate and torment his face like a police interrogation light, probing for a confession.

The boy, Rick Morrissey, was a 31 year-old man, in a 22 year old's body, with an 18 year old's psyche. He was single, immature, slightly muscular, and was considered attractive by his peers, though he seldom felt so when comparing himself to others. He was a successful lawyer for one of the largest law firms in Chicago, and he abhorred his work.

Perhaps his employer didn't like him much either. Single lawyers in Chicago were considered loose cannons, and Rick was no exception. Single lawyers could flee their jobs more easily than the married ones who sink themselves into debt so far that they can't afford to quit their jobs for fear of losing their homes, their foreign cars, their wives, and, for some, their paramours. Rick never took on life-long responsibilities if he could avoid them. Though he made an excellent salary, he knew that the money never lasts, especially when it's given away as quickly as he did. He didn't embrace materialism and he pissed most of his money away on foolish gifts for his friends and family, or on weekend jaunts to the Caribbean whenever he had cabin fever, spring, summer, winter, or fall.

He was munificent in giving both his time and money to charities, strangers, and, especially, family and friends. This was done, in part, because he felt the need to share his good fortune with those who had less, but more so as an act of attrition for his own selfish lifestyle. He was raised in a small town in Wisconsin a couple of hours northwest of Chicago where he was taught the Christian maxim that a man should never be judged until the end of his days.

Rick had been lured to the big city from his hometown in Calida, Wisconsin, because Chicago offered him a chance to do legal work which he considered challenging. After becoming a member of the Wisconsin and Illinois Bar Associations at age 26, Rick discovered that Chicago sucked, and so did the practice of law in the big city. As a result, his refuge lay in drinking at local bars and meeting attractive women with hopes that one of them would be just the girl that fate had planned for him to meet. He knew he'd not met her yet, and he knew she probably wasn't waiting for him in a bar, though bars were the only place he looked. He was a hypocrite, and he knew it. His latest female encounter was now resting next to him in his bed, and that fact was nothing out of the ordinary. As he lay awake in bed, he recalled the events of the previous night with abject guilt.

Rick had started and ended his night drinking at Vince Planet's Bar. He was a regular there and knew most of the help personally. Vince Planet's was famous for not being a tourist hang-out. It was a true neighborhood bar and no ties were allowed after work. Ties were allowed, however, for weddings and funerals. Vince Planet had always remarked that they were one and the same anyhow. The bar was vintage 1920's with mahogany wood liquor shelves and bar stools. Brass railings lined the foothold of the bar, and the walls were decorated with old tins and pictures reflecting an easier, more innocent time for America, or so it seemed to those living in the new millennium.

Vince Planet's Bar served Guiness and Bud Light on tap and had a full selection of canned beers and all grades of liquor. Rick drank them all, and unlike many of the other regulars, he didn't have a "usual." In fact, Rick didn't even know what he was drinking until the bartender asked him twice. If his flavor was bourbon, he was bound to tie one on and be in rare, though considered usual, form. This night was Maker's Mark Bourbon, 45% alcohol by volume, 90 proof.

Rick's best friend from childhood, Jeff Wilhelm, also lived in Chicago and, since Rick could never seem to make close friends after he entered the professional work world, the two would often meet at Vince Planet's and drink together. Out of boredom, self-pity or plain spite for the opposite sex, Rick and his buddy would often engage in a ritual with one another they called "glory daying." This was a puerile and overly used technique of trying to impress women, and themselves, by talking up the glory days of each other's collegiate athletic career. Though they still relished in the glory daying themselves, the idea had become geared more toward picking up women, or, if anything, as an ice breaker. Typically, if one friend saw another talking with a woman, he would get together with the new couple and magnify his pal's athletic prowess. Rick was growing tired of this stupid, but amazingly effective technique on the more naive female clientele of the bar. Jeff Wilhelm, however, still relished the fact that the two men played together at FSU on the football team when the university entered its hay day in the late 80's. Last night was a classic repartee between Rick and his old college classmate, and closest friend.

While lying in bed, Rick remembered that Jeff came up to the bar when Rick was wooing the still unaware woman who had become his focus and soon-to-be latest bed partner. Jeff was an FBI man who was stationed in Chicago for the past six months heading investigations on political corruption of aldermen and Cook County office holders. Most of his job concerned uncovering travel scams and funny bookkeeping schemes aimed at greasing local business officials. He also investigated corporations that would get tax holidays and other financial breaks from local politicos who were using money channeled from the public coffers, all at the expense of the taxpayer. Nothing new. Jeff was red-haired, bold, handsome, articulate, and an admirer of Rick, though Rick never understood quite why.

Normally, Jeff didn't need glory daying to get his girls. He would pick-up girls by approaching them from behind, acting like an old acquaintance, grabbing them by the shoulders and yelling, "Jane! How ya be. . ., oh, gosh, I'm sorry, I thought you were someone I used to know." If they bit, he was set. If they didn't, Jeff would just touch them on the shoulder gently and say softly, but directly, "Fuck me if I'm wrong, but is your name Mary?" Half the time, her name *was* Mary, or Jennifer, or something common, and if they had a twisted sense of humor, it didn't matter, they warmed up to him. Jeff, however, was even more at his best when he was glory daying for Rick. This night Jeff was in his customary form.

"Hey Rick, what you been up to, man?" Jeff said to Rick while on his way toward the bar. "And who's the pretty girl you're playing host to?" He approached both of them, beer in hand, smiling.

"Just the usual, Red," as Rick had called his red-headed friend since grade school. "This is . . .What's your name again?" Rick inquired.

"Jackie, but I like Jack-O," the beauty replied.

"It figures," Rick said to himself.

The three carried on a conversation for fifteen minutes while watching a college football game on the big screen and commenting from their bar stools about a horrible play called by a coach, or a fantastic catch by a receiver. Then the glory daying commenced.

"Say, Rick, that play reminds me of you. You remember that game against Louisiana Tech our junior year when you caught that last minute touchdown? Man! What a swan song victory that was." Red started in.

"Oh, you guys play football?" Jack-O asked.

"Played." Rick said, correcting her and feigning modesty. "It's just that Red here can't stop talking about it a decade later."

"Shit, how can you stop talking about the event of a young man's lifetime." Red explained. "This guy was an all-conference receiver. Broke a couple of records at our school."

"Ten years ago? Wow. You could've fooled me. You guys don't look a day over twenty-four." Jackie said. "Are you really a college football record holder, Ricky?" she asked, using the name Ricky now as an endearment. Typically, Rick only accepted being called Ricky from close friends and family. Jack-O was trying too hard.

"Well, I think I still hold the record for the most fumbles by a receiver, if that's what you mean." Rick said, feigning self-deprecation, but knowing what was next. "And it was more like twelve years ago. It's just that my friend Red here never quite matured since leaving college."

The girl knew football and figured Rick was being modest. "Tell me about your career as a football stud," Jack-O inquired.

Rick thought to himself that this routine was becoming boring. Nevertheless, he looked at Red with a half-smile smirk and a wink of his eye. Red went on to explain Rick's heroics of the night, and it worked like a charm, or so it seemed at the time, considering that alcohol and poor judgment had combined to put both Rick and Jack-O in their current position.

Lying still in his bed next to Jack-O, Rick stared at the ceiling in disgust over his un- fulfilling lifestyle. Being a slut lawyer was losing its charm, but it was all Rick knew. Admiration from others had come at a personal cost to Rick and he was pensive over the thought of his individual fate. He sat up and stretched an enormous stretch which caused him to involuntarily release a low pitched, hollow growl.

"Morning crackerjack," the cigarette-scratched voice of a woman said.

"Crackerjack. What?" Rick turned his head toward the young woman next to him. "Who are you talking to; why are you calling me 'crackerjack?'"

"Because you're a crackerjack lawyer, aren't you?" Jack-O said.

"Who told you that? Didn't I tell you I sold Port-a-Potties?" Rick asked.

"Yes, but who could believe that crock of shit. No pun intended. Besides, I had a pretty good clue you weren't in sales when the bartender, the cocktail waitresses, and about a dozen other people in the bar told me you were a crackerjack lawyer. What's that mean anyway? 'Crackerjack?'" she asked.

"If I told you I'd be pattin' myself on the back, and right now I think that would be a little more than I could handle, considering my current position."

"What's that supposed to mean?"

"Nothing. It's just that I'm a little weary of meaningless nights on the town." He knew he'd said too much.

Jack-O sat up as her jaw dropped open. "Why, you are an arrogant son of a bitch. Crackerjack must mean asshole," her voiced swelled as she jumped out of bed.

Rick, noticing his blunder and feeling bad for saying what he did, offered, "I'm sorry. I didn't mean to say that."

"I thought we might have had something, but I definitely don't want any of your fucking games," she tried to talk like a sailor and meant every word.

Women love to say shit like that, Rick thought to himself.

Jack-O jumped from under the covers, wearing nothing but white socks and stormed the apartment looking for her clothes. For a fleeting moment, the boy, who should be a man, imagined another opportunity of feeling the woman's soft tanned skin and wonderful curves one more time. Indeed, she was beautiful. A knockout really, but love, or even the thought, had not entered his mind. Although he was an unselfish lover, he was selfish to the extent that that was all he did. He was a lover, he couldn't possibly love her. His imagination was interrupted when Jack-O slipped on a puddle of water left over on the kitchen floor from the boiled peanuts Rick had made around four o'clock that morning when they got to his condo.

"Shit!" she exclaimed. "Where are my clothes, dammit?!"

"I do believe they are on the balcony, left over from your hula dance and strip tease you performed for the neighbors and me last night," Rick caustically enunciated each word.

She said nothing and silently, swiftly, retrieved her jeans and tee shirt from the veranda and put them on.

"If the phone doesn't ring, it's me," she said on her way out.

He had a snappy come back for her, but figured she was doomed already from listening to too many Jimmy Buffett albums as he recognized her line from one of Buffett's songs. He let her go, put his own B-side Buffett mix in the C.D. player and headed for the shower.

Actually, the boy, who would turn 32 that winter, enjoyed Jimmy Buffett's music, mostly the old stuff, and he cursed the girl for putting that song in his head.

"Shit, she has no idea how good Buffett was," Rick said out loud. Jack-O along with the rest of generation X appeared to Rick to have no idea Buffett sang anything but "Margaritaville" and that was definitely not his best, in Rick's estimation. It may as well be titled, "Marijuanaville" for the stoner effect it had on the audience. Indeed, Rick longed to see a Buffett concert where not one of the so-called hits was played, but instead, only the B-sides, or less known songs. Rick vowed to spend most of the afternoon working around his condominium and listening to the Caribbean music of Buffett while he contemplated another of what had become many escapes to the tropics. Rick's love for the beaches and the salt water made him contemplate why he ever moved back to Wisconsin after spending his formative years in the Florida panhandle. He poured shampoo into his hands and lathered his blond hair.

For Rick, the only southern location he truly loved was the semi-tropics of the Florida panhandle. The Emerald Coast. His journeys began there when he was 18 when he, and his best friend, Red Wilhelm, left their home in Wisconsin and started school twelve hundred fifty miles away at Florida State University in Tallahassee. At the time, Rick thought the school would be right on the coast of the Gulf of Mexico, but the nearest coastline was 30 miles away in a fishing village on the intercostal waterway, in a town called Panacea. His favorite beach was Beacon's Point, a secluded beach town located fifty miles between Panacea, a fishing town, and Panama City Beach, a tourist trap. Beacon's Point was the most magnificent coastline with its sleek white beaches and sand dunes bordering the emerald salt water. Panacea, on the other hand, didn't offer much by way of aesthetics, but it boasted the most delectable fresh sea food in the state of Florida. Rick had shucked oysters at a local bar there to help pay his way through college. He now considered that a return trip to the panhandle might be just what he needed and he vowed to take a vacation in the next couple of weeks.

2

The young woman, who never had a chance to be a girl, woke up alone to a sun-drenched morning in the Florida panhandle craving her two cups of coffee and a twinkie. The panhandle was heating up as usual for late September with the night time low of 72 degrees Fahrenheit expected to rise to 85 degrees by midday. The beaten down antebellum home in which the woman awoke was replete with pictures of family, now gone, and paintings of the gulf landscape done by her mentally ill, but talented, mother.

Delaney Chase had been a resident of Panacea, Florida, her entire twenty-one years on earth. She was born a young woman, missing out entirely on her little girl rites of passage like Barbie dolls, jump rope, E-Z bake ovens, hop scotch, fancy dresses, and daydreaming. Born under the guidance of a midwife in the same bedroom she now occupied, Delaney had become used to living alone, and enjoying the solitude. Before Delaney could understand she was a child, her mother, Meredith Chase, had begun her bouts with alcoholism and depression.

Delaney struggled throughout childhood searching for her mother's stashed liquor and mouthwash bottles and dumping them down the drain before they abetted Meredith Chase to a point of intoxication. Though the home and lifestyle in which the Chase family lived appeared regal, there were troubled times financially, and the home now reflected that era.   Fortunately for the family, the large home they occupied was owned free and clear by Meredith Chase, who'd inherited the property from her parents. Meredith now resided in a home for the mentally ill near Atlanta. Delaney drove the four hour trip there to see her mother once a month.

Delaney was only ten years old when her daddy, Pally Chase, had died.   Mr. Chase was a commercial shrimper, and a well-renowned political activist who perished tragically in 1988's Hurricane Gilbert pursuing his one occupation which was his one and only love, besides his daughter. Prior to his death, Chase had been active in political causes such as preservation of the Gulf of Mexico from oil drilling and industrial shipping and development along the coast.   Mr. Chase's life was an inspiration to Delaney, as she admired her father and embraced his political beliefs.

Delaney now occupied the family home by herself, while she studied at Florida State University in the College of Education. Delaney's weekdays always started the same. With the coffee maker on timer for six a.m. coffee, Delaney awoke to a fresh brewed morning blend around six thirty.   After consuming her two cups of coffee while reading the Tallahassee morning paper and eating a single twinkie, usually just the inside filling, Delaney drove her car to Tallahassee, as she commuted every day to FSU.   Typically, on Monday, Wednesday, and Friday, Delaney would finish school around four o'clock and return to Panacea and Captano's Restaurant where she served food from dinner until close, usually around nine o'clock at night.

Today, Delaney left for college early to meet with some classmates who were all members of a student-based coastline preservation group.   Delaney had joined Save Our Shorelines, better known as S.O.S., during the previous spring semester.   S.O.S. had been started a year earlier by an adjunct faculty instructor who worked in the Biology Department at FSU.   The group's mission was to increase public awareness of the fragile condition of the panhandle shoreline and the industries that were responsible for its decay.   Although the group membership was small, only thirty-five students, it was effective in placing banners around Tallahassee and writing letters to the newspapers condemning the cruel greed of the shipping and oil companies who exploited the reserves of the Gulf of Mexico.   Delaney felt as though her father would be proud that she was involved in protecting the Gulf waters that fed his family for so many years.   To most adults in the community however, S.O.S. was simply a group of liberally minded tree-huggers who enjoyed smoking pot and philosophizing over the greater things in life, like nature, and how mankind seemed to disregard the good mother earth.

S.O.S. didn't seem to be taken seriously until six months earlier when Copperhead Oil Company announced plans to drill for oil in the Gulf of Mexico within the authority of a federal government lease proposition.   Copperhead planned to begin its drilling operation in the spring of 2001. When S.O.S. heard of the proposal, the group agreed to focus on Copperhead and to try to lobby the legislature to terminate the lease area granted by the government. S.O.S. believed staunchly in their resolve, but agreed from the onset that the group's demonstrations and activities would always be peaceful.   Unknown to the rest of the membership, however, two of S.O.S.'s members vowed through an anonymous letter to the Tallahassee newspaper to sabotage the operation by explosive means.   The letter smacked of terroristic acts of violence with explosives, and it got the attention of law enforcement and executive officers at Copperhead Oil. It didn't matter that the letter could have been just silly kid stuff from a group of college students too liberal to think clearly. Copperhead considered the threat seriously and embarked on a mission to determine whether the culprits of the letter were their competition or Greenpeace-types with nothing to live for except blocking the corporate expansion of the oil world.

Delaney's ambitions in life were well-focused for a woman her age as she was determined and comfortable in knowing that she would be a school teacher one day and remain active in social causes like S.O.S. She would make herself and her family proud. Although she enjoyed fishing and was excellent with a rod & reel, she knew it would never be a good career choice for her to take over where her father's legacy left off. As Delaney drove away from her home and headed up Route 319 toward Tallahassee, she reflected on the years that had passed since Pally Chase died and how she was becoming a grown woman of whom her father would have been proud. She was only twenty-one and she knew what she wanted in life. What she didn't know was that she would soon be heir to several million dollars and that, for the twentieth day in a row, she was being followed.

3

The Washington, D.C. based firm of Wallace, Nieson, and Carson was comprised entirely of three men and two full-time secretaries. Bill Wallace, Ray Nieson, and Ned Carson had all attended the University of Florida back in the 70's and, after seeing the light, converted from Democrat to Republican upon their graduation. They all agreed that Democrats had more fun and that everybody should enjoy being liberal at some point in their lives, but there was money to be made, and Republicans made the most. They moved to Washington, D.C., together and, with the assistance of their parents' money, opened a lobbyist firm that catered to conservative issues like gun ownership, insurance company rights, land development, and corporate industrial expansion. After twenty-five years in the business of rubbing elbows with the lawmakers, Wallace, Nieson, and Carson was considered the go-to firm for any company seeking a chip, or a vote, from a congressman.

It was a rainy late September morning in D.C., and the firm began its busy week with its usual conference of partners. The three men gathered in a locked conference room and drank coffee while discussing the weekend fun they had cheating the government, their wives, or their neighbors. They could hear the phone ring but ignored it as usual while the secretary picked it up. The three founding partners were in the middle of laughter when the intercom buzzed into the conference room.

"Carl Pagan from Copperhead Oil is on line one, gentlemen," came the voice from one of the secretaries. Typically, the secretaries knew not to interrupt the morning meeting unless it was important. Today's call was expected by Bill Wallace who had drunk scotch with Pagan three nights earlier at a Nevada strip club.

"I'll take it," Wallace said, and picked up the receiver. "Hello, Carl, this is Bill."

Ray Nieson and Ned Carson looked at each other trying to figure out what Wallace was up to with the man on the other end of the phone. Wallace, Nieson and Carson had lobbied on behalf of Copperhead Oil in the mid 1990's when Copperhead secured permission to drill for oil off the coast of Florida - Atlantic side, and in a failed effort to drill in the Gulf of Mexico in 1988. Neither Carl Pagan or the Copperhead name had come across their client list since then. The two men stared at Wallace for his input from the phone call.

"Yes, C.P., I remember the conversation. You must not know that I'm an experienced drinker. Besides, I get pretty sober when talking about money," Wallace said into the phone. Wallace looked at his partners and gave them a wink with a thumbs up gesture which transformed into a rubbing of the fingers and thumbs representing the lobbyist firm's universal symbol that cash is on the way. Nieson and Carson grinned back at him.

"Tell you what, Carl, I think the boys and I would enjoy a little sunshine. It's raining to beat hell here," Wallace said. "I'll let them know the deal and we'll give you a report after we make contact with Billy." He paused. "Other than airfare and a house on the beach, I don't see our bill going much higher than two hundred. Very well. Thank you." He hung up the phone. "Fuckin' 'A,' boys!" Wallace said to his partners.

"I - I - I like the s - s -sound of that," Ned Carson said in a stuttered voice he could never correct since childhood.

"Two-hundred thousand for what?" Nieson asked. "And how long do the three of us get to suntan before it's earned?"

"That was Copperhead Oil fellas. We've got a job in Tallahassee for a month or two. Apparently their cool-hand Luke down there isn't getting the job done and they're expecting to drill for oil by spring," Wallace said.

"Who's their cool-hand lobbyist?" Nieson asked.

"Billy Barute," Wallace said.

"No way. That sonofabitch got a job?" Nieson said.

"He's come a long way since graduation," Wallace said. "Hell, everyone thought he'd be a politician since he was student body president at U.F."

"I - I - I d-d-didn't," Carson said. "He was j-j-just not g-g-good looking enough."

"You're just pissed at him because you were his flunkie in student government," Wallace replied.

"L-l-like hell!" Carson responded. All three of the men laughed.

"Well, Ned, you are right about one thing. He wasn't a looker at all," Wallace said. "Probably still weighs more than the three of us put together. But he became a helluva lobbyist. Knocks down three hundred grand a year, with benefits."

"D-d-d-damn!" Carson said.

"Poor son-of-a-bitch probably spends most of his money feeding his cocaine and hooker habit," Nieson said.   "How'd you know what Barute is up to?"

"Saw him in Vegas last weekend," Wallace replied. "And, Ray, he was having a tryst with a hooker, so good call.   Anyhow, that's how I got reconnected to Copperhead.   Billy said he could use some help down there because the public is starting to scream about the shorelines being ruined by the oil industry," Wallace said. "Apparently, some of the state reps and senators are listening and they are drafting a bill to terminate the federal government lease option on the drilling zone. That's where we come in. Gotta save the oil company. Copperhead's got four million in this project already, from political contributions to research. They're not about to let this one get away," he continued. "So, the sooner we change their minds, the sooner we'll get paid and be relaxing on the beach."

"I don't know, Bill, maybe would shouldn't go sunbathing on the beach after this is all through," Nieson said.

"Why n-n-not?" Carson asked.

"Whatcha' gettin' at Ray?" Wallace said.

"Well, I'm thinking we should go fishing instead," Nieson said.

"Good point, Ray," Wallace said as they looked at each other and chuckled. "The sun will always be there, but the fish might be gone after Copperhead comes to town."

4

The work week began busy for Rick and it was almost four o'clock in the afternoon at the mega firm of Sloan & Jasper, P.C., by the time he realized he was so sunk into his work that he had not eaten breakfast or lunch. Rick decided that his first meal of the day would not be cold milk and oat bran cereal, which was his weekday usual, no matter the time of day. Today, Rick would dine at Vince Planet's on steak and beer. Though Vince Planet's Bar did not boast the best food in town, Rick always enjoyed the late Monday afternoon crowd because they were usually animated with stories, some sordid, from the weekend before. Though Rick never shared his own exploits, he was oddly comforted in hearing that there were plenty of people in the world who shared his lascivious and unbecoming lifestyle. Besides, the filet mignons at Vince Planet's weren't half bad.

Rick had been a friend of Vince Planet's up until his untimely death almost two years earlier. He first met Vince during Rick's first week in Chicago in 1994. Rick was having a cocktail when Vince approached him for legal advice. Vince was a defendant in his third drunk driving charge in ten years and he wanted Rick to represent him. It didn't matter to Vince that Rick had never tried a criminal case. All that mattered was that Rick drank the same brand of bourbon as Vince, and he thought Rick had the panache for convincing a jury that Vince was not guilty.

Days before the jury trial Rick had diarrhea and stomach cramps so severe that he had to see a doctor for prescription muscle relaxers. Rick knew that when he cared too much about the outcome of a case or a trial that it would exact a hefty toll on his physical and mental health. Vince, of course, laughed hysterically when he found out Rick's constitution wasn't as tough as Rick appeared. However, in the courtroom, Rick was daunting.

Much to the delight of Vince and the patrons of his bar, including a dozen who attended the two-day trial, Rick obtained a not guilty verdict in what had been previously termed by the prosecutors, and Vince's friends, an unwinnable case for the defendant.

After the trial, Vince bought the house free drinks from 7 p.m. to close. One of the bailiffs from the trial even made it over for a nightcap. When the bailiff asked Vince how he got off the charge, Vince looked him dead in the eye and said, "Well, Mr. Bailiff. It's simple. Although I had a good attorney, the real reason I got off is the State had only a half a case and I had a full one." The bar was up for grabs after that.

Vince had been the epitome of a bartender who had a quick line for everything, and was a friend to all, a best friend when he was drunk. From his drinking, Vince had confronted and defied the jaws of death on numerous occasions, and had even escaped an inadvertent suicide once, though he later contested whether it was a suicidal or accidental attempt. He drank way too much, but that didn't kill him, though it almost did. Rick never forgot the event or Vince's explanation of how his life got turned around when he realized how near to death he had come. After celebrating his 30th birthday until four in the morning, Vince drove himself home, post twelve shots of Yagermeister Liqueur and umpteen beers in a 8-hour time slot. Most of his drinking friends were hammered, but had the sense to know that Vince shouldn't drive and, though he did make it home alive, he passed out in his garage with the motor running, car windows down, and the automatic garage door shut tight, trapping the carbon monoxide in the garage. The poisonous gas gradually made its way to Vince and he had been asphyxiated for nearly three minutes when the early morning newspaper boy arrived to deliver the paper. The newspaper boy heard the car running and walked around to the framed door entrance of the garage to find Vince nearly cold. Vince's life was saved, though it did cost him a bit of dignity.

Rick remembered Vince's recollection of the event which he eventually learned to enjoy telling. After all, Vince could make fun of himself as well as anyone. Until Vince nearly died from it, Rick never knew what carbon monoxide poisoning was or what it did to the human body. Vince explained with ribald humor the doctor's report that Vince's larynx was the biggest he'd ever seen. It was so swollen that Vince's source of oxygen was nearly cut off completely and the poisonous gas had caused him to go into a near cardiac arrest. According to Vince's doctors, carbon monoxide poisoning was one of the worst ways to die, but, as in Vince's case, being drunk alleviates a lot of the discomfort in death. Vince's life was saved by merely seconds as full cardiac arrest was imminent if not for the paper boy's discovery.

Vince stayed in a coma for only 2 days after the carbon monoxide episode and came to life when his girlfriend, Donna, came to his bedside to tell him she was breaking up with him because of his drinking habits. Immediately he snapped to life and vowed never to drink again. Even though his promise lasted only a few days, Vince had meant well and Donna stayed with him through the drunken years until they married a year before his death.

Instead of dying from liver disease or an alcohol-related blackout, as would be expected, Vince died in a car crash, and he wasn't even drinking. As fatal car accidents go, the highway department had put up a flashing yellow light at the intersection where Vince died one year to the day after his accident in 1998. Before his death, Vince always marveled at the fact that the highway department didn't know an intersection, or a curved roadway, was dangerous until someone died there. Vince always derided the highway department for its insincere effort of healing the wounds of the surviving family by placing a blinking yellow light up in the deceased loved one's honor.

Vince Planet might have changed his mind and been proud of his yellow light as it accompanied a similar yellow sign that read "Dangerous Intersection" where Vince met his Maker. Vince was an All-American Midwesterner cut short from his stay on this planet. He'd been a rebel most of his 39 years but had recently turned to Catholicism and was on his way to church when a semi-truck overturned on him and his 1982 Dodge Truck at a rural highway intersection in Wheaton, Illinois. Vince had named his wife, Donna, the full beneficiary under his will and, since his death, Donna continued Vince's bar business and kept the name of the bar in his honor.

Rick ate his steak and vowed to drink at Vince Planet's every night that week, promising himself he'd take nobody home to bed. A good start at redemption, he thought. When Friday morning finally came,

Rick awoke and went through a rigorous morning at work beginning at seven o'clock which included hearings, legal research, and the deposition of an opposing party's neurosurgeon. Unfortunately for the neurosurgeon, who had previously disagreed with Rick's injured client's position, Rick was in an aggressive mood. The deposition was in Lisle, a suburb of Chicago, and the 59 year old specialist was discredited and humbled by the crackerjack lawyer nearly half his age. Normally, Rick would be assertive and fair, but he advocated fiercely this afternoon out of spite for these "insurance company whores" as they had become known. They were merely experts paid exorbitantly to say someone's injuries weren't serious or related to an accident in order to benefit the insurance company. Rick learned much about medicine in his role as a lawyer, and he could keep pace with any conversation involving internal medicine and orthopedics.

Rick headed back into the city to finish his day at the office and then resort to happy hour at Vince Planet's with some other attorneys. Rick didn't drink the whole night, but stayed until closing, listening and watching with cleared vision the other bar patrons who, like Rick a thousand times before, wasted their days and nights without any genuine reward.

When he awoke early Saturday morning, Rick considered that he'd become far too cynical in his work and overbearingly particular in his life when it came to personal relationships. He had dedicated his early career to work and now thought work was all there was that held meaning. He was growing intolerant of the idea that this was all his life had to offer. While Rick didn't hate the idea of a relationship with a woman, he did fear that he would marry for all the wrong reasons, without being patient enough for fate to lend a hand. To Rick, compromising fate for the sake of convenience and comfort was taboo. He would rather wait than compromise, though he was resenting the dreamer in him who felt that way.

Work, as it was turning out, proved to not harbor the answers to life it seemed to hold five years earlier. Rick was beginning to dislike his work, and he loathed the one-nighters. He felt himself a bit shallow, holding everything worldly, but nothing to show for it metaphysically or spiritually. An intangible, and imagined, disease thrived within him, and it was apparent the cure did not rest in Chicago, or the practice of law.

As Rick read the Sun Times while drinking his coffee, an ad in the travel section caught his eye. "Florida Panhandle's Emerald Coast - Cure for the Common Cold (or whatever ails you)," the ad read.

Rick had spent years along the Florida panhandle when he was younger and thought the area as good as any for a getaway - be it temporary or permanent. Without much thought for the future, he vowed to give two weeks notice at work that Monday and then he would fly south to the Florida panhandle. He would go for a break, for a change, for a cure. There, he would rest, regain his composure and, possibly, his sanity. He hoped.

"Fuck it!" Rick said, as he looked out the window toward Lake Michigan. "A hundred years from now, it all won't matter."

5

The weekly meeting of Save Our Shorelines began with an update of current events and proposals from the corporate industrial world. Delaney Chase had been appointed secretary *pro tem* for this meeting and she was diligent in recording the minutes of the meeting in her own version of college shorthand. The group met at the Diffenbaugh building on the campus of Florida State University. Today, Copperhead Oil was the subject of interest as S.O.S. learned of previous drilling initiatives advanced by Copperhead on the Atlantic side of Florida. According to the president of S.O.S., Joe Sherman, five years earlier Copperhead had convinced the Florida legislature to vote to create a lease area just outside of St. Augustine for the drilling and manufacturing of crude oil. This, of course had been at the consent of the federal government. Florida Senator D.D. Amato was the author of the bill which was passed by a mere four votes in the conservative-run senate. The Republicans dominated the House of Representatives and the measure passed without going to committee. It was legal and acceptable to drill off the Florida shoreline.

"D.D. Amato is now presenting a bill to allow Copperhead to drill off the panhandle," Sherman announced. "We need to apprize the public of the dangers of this operation and the likelihood of an oil spill ruining our shorelines for generations, not to mention the fish and aquatic wildlife that would suffer indefinitely."

Sherman went on to explain the Coastal Impact Assistance program which was created by the federal Congress to offset environmental damage caused by decades of off-shore oil and gas exploration. The federal government had offered $142 million dollars to the coastal states and Florida was receiving a large chunk because of damage to the Florida peninsula because it is surrounded almost entirely by water.

"Six counties in Florida have received most of the money from our federal government to assist in the clean up for the injuries that the oil industry and corporate greed have inflicted upon us and mother nature," Sherman declared. "And what's not so funny about it all is that the money comes from the offshore drilling industry itself."

In fact, the offshore drilling industry paid over $9 billion dollars in royalties to the federal government in 1999, which was a mere fraction of their own profits. Florida's receipts from the Coastal Impact Assistance program would be used to cap off already abandoned and leaking oil wells, along with some infrastructure assistance to the counties that received the monies.

Delaney listened with great interest to Sherman's speech. She was beginning to understand the impact these companies had on people like her father. She also understood how important it was to be a part of a group that opposes such destruction.

Sherman called for action and a formal protest to be held in Pensacola, Florida, where Copperhead was planning to announce their intention to take advantage of a lease area in the Gulf of Mexico for oil and gas exploration. Pensacola was the nearest city on the panhandle to the lease area and Copperhead intended on showing them a nice check for their being so gracious and kind during the drilling initiatives. More checks would follow for cities like Destin, Panama City Beach, Panacea, and Lanark. Oil and Gas Lease Sale Area 181 was the first proposed government sale area for oil and gas exploration in the Gulf of Mexico since 1988. It was in that year that Pally Chase was most ardent in fighting the drilling and, unfortunately, the year he met his fate in the hurricane.

The area itself encompassed over 1.5 million acres, located as near as one hundred miles off the panhandle shoreline. The U.S. Department of the Interior, Minerals Management Service for the Gulf of Mexico Region, was handling the offers to drill for the oil industry. MMS would also oversee the collection and disbursement of mineral revenues which would later end up in the hands of local governments needing assistance for environmental relief.

"Nobody get crazy here," Sherman said. "This is a peaceful demonstration. I know a few of you who are harassing Copperhead in ways that might get you arrested. And while I may care about your sorry asses, I don't want our organization to get a black eye because of some people who went beyond our mission and philosophy."

"When is the demonstration?" Delaney asked.

"It's October 12. Thursday. Let's have everyone there around noon," Sherman said, as Delaney took the minutes. "We need some letters to the editor, hand bills, and some posters. Bring all the people you can find. I know a few other groups will be there and, hell, the whole town of Pensacola will probably be there showing their disapproval as well. This is our shoreline, folks; let's make sure corporate America and our own government know it!"

6

Rick put in his notice at Sloan & Jasper, P.C., and went through two exhausting exit interviews where the head partners try to grill the exiting associate into staying and making him feel guilty for leaving, after all they've done for him. After almost two weeks of organizing his files for the next sorry lawyer to succeed him, Rick packed up most of his office belongings, including his diplomas, on Thursday, October 12, and began to head back to his condominium around noon. Rick smiled with inspiration and wonder when he reached for his day-to-day desk calender only to see that under the date read the declaration that October 12 was "Destiny Day."

Rick left the office saying goodbye only to his secretary. He felt sorry for her and frowned at the prospect of her next twenty years of breaking in new associates for Sloan & Jasper, P.C. He gave his secretary a gold necklace in thanks for her service to him and then he walked out of the building. Rick had previously arranged for a rental car to be waiting for him at his condominium. When he got home, he changed clothes, grabbed a beer from the refrigerator, and took off in the car for Calida to discuss his plans with his parents.

On the northeast tollway, Interstate 90, from Chicago to Madison, Wisconsin, Rick drove his rented Chrysler 300M ninety-five miles an hour. His rationale for this reckless speed was that, should he die on the interstate, then his change of course in life was never meant to be. He thought himself a man possessed, but of what, he couldn't discern. Just outside of Rockford, Illinois, Rick passed an Illinois State Trooper traveling in the same direction, and, with tunnel vision, he never even noticed the squad car. Oddly and propitiously enough, the trooper didn't pay attention to Rick, other than just shaking his head, as Rick noticed when he looked up into his rear view mirror after passing the marked car. "Must be the end of his shift," Rick thought, as he pressed the accelerator harder. Turning north on highway 51 in Wisconsin, Rick made the 140 mile trip in just over an hour and a half.

Calida, Wisconsin, had four stop signs on the main strip going through the heart of town and no electronic traffic control devices located anywhere. Its downtown area was dilapidated but not vacant. Many of the old buildings that used to house clothing stores, hotels, bars, and department stores were now filled with candle shops, fudge factories, cheese houses, and antique stores. Most of Calida's downtown businesses attracted out-of-towners who were merely passing through. The locals usually didn't shop downtown as they found life's necessities at the Fleet Farm or at the Wal-Mart which were located on the outskirts of Calida. Rick was disgusted with change, especially the type that converted his boyhood hometown from a mecca of childhood innocence to a wasteland of a simpler time.

Rick first stopped at his father's home on Sunset Lane to discuss his decision to leave Chicago for no good reason other than to get away. To his father, Rick knew this would sound like a pretty immature decision to be making on a whim. Rick didn't want to explain the fact that this decision was being made since he graduated law school.

| PANACEA |

Rick's father was a kind man of modest wants and means. He held family dear and liked everyone to stay close to home. Sean Morrissey was a union laborer by trade and a talented mechanic on the side. Rick always encouraged his father to charge a fair price for the labor he did on cars after normal working hours but Sean Morrissey gave his services away. Only occasionally would Mr. Morrissey even charge for the spare parts that he would buy himself at the local auto parts store to fix a friend's, or a stranger's, car. As a union laborer in Wisconsin, Mr. Morrissey earned only around $30,000 per year after 36 years in the trade as a journeyman.

Because Wisconsin was a "Right to Work" state, a legislative imposition sponsored by conservative Republicans, Mr. Morrissey was forced to accept much less than a prevailing wage for a man of his skills when compared to states like Illinois which didn't have Right to Work legislation. Right to Work was a cozy term introduced by the conservative movement that had nothing to do with a person's right to work but the right for companies to employ skilled union labor at the same cost as hiring unskilled people to do the same work. In essence, all right to work legislation did was eliminate a good salary for skilled union members and give the companies a higher profit line. The only other benefactors of the legislation were the unskilled men and women who took any job they could find with their minimal training and consequently earned more than they should when compared to the better skilled and trained workers.

The Right to Work legislation, among other things, also compelled Mr. Morrissey to raise his children as Democrats. The Morrissey children were taught the belief that corporate America never gave a damn about people or the environment.   To Sean Morrissey, sticking up for the little guy was a noble occupation, no matter what work one did.   Sean Morrissey was an honest man and a hard worker.   Rick learned politics from him and focused part of his legal career on representing union workers in disputes with big business or in workers' compensation.

Rick found his father working on a neighbor's car in the old garage that stood next to the home Rick and his dad shared from Rick's graduation from junior high through high school. Sean Morrissey heard Rick enter the garage and looked out from underneath the hood of the 1984 Chevy Impala he was repairing.

"Hey, buddy," Rick said.

"Rick, what a surprise. You moving back home?" Mr. Morrissey said, skipping straight to the thought that passed his mind every time he thought of his son.

"Sure am," Rick said.   "You got my bedroom shrine still preserved."

"Aw, sorry son. Your step-mother painted it baby blue and put pictures of little ducks and teddy bears on the wall," Mr. Morrissey said. "Suppose she's waiting for you to have a baby?"

"Could be," Rick said. "It's just that I'm not pregnant. At least, not that I know of. Guess I'll have to pass up returning home to live." Rick took a pack of cigarettes from his right front jeans pocket and lit-up.

"I thought you quit," Sean Morrissey said to his son.

"I did, Dad. Now, I only smoke after sex. I'm just catching up." Rick attempted a stupid joke, which bore some truth, knowing the reaction wouldn't be the laugh he was hoping for from his father.   Sean Morrissey rolled his eyes and looked disappointed for a brief moment.

"Big town lawyer losing his scruples," Mr. Morrissey said, pausing and continuing. "And his marbles. I don't know how you lead a perfectly healthy lifestyle through college and then decide to pick-up that nasty habit."

"It's called law school, Dad," Rick said. "So what was your excuse for starting at age 17?"

"It's called marriage. But you wouldn't know anything about that," Mr. Morrissey said.

"Well, maybe when I get married, it'll cause me to quit," Rick said. They both laughed.

"How are you, Son?" Sean Morrissey asked.

"Good Dad. And not so good," Rick said. Rick went on to explain that he was leaving his job in Chicago for a temporary period to visit Florida and maybe look for less strenuous, more fulfilling work there. To ease his father's nerves, Rick intimated that if the whole Florida thing didn't work out, he'd probably end up back in Calida working as a sole practitioner handling wills, trusts, real estate, and a variety of life's simple legal pains in the ass. Sean Morrissey always wanted Rick to live at home, or at least near home, and the last of Rick's plans pleased Mr. Morrissey's ears. He encouraged Rick to leave the job in Chicago.

"Got time for supper tonight?" Sean Morrissey asked.

"No thanks, Dad. I've got to go tell Mom and then get going before I change my mind," Rick said. "I appreciate your always supporting what I want to do. Thanks."

"Sure, you know I've always supported your decisions," Mr. Morrissey said. "Unless you refer back to the birds and the bees speech I had to give you when you turned 15. Didn't want to support what you wanted to do then."

"Speech!?" Rick said with eyebrows raised and a smile on his face. "Dad, all you told me was not to let the girls stick their tongue in my mouth. What the hell kind of advice was that?"

"You didn't get pregnant, did ya?" Mr. Morrissey said and smiled.

"No, I guess I didn't. You are smarter than you do know, Dad." They both laughed and embraced.

Rick's mother lived in a three bedroom cape cod home which appeared modest on the outside, though it was landscaped artfully, in light of the fact that Rick's mother was an environmental artist who worked mostly with oil paints. Rick pulled into Helen Morrissey's home on Plainfield Avenue around 4 p.m. She had kept the Morrissey name because most of her paintings had become known by it. Ms. Morrissey didn't greet her son at the door and Rick walked in unannounced. Rick found his mother in her drawing room painting a scene of a mischievous beaver building a dam on the Wisconsin River in early Autumn. Her back was to the door of the room and Rick announced his arrival.

"Hello, Mrs. Rockwell, would that be a self-portrait?" Rick said, kidding his mother.

Ms. Morrissey turned, smiling. "Are you calling me a beaver? That's a little sexist, don't you think?"

"Mom, I think you've got a dirtier mind than me. I wasn't even thinking along those lines," Rick said.

"On the contrary, my dear son. Those are the only lines you think along." She smiled and rose. "Rick. What a great surprise. What brings you home?" Ms. Morrissey hugged her son and kissed him on the check. "It's so nice to see you!"

"Great to see you mom," Rick said. "How's the artist industry?"

"Oh, I never charge enough money. You know that," she said.

"Thank God you have modest wants, Mom." Rick said. "Except for that brand new Ford Expedition in the driveway."

"Well, I'm fifty-nine years old, honey. I've got the Ford Expedition coming to me," Ms. Morrissey said. "How about a bourbon?"

"Sure, I'll get it," Rick said. "You want a glass of wine?"

"Yes, but take this glass and add a couple of ice cubes too, would you?" Helen Morrissey gave Rick a half drunk glass of white wine and Rick made his way to the kitchen. It wasn't unusual for his mother to drink while she painted and Rick wondered how many she'd had at this point. Typically, Rick's mother wouldn't drink unless she was creating something, be it a painting for herself or food for a party she was hosting. Helen Morrissey loved entertaining and, though she guised her get-togethers as opportunities to sell her paintings, Ms. Morrissey relished the company of others and she was a perfect host to any occasion, including post-funeral luncheons. Rick's mother was a friend to all and she lived her life selflessly. Rick went for the cocktails in his mother's kitchen.

Returning to his mother who was now picking up the mess in the drawing room, Rick offered her the glass of wine. "Your painting looks great, Mom."

"Thanks, Honey," Ms. Morrissey said. Helen Morrissey had no need to rely on her paintings for sustenance as her mother and father left her financially independent after their death. As an only child of a real estate investor, Helen kept some of her parents' rental properties and managed them for "something to do" when she wasn't painting or volunteering her time with various charities.

Rick lit a cigarette. "You'll be glad to know that this is only my fifth cigarette today, mom," he said.

"Good for you, Rick. When you gonna quit?" Helen Morrissey said.

"Won't be long now, mom," Rick said. "I quit the occupation that got me started in the first place."

"You did!" Ms. Morrissey said. "I'm glad. Those people don't give a damn about anybody. You'll live a lot longer and be happier without that firm." she paused. "Well, knowing you, you must have a plan. Who you gonna work for now?"

"I'm thinking about living under a thatched roof hut on the beach in the tropics and selling frozen drinks." Rick said. His mother looked a little bewildered. "Don't worry, I'd like to do that but I'll try something a little more responsible first. I'm taking a trip down to Florida to find some work and hang out for a while. Who knows, I may be back here practicing law in the next few months. I just need a break."

"I think that sounds great," Helen Morrissey said, always one to support her son. She didn't have any desire to know her son's motives for leaving Chicago because she trusted his judgment. "Do you need any money?"

"No. Thank you though, Mom," Rick said. Just then the front door of Helen Morrissey's home opened and a voice called to Rick and his mother.

"Hello. Mom? Rick, are you here?" came Rick's sister, Rachel

Tilton's, voice.

Rick's sister was thirty-seven years old and looked younger than Rick. She had recently married for the first time and was now six months pregnant.

"In here, Rach," Rick said. He rose to meet his sister at the threshold of the drawing room. They embraced.

"Whoa, is that a baby in your stomach or are you just happy to see me?" Rick said.

"Nice try. Wrong gender, baby brother," Rachel said.

"You're looking great, Sis," Rick said. "How much longer?"

"I'm inducing labor in ten minutes. Just came by to see if you two wanted to watch." Rachel said. "Why are you in town? Those creeps finally fire you for being the most tan lawyer in the off-season?"

"I wish," Rick said.

"Rick's going to Florida for a while. He quit working for the firm," Ms. Morrissey said.

"Oh, great, Rick. Good for you," Rachel said. "You were starting to look a little old from working all those hours," she kidded him. "How long will you be gone?"

"Don't worry, I'll be back when you have the baby," Rick said.

"That's not what I'm worried about," Rachel said. "I want to come visit and have my first Margarita after the baby's born while tanning on the beach."

"I can arrange that," Rick said.

Rick, his mom, and Rachel visited for another hour while Rick and his mother had two more drinks. Feeling a comfortable, yet adventurous buzz from the alcohol, Rick announced his departure and promised to call when he got to Tallahassee. Rick gave his mother and sister a kiss and headed back to Chicago where he planned to finish packing and make one more stop at Vince Planet's before bed and the next day that would begin the rest of his life.

Rick made it back to Chicago around 9:30 p.m. and left a message with the realtor who had sold him his condominium two years earlier. Regardless of the outcome of his trip down south, Rick was not returning to Chicago and he hoped his condominium would sell quickly. He examined his plane tickets which reflected a round trip ticket to Tallahassee departing at seven o'clock from O'Hare International Airport the next morning. He didn't turn the page to see when his return date or time was. By this time, Rick was too tired to go to Vince Planet's and he opened a beer and put Jimmy Buffet on his stereo with all the lights down and his living room illuminated only by the outside twilight of Chicago. Rick wondered if any of the regulars at Vince Planet's would miss him and then he thought to himself with some degree of guilt that he wouldn't miss them. He may miss the people, but the life they represented was something Rick was comfortable in never revisiting for the rest of his life.

Rick finished his beer and had another one. He packed all the shorts and tee shirts he owned, along with one pair of blue jeans and a pair of sandals. Reluctantly, Rick packed one of his suits along with the expected accessories. By midnight, Rick had finished his fourth beer since he got home and he fell asleep on the living room floor listening to the tropical music of the Caribbean crooner with whom he'd started his night.

It wasn't a conscious decision at the time he fell asleep, but by

| PANACEA |

daybreak Friday morning, Rick was pleased that he avoided sleeping in his bed which had played host to so many nights of which Rick was, now, no longer proud.

7

The plane ride to Tallahassee, via Atlanta, was bumpy, and Rick watched with childlike wonder the southern "boomers" as he called them, or thunderstorms, beneath him, somewhere over Tennessee, he thought. They lit the clouds like a strobe light inside of a balloon. It was a magnificent display of nature. Beautiful, yet potentially deadly to those below. . .or to those flying through it. Rick never liked to fly and these distractions were amusing enough to keep his mind from worrying too much. Rick had an unreasonable fear of flying. Often when he flew, he would take a look around the plane and study people's faces before take off. He would try to determine if any of the passengers looked like someone who would be missed, who could likely end up in a plane crash. He also looked for people who might be considered fictional, just nameless faces put on the plane for the sole purpose of perishing.

"Is destiny on their faces today?" Rick would ask himself. He was always comforted when he saw a young mother with a baby. "Those people aren't dying today, their life has just begun," he would console himself and pray hopefully to God. Rick wasn't too sure that God appreciated man's taking flight off the good green earth he was made to roam, and his prayers were apologetic, yet beseeching.

As the odds would have it, Rick's plane landed safely in Atlanta where he made a connecting flight to Tallahassee and flew uneventfully to Florida's capital.   After landing at Tallahassee International Airport, Rick could smell the salty southern air as the plane taxied to the terminal.

He made his way to the luggage check, retrieved his suitcases, and headed for the car rental office. Rick rented a dark blue Chrysler Sebring convertible, ran some errands to buy provisions for his stay, and headed for the Radisson Hotel in Tallahassee, where he knew he'd have plenty of time to relax and think. His first few hours were somewhat lonesome and he fell asleep with no plans other than beaching it for the next couple of weeks or so.

His first full day started out with beautiful sunshine and Rick didn't bother to check the forecast. He was headed for St. George Island seventy miles from Tallahassee to relax and grill out on a portable Weber Grill he had purchased at a Tallahassee hardware store the night before.

He was forty-five miles down Route 319 when the rain began to trickle down.   Within ten minutes it was pouring torrentially and Rick, disappointed, turned the car around. He was near the intersection of Route 98, just after passing Lanark Village, when he thought of one of his favorite seafood spots, and turned for Captano's Restaurant near Panacea for a light lunch of boiled shrimp and raw oysters. Since the Gulf waters had cooled with the autumn weather, Rick didn't have a problem eating the oysters out of Apalachicola Bay.   Over the past several years, the bacteria in the Gulf waters in the summertime had made some of the oysters deadly. This was due, in part, to a failure to adequately protect the waters from commercial shipping which spilled trash, debris, sewage, and other bacteria into the water. Being a person who appreciated preservation of the environment, Rick anguished at the thought that big commercial business was to blame, all at the expense of the people and nature.

Rick walked into a surprisingly busy lunch at Captano's and could hardly focus in the dimly lit atmosphere. Rick's eyes were slowly adjusting when she appeared across the restaurant carrying a mother-lode of seafood platters and fried Gulf crab claws. She was a vision.

An eager and less attractive hostess interrupted Rick's focus. "Table for how many?" she said, as Rick stared at the waitress across the room who'd caught his eye initially.

Rick turned to the hostess. "Just one, smoking," Rick responded.

"They're all smoking, Honey. Right this way, Sir," the hostess invited Rick respectfully.

"Sir? Do I look like a 'Sir?'" he thought to himself, dejected that his youth was slipping away in the eyes of the older hostess.

Rick sat down in what he had hoped was the section of the young woman he'd noticed when he walked in, and he soon learned that it was. As she approached, Rick observed her name tag said "Delaney" and she was wearing a grease-smeared apron, stuffed with what must have been a Missouri bankroll of ones and fives from generous customers. Rick's eyes were locked on her for only a second but, even as he turned away to look at his menu in feigned indifference, her image was frozen in his mind.

"May I get you something?" she asked.

Rick turned to look back at her. "Is a sunny day at the beach on the menu?" Rick asked.

"Not today, unfortunately," came the reply. "Tropical weather down in the Gulf is supposed to stir things up here for a couple days," Delaney said.

"Then a rainy day at the beach is only fit to be capped off with a pot of boiled shrimp and a beer," Rick said. He hoped and thought he had spoken like a true southerner.

"Sounds like you had a rough day. That order should just about set you straight," Delaney smiled and said. "Were you caught on the sands in the rain?"

"I only made it half way to St. George," Rick said. "I was thinking by the way the day started out, it would be beautiful. I guess I'm a fair weather beach nut."

"Fair weather, huh?" Delaney said. "When it rains on the way to the beach, true beach goers know that you throw your bumbershoot in the back of the car, turn around, and head for a beer."

"Nice to know my way of thinking is accepted," Rick responded, pretending to understand the regional slang used by Delaney.

"Accepted and appropriate," Delaney said. Rick was enchanted.

Delaney asked how Rick discovered St. George and what he knew about the island. She seemed overly inquisitive at times, and Rick was wondering about all of her regular customers who certainly could use their food or a drink by now. She stood and chatted with Rick for three or four minutes. Rick was amazed by the amount of time and genuine courtesy given him by Delaney. He thought that, perhaps, he'd just been up north too long and grown accustomed to the people there and their lifestyles that rarely left any time for common courtesy to others.

"Ever since I was a kid, I've always enjoyed the Gulf," Rick said. "I learned to swim, fish, sun tan, and, in my later years, drink, right along this coastline." Delaney laughed.

"Sounds like my life," Delaney said.

| PANACEA |

Rick didn't offer the fact that his mother previously owned a timeshare in St. George or that he was once an overpaid, overworked lawyer. He enjoyed the prospect that Delaney was genuinely kind to him without knowing what he did for a living, or what his net worth was. Though Rick wasn't a millionaire, he did have some money, and potential for earning, and, besides, he relished the concept of a woman falling for him just for being himself, unlike the now countless others in Chicago who were looking to hook-up with a good earner, et cetera.

Rick chided himself for even thinking Delaney was interested in anything more than a fair tip for her waitress duties, but he couldn't help feeling he was actually very interested in her.

"St. George was my favorite place in the world," Delaney said with some apprehension.

"Really? Was?" Rick asked.

"Until a bunch of money hungry folks built time shares all over the whole island," Delaney said.

Rick was now thrilled that he didn't proffer his assets for pleasantries. He was far from being a materialist, and he delighted in her position, but now wasn't the time to explain his love of nature and the Gulf of Mexico and to rationalize his wanting a house built on its shores.

"I know you want beer and shrimp. Anything else?" Delaney ended the conversation.

"No thanks, but you are welcome to join me if your shift is nearly over," Rick said, only half-joking. Then he thought he sounded desperate, and he probably did.

Nevertheless, Delaney's smile broadened and she said, "Well, I've got four more sets and it'll probably be about forty-five minutes.

How about a drink after I get through cleaning my section?"

Rick swallowed visibly and smiled, somewhat bewildered. "Sounds good. In the meantime, I'll peel and eat."

"Great, I'll set your order." Delaney turned to walk away and then looked back, pensively. "By the way, I'm Delaney Chase," she extended her hand with confidence.

Rick rose half-way out of his seat, extended his hand, and shook hers firmly. "Rick Morrissey, Delaney." He smiled. "It's nice to be meeting friendly people again. The north can't hold a candle to the south," Rick said, reminded of how refreshing it was to be away from some of the cold-minded people he left behind in Chicago. Delaney smiled and walked away.

Rick couldn't believe the exchange that just took place and could only raise his eyebrows and look out the window over the Ochlockonee Bay with a shit-eating grin that would certainly have ended his chances of ever being taken seriously if he were caught.

Rick occasionally glanced at Delaney while she was away waiting on other tables. She was dressed in tan shorts with a cash apron wrapped around her waist and she was wearing a white Captano's tee shirt. Though she was wearing only running shoes, Rick thought she appeared tall. Her figure was attractive and her measurements were proportionate. Her physique was far from bold and Rick was astonished in himself for being so impressed with her modest features. She had all the right physical curves and features, but none of them commanded more attention than her face and eyes. With her dark hair in a pony tail, Delaney's brown eyes stood out, reflecting a kindness and sincerity in her spirit. She had a mellow expression as she walked to and from her tables; but whenever she came into contact with a customer or a co-worker, her smile appeared effortlessly and spontaneously. She was natural, affectionate and gregarious when greeting her customers. When Rick caught himself staring too long, he shook his head and tried to stare out the window which overlooked the water.

Delaney brought Rick's food and beer at the same time and politely dismissed herself from further conversation to attend to her other tables where she had fallen behind by talking to Rick earlier and then finagling the cook to add a few extra shrimp on Rick's plate.

Rick gratefully acknowledged her efforts and peeled the shrimp too delicately to be a proper southerner, but he felt like a gentleman. Delaney was busy for the next half hour and Rick got up to get his next two beers himself at the bar. Once he had finished those and the shrimp, he cleaned his hands and mouth with the extra lemons placed on the table and patiently watched and waited for Delaney to finish and join him.

Nearly an hour later, Rick was staring, smiling actually, at his fourth beer and Delaney approached him with a beer of her own and sat down. By now it was two o'clock in the afternoon and Rick was in wanderlust, if not nearly drunk. The restaurant was clearing out.

"Hi. Sorry I took so long," Delaney said. "I'm already getting teased by the cook for coming over to have a beer with you. I told him you were my cousin to fend him off."

"No problem. I'm a pretty good relative. Just ask one of my cousins," Rick said.

Delaney was still smiling. "So, where did you say you were from? Chicago?" Delaney asked.

"Kind of, I worked there for a year and a half, but I'm from a small town in Wisconsin."

"How do you know the area so well?" Delaney asked.

"I vacationed here as a kid and then spent four and a half years trying to get through undergrad at FSU. Unfortunately for my student loan balance, the beach was my favorite classroom," Rick said.

"Can't blame you there. This area is beautiful, isn't it?" Delaney said.

"Indeed," Rick said. He thought he sounded too educated and pompous. "It sure as hell is." He had gone from academic to guttural. "Shit," he thought. His mind was racing pitifully.

"Are you staying long?" Delaney asked.

"Until I find what I'm looking for." Rick responded.

"And what would that be?"

"I don't know. Fun. I guess until it's not fun anymore?" Rick said.

"Fun?" Delaney replied inquisitively.

"Yea, fun. Isn't fun the best thing to have?" Rick said.

Delaney laughed, and agreed.

The two talked on for an hour. Delaney explained how she was born to a shrimper and a commercial fisherman who was "one helluva sailor" and a good father, albeit a hard drinking one. Delaney's mom, Meredith Chase, was a southern woman and a debutante. She was elegant, refined, and a good Christian by strict Southern Baptist tradition.

Delaney continued to explain that just over ten years ago, her father, Pally Chase, had disappeared in a storm spun from Hurricane Gilbert's deadly winds. Pally had gone to help a fellow fisherman in need, named Coatie Gillen. Coatie's shrimping business had gone sour and he'd opted to cut down staff and fish for grouper and dolphin by himself. Mr. Chase provided his own boat for this particular excursion and he and Coatie were about 12 miles out in the Gulf when their last radio communication was heard. Chase had called in a distress signal and indicated that the storm had sporadically cut their instruments off, and he could only give an approximation of where he and his friend were. They had last been spotted off Alligator Point, but, because of the weather, and loss of connection from Chase's radio, the coast guard couldn't even begin its search until twelve hours later. Pally Chase and Coatie Gillen were found floating in the Gulf sound waters nearly 20 hours after Pally had radioed for help. *"My Fair Delaney,"* Chase's boat, was never found.

Rick remembered the storm well, but not its tragic effects. He told Delaney of his experience with the storm. He was in his last year of undergrad at Florida State when he and his friend, Barry Bossanova, heard about the great waves generated on the usually calm coast of Florida's panhandle. Neither of the two had ever surfed before, being from the midwest, and they saw a shining opportunity to try something new. Barry borrowed a friend's surfboard and the two skipped school to drive two hours from Tallahassee to Panama City Beach, where the waves were reported as enormous, from eight to ten foot swells. They had no idea how dangerous the sport could be for beginners.

When the two young men arrived at the Panama City Beach KOA campground convenience store to pick up the usual beach provisions, beer, ice, cheap sandwiches, and AA batteries for their walkmans, they were confronted by the store clerk.

"Ya'll fellahs don't plan on goin' out in that surf do ya?" the clerk sounded parental.

"Sure, it isn't every day you can surf on the Gulf. Why?" Rick replied.

"Three people were eaten by sharks at the cement pier just yesterday," said the clerk. "Surf boards look just like a seal lunch to those hungry tiger sharks in a hurricane," she finished.

"Yea, right, you old bag of bones," Barry responded under his breath but with enough volume that the clerk thought she heard Barry right.

"I ain't shitten' ya boys, it's in today's paper. Look," the clerk held up the morning telegraph and the day's headline: "Shark attacks two surfers and a pair of scuba divers." The shark, or sharks, had spared the life of one of the scuba divers, but ate the entire bodies of the other three individuals, leaving behind only the surfboards and scuba gear.

Barry became concerned, but Rick had always been cavalier in the face of danger. "Well, I guess that means the shark is full, having left behind one of those guys. We'll be surfin' today," Rick said. Barry could only nod in silence. It wasn't cool to look afraid in front of his death-defying friend. The two headed for the beach at cement pier.

When they got to the beach, they were both relieved to see as many as 30 other guys as reckless as they, all out there surfing and ignoring the threats of mother nature, animal and mineral. Rick decided to go first. Wanting to prove his courage to Barry, he grabbed the surf board and headed out to the sea. Rick fought the waves trying to get out to the main swells for twenty minutes. Dejected and frustrated, he came back to shore. "I don't know how those guys get out there. I'm fighting the waves and the current and can't get out 30 yards; even trying to go under the waves doesn't work," Rick told Barry.

"I think that going out alongside the pier helps break up the wave force. Look at how these other guys are doing it," Barry instructed Rick.

"You try, I'm beat," Rick responded.

Barry took the board and fought his way out into the surf alongside the pier and some well-wishing surfers. "Hey poser, hey buddy, keep it up! First time on a board? Follow us," came the surfers' replies. To them, Rick and Barry were beginners, or "posers" as the surfers liked to say.

Barry made it out and began to surf, sort of. A wave did, in fact, take his board and carry it back to shore, but Barry was not on it. He had forgotten to latch the ankle strap and the waves threw him and the board in different directions. Barry didn't seem to mind and came rushing into shore and to Rick with a childlike enthusiasm.

"Man, you got to try this, that was a rush!" Barry exclaimed.

"Okay," Rick said as he thought he could at least do what Barry did.

Rick grabbed the board and headed out along the pier while Barry lit up a Pall Mall non-filtered cigarette and opened a beer. The waves were powerful. They reminded Rick of the current generated in an above ground circular pool he and his friends would swim in as children. Five or six kids would walk the perimeters of a three feet deep circular pool for several minutes until a manmade whirlpool was created. Then they would turn around and try to walk in the opposite direction, which was usually impossible for a few seconds.

Fighting the heavy current successfully, Rick made it out nearly

100 yards off shore and began the wait for the big wave. It was exhilarating to consider all of the variables. Here was a beginner surfer, on top of hurricane generated swells. Rick considered the ominous look of each approaching wave, gently lowering Rick and his surfboard below sea level and then back on top of the swell, all without the waves cresting. Rick considered what he must look like to a shark from underneath. A torpedo shaped body with little arms draped over the board. A seal. "Shit," Rick said to himself as he brought his arms out of the water and held them behind his back. "Please don't let me get eaten," he prayed.

Before too long the wave had appeared. Rick saw it coming from thirty yards away and knew that it would begin to crest at Rick's position in the water. Rick maneuvered the board so that the head would face the shore and he paddled gently to allow the wave to meet his momentum. The dark colored wave drove silently into Rick, with a deadly swiftness. Rick felt the rush and he placed his hands on the edge of the board to prepare to get on his hands and knees with the hope of standing on the board. The wave boosted Rick up and he performed as well as any amateur. He made it to his hands and knees and felt the power of the wave's thrust. It began to crest and white caps showered Rick and the board. Rick went to stand on the board and realized for the first time that he couldn't see. The salt water was spraying him copiously. He did stand up for just over a second before the wave pounded him back down. The mighty wave rushed over Rick with a tremulous force and violence and Rick first realized he was ten feet under water when the board was thrust up behind him and cracked him on the back of the head. He'd thought his life was over. Spinning in the undertow, with his head bleeding, Rick wondered how he could've forgot about this danger in the wake of considering shark attacks. He spun in circles two or three times and crashed on the sand below. He was still alive. All he had to do was find which way was up. Just when he felt his held breath about to give, he surfaced.

Shaken, Rick thrashed into shore to find Barry with the headphones on and eyes shut, enjoying the beach music. Rick bumped him.

"Hey, man, that was great!" Rick lied. "But I'm done, how about relaxing for a while?"

Barry nodded, and they didn't surf again.

At Captano's, Rick described his experience in the storm and with surfing much to Delaney's delight. Barry Bossanova never graduated college, but went on to make it big in boat sales. Rick spoke of his most recent career change, which was from lawyer to layman. Delaney was particularly interested in Rick's sometimes comical tales of practicing law in a big city. Rick was intrigued by her interest. She was only twenty-one and yet her curiosity was stunning considering the fact that she'd never been involved in the court system, except to settle her father's estate, Rick presumed. Rick talked about lawyer jokes and how a large majority of lawyers have earned all the reputations described in them. Other lawyers had tried to bribe him, he'd been winked at by judges ruling in his favor, sexually assaulted by female clients in the middle of a divorce he was handling, and offered illegal gifts of drugs for legal services from clients, some of whom were not even criminal defendant clients. Though Rick didn't cross ethical boundaries, he was still disappointed with the lack of consciousness of the lawyers and upper class, and he was not satisfied with the career. He even felt unethical for being a part of the whole picture, though he didn't participate in it.

Delaney was soft-spoken, but described her very happy and meaningful formative years. When her father died, she was only ten years old. She explained to Rick that she lived with her mother and grandmother until she was seventeen. Her grandmother had left to be in a life-care nursing home in Atlanta when Delaney turned 18. According to Delaney, her mom was spending every autumn with her mother's older sister in Atlanta, since the death of Pally. Delaney was lying about her mother because she didn't want to get into the mental instability and heartbreaking episodes of Meredith Chase's daily life, which not only included depression, but schizophrenia. In fact, Meredith Chase hadn't resided in Panacea for nearly a decade.

Delaney began waiting tables when she was eighteen and bounced around with her high school friends from party to party, usually college parties at FSU. She grew up after a couple years of irresponsibility and decided on college. She was studying to be an elementary education teacher. Delaney had a lot of freedom and was an only child. Their conversation went from meaningful to playful.

"Aren't bars and restaurants amazing places to work?" Rick said.

"Yes, except when you wait on women, they never tip. Except, maybe, they tip for good looking male servers," Delaney said, correcting herself.

"I bartended for six years to get through school. I think my degree should have been in the study of dipsomania."

"That's quite a word, the art of craving drinks all the time," Delaney responded, as she demonstrated an understanding of vocabulary beyond what Rick knew at her age.

"Okay, I tried to stump you. You win. What the hell is a bumbershoot?" Rick had acquiesced to his better read companion and could tell Delaney relished the compliment. "You threw that one at me earlier, and I'm a little out of practice in southern slang."

"Bumbershoot is southern for umbrella," Delaney said. "But you probably knew that. You're just putting me on."

"Sure I am," Rick said, smiling. "And I would have thrown mine in the back of my car if I'd have thought about bringing one, or known what one was." They both laughed. "Actually, I should have bought one when I arrived in Tallahassee since there were some pretty heavy thunderstorms all over the south," Rick said.

"You mean thunder boomers?" Delaney said smiling.

"You know what? I did mean thunder boomers! I actually learned that word when I lived down here," Rick said, feeling relieved he hadn't forgotten all of the southern regionalisms he had previously acquired.

"So you flew down?" Delaney asked.

"Yes, it wasn't bad really, except we had to layover in Atlanta," Rick said.

"Ah, Atlanta. My mom always said if you want to get to heaven or hell from the south, you had to go through Atlanta," Delaney said, referring to Delta Airlines main hub in Atlanta and the fact that they were the major carrier for Tallahassee travelers. Most airline passengers serviced by Delta in the south were required to layover Atlanta before continuing on to a final destination.

Rick smiled at her. "I think your mother was right because, for me, it's hell going back home to Chicago and its heaven being here on the coast." Delaney laughed and raised her bottle to Rick's. They toasted and each took a drink.

"I bet you probably got a lot of tips from women when you were a bartender," she said.

Rick appreciated the compliment and thanked her, but disputed that women tipped him any better. "I think the only tip I got from them was that no two women drink the same drink at the same time. I think I ran ten miles a night from the blender to the beer cooler."

"Well, don't worry about me," Delaney said. "I'm pretty much a beer girl. Though an occasional daiquiri isn't bad." she smiled.

"That's just fine," Rick said. "Maybe I can make one for you sometime."

"You can try, but I'm pretty particular," Delaney said, smiling.

"Particular?" Rick responded. "I can make a daiquiri that'll freeze your lips, frost your gums and give your tongue a sleigh ride." Delaney laughed at Rick's remark. "You know, Delaney, we're about the last ones here," Rick said.

"Not for long," Delaney said. "The dinner crowd will be pouring in soon. Would you like to take our beers out on the deck over the water to let these folks clean up?"

"Good idea," Rick responded.

They went out the french doors at the rear of the restaurant and sat in wicker rocking chairs under the overhang of the porch and its twenty year old ceiling fans. "We come out here after work sometimes and drink beer 'til four in the morning," Delaney said.

"I remember the service industry days that way too. I never drank so much, nor spent so much cash and couldn't show anything for it," Rick said. "This is really great, though. Thanks for joining me. I always tell people back home that southerners are different. There's a genuineness to them you can't find in Chicago," he said, and he meant it.

They spent an hour on the deck and Rick, not wanting to overkill the extraordinary feeling he had inside, told Delaney he had some things to tend to back in Tallahassee.

"I've enjoyed it. Too bad you have to go. Probably see you next time I'm working?" Delaney asked.

Rick was now wondering if he should have offered to leave so soon. Delaney walked him to the front door of the restaurant and, as he left, he could hear Delaney's co-workers whistling and jostling Delaney. He blushed on his way to the car and replayed the entire lunch in his mind over and over on the way back to Tallahassee. Rick dined at Captano's again three days later and got up the nerve to ask Delaney to lunch away from her work place.

She accepted.

8

Rick and Delaney's first lunch date was veiled in platonic surroundings at Sharpe's Café in downtown Tallahassee on Friday. Delaney planned to introduce Rick to some lawyers and lobbyists she'd waited on at Captano's to help Rick land some type of job before his money ran out. Law may not have been his first choice, but an experienced attorney is paid well and Rick could make most of his own hours, provided he got the work done. In Tallahassee, any legal service Rick would perform would have to be behind the scenes as the Florida Bar Association frowned upon lawyers who did legal work in the state without being admitted to their Bar.

Rick and Delaney dined at the upper class Sharpe's Café which was located near the Capitol Building. It was elegant and ostentatious, and, by admission, not Rick nor Delaney's type of hang out. However, it was where all the political clout hung out. The brass of Tallahassee could be spotted here or at Barker's tavern just a stone's throw away. In either place, the lobbyists and legislators could be found absorbing their favorite single malt whiskeys and martinis, along with each other's egos. Delaney knew several of the men from Captano's. She was unaware of any women who held similar positions of power. Seldom could one spot a female legislator or lobbyist in this Florida city which was virtually a southern Georgia town, being only 25 miles from the Georgia border.

| PANACEA |

Although Tallahassee was Florida, no one could tell with its beautiful swaying pines, rolling hills, and cypress trees. Tallahassee was not what someone would consider Florida; it was still in the Old South, replete with antebellum homes and confederate era architecture for its government buildings. Most pick-up trucks had confederate flags hanging from the rear window and the town's black citizens still seemed oppressed, but they appeared much kinder and more sincere than northern blacks, an irony Rick never quite understood when he had lived in Tallahassee. Not many buildings in the capital could be considered modern in architecture, whether built a hundred years ago or the night before last, as the town takes pride in its southern heritage.

Rick was introduced to a state representative nick-named "Buddy Bear" who was from Pensacola. Buddy particularly took a liking to Rick's knowledge of the law and apparent interest in Delaney. Rick never got the Congressman's real name, but Buddy Bear was a friend of Delaney's father and had been on vacation with the Chase family just two years before Pally Chase disappeared. Buddy was the family's best friend during the loss of Mr. Chase and he'd been a mainstay of family support since the hurricane. Buddy introduced Rick to a lobbyist named William Barute. Within an instant, Rick knew he didn't like Barute.

Billy Barute was an obese man who was smoking Cuban cigars and double fisting scotch on the rocks when he was first pointed out to Rick. He had an inimical spirit and was boisterous in conversation. He set one of his drinks down on the bar upon introduction.

"Billy, this is Rick. . ." Buddy paused. "What's your last name again son?"

"Hi, Sir. Rick Morrissey." Rick responded with confidence and an extended hand.

"Rick's a fine young attorney sent down from Chicago by the cold weather. Ain't that right Rick?" Buddy said, chortling.

"I guess he's right," Rick smiled, and continued. "What do you do? (besides ingest pizzas)," Rick said and thought as he examined the man's waist line and met him again at eye level.

"I'm the damnest lobbyist this side of the Mason-Dixon line, old boy," came Billy's response. "The 'Terminator!'" Barute bellowed, laughing to himself and looking around for support, none of which was apparent. "Do ya'll sombitches even have lobbyists in Chicago or do ya just pander to the minorities, environmentalists, and special interest groups without considering the consequences?" Billy was in his usual, garrulous form. Rick knew now why he didn't like him.

Rick smiled at Barute's mordant remark though he personally resented it. "Republican dickhead," Rick thought. He then said out loud, "Shoot, I don't reckon I can answer that one Billy, uh, Sir, I'm not a lobbyist like you, never really knew what 'dem rascals do." Rick's sarcasm and fake southern accent went over the good ole boy's head.

"You're not a Democrat are ya, boy?" Billy chuckled, his belly continuing to shimmer after he spoke.

"Not only am I Democrat, I'm a yellow dog one. You know there's really not much difference in a Democrat and a Republican. Mostly, we all want the same things, economic growth, security, international expansion, and individual liberty. It's just that Democrats are set apart by compassion," Rick stated, as if a candidate for the House of Representatives.

"Naw, you old tree huggers never understood economics or,

especially, individual liberties," Billy said. "Take the Second Amendment for instance. You think guns kill people. Hell, ever'one knows that people kill people. . . and deer, and coyotes, and lots of pests we don't need in our society."

Rick paused, knowing he shouldn't speak his mind in a strange crowd, but deciding differently. "Well I agree that guns don't kill people," he paused, "they just make it a whole lot easier."

The two exchanged intellectual barbs until Rick grew tired of the conversation. "You know, my grandfather always told me there's not much difference between a Republican and a rooster," Rick said.

"What do you say, boy?" Barute said, still enjoying the clever repartee of which Barute thought he was the center.

"Well, a Republican's a lot like a rooster."

"Go on, son, what's you're punch line."

"Well, we all know a rooster is a fowl thing." Rick paused.

"Yes, what's your point." Barute said, smiling with arrogance.

"And just like a rooster, he'll fight his father, fuck his mother, eat shit, and vote Republican." Barute's smile left his face. Rick was out of line. He had remembered the quote from his grandfather who'd said the same line on numerous occasions in Calida area bars when he was out campaigning for local candidates. Most of such "campaigning" consisted only of sitting around a bar and speaking lines that could only be forgiven by the influence of alcohol.

"Boy, you're the damnest fool I've had the pleasure to meet. How bout a drink on me?" Barute laughed loudly and seemed amused, though Rick thought he shouldn't have been.

Rick was suspicious of Billy. He had that used car salesman aura about him and topped it off with a little insurance man's stuffiness. He even emanated a body odor that repulsed Rick. Rick was actually trying to offend the large man and couldn't do it. He rarely underestimated people and this time he overestimated, or so he thought.

After lunch, Rick and Delaney went for a Heineken beer at Tycoon's Tavern, a basement bar on Copeland Street. They had every intention of getting drunk. When they arrived, they ordered their beers and took their free spin of the bar's signature color wheel for complimentary drinks. They each won another import when the arrow landed on the color green. "Auspicious," Rick said out loud as he looked at Delaney. They both laughed in recalling that the color green is typically associated with the word "horny" to most adolescents, and some adults. Their laughter was almost childlike as their facial expressions and mental impressions mirrored one another.

Unknown to the beaming twosome, one of Barute's guests from Sharpe's café walked into the bar and ensconced himself into a corner booth and discreetly observed the two.

Rick introduced Delaney to Snowshoes from the north, a drink consisting of peppermint schnapps and brandy. They drank shooters of Snowshoes and chased them back with small glasses of beer. While playing darts, Delaney impressed Rick with her flare for the game and her sometimes unbelievable luck. Rick thought about kissing Delaney during the games after the high-fives had become commonplace, but he had the composure and good sense to wait for a better moment.

Between throws at the dart board, Rick, buzzing from the alcohol, inquired about Delaney's father's demise. "So, was your father out there without a good radio?" he asked.

"It was a brand new radio, but it just wasn't working in the storm," Delaney said.

Delaney described her father over a draft beer. He was a strong southern Democrat who had much more depth than Delaney initially led on. He was a fisherman by trade, but a firebrand by the grace of God, promoting the preservation of the natural landscape and protecting the less fortunate. During the Reagan presidency, Pally Chase had become active in Panacea city government and, later, Wakulla County government. Mr. Chase's commercial fishing business had taken a turn for the worse when then Florida Governor Marshall Rodriguez announced a plan to open bidding for companies to drill for oil off the Gulf Coast, from Panacea to Pensacola. Most of the contracts previously went to Copperhead Oil Company for their bids to drill off the Atlantic coastline. The governor had already allowed oil companies to spot check the continental shelf in the Gulf of Mexico several miles off the panhandle for potential drilling sites, including Copperhead. Pally knew he could manage to get by on his own, but several other smaller fishing businesses approached him hoping his bigger business influence would carry some clout in the Florida legislature, and even in Washington, in trying to stop the drilling by big companies like Copperhead.

Chase had never set foot inside City Hall at Crawfordville, the county seat of Wakulla County, Florida, until October of 1986. At that time Pally had been persuaded to attend a town meeting where the council was discussing the drilling proposals and a voter initiative sponsored by the Republican party platform to permit oil drilling in hopes of bringing the almighty tax dollars and jobs to the county. It wasn't as if Panacea couldn't use the work or the money. In fact, the county's unemployment rate was seventeen percent, drastically higher than the national average of six percent. However, most of the people there who didn't work, didn't want to. They enjoyed life in their mobile homes and secured money through odd fishing and construction work. Most of them were content with their money, considering they didn't report much of their income to the government. This, of course, was in addition to the supplemental income they received from social security and the department of employment security.

Nevertheless, the virtue of blocking the oil drilling rested upon prevention of the risk that the drilling could pollute the Emerald coast for generations to come with just one oil spill or explosion. It was too much for the fishermen to contemplate and, unfortunately, there weren't enough tourists dollars coming to the county since Panacea, as well as most of Wakulla County, was a fishing coast, bereft of white sandy beaches and condominiums. Yet, Chase had the rest of the coastline to argue about and the possibility that multi-million dollar properties closer to Panama City and Destin could be eliminated. While this didn't involve Wakulla County, it did affect the overall scheme of the Florida panhandle. A huge imbroglio erupted over the controversy with Pally Chase and the mayor of Crawfordville as sparring partners.

Harold Baker was the mayor of Crawfordville, and he was a conservative. Chase, along with his friends and colleagues, simply called the mayor a cheating bastard. Mayor Baker had once sold his family's estate, near Shadeville in Wakulla county and held for generations, to a toxic waste disposal company without regret. Baker made over a million dollars in the single transaction, bilking his own relatives out of their fair share. Though his fellow citizens resented him for it, they revered the man for his power and influence in the county. At city hall, Baker was the man to be reckoned with.

In his first public speech, Mr. Chase challenged the commission and Mayor Baker over the prospect of destroying wildlife and the coastline by supporting initiatives for drilling. According to Delaney, her father's speech was from the heart and, with five hundred vociferous citizens of Wakulla County in attendance supporting Pally, it struck home. After Pally's presentation of the consequences of oil drilling, Ted Robinson, a septuagenarian friend of Chase and former World War II veteran, stood up and played "America the Beautiful" on his trumpet. The whole audience began singing,

> Oh, beautiful for spacious skies, for amber waves of grain,
> for purple mountain's majesty, above thy fruited plains,
> America! America! God shed his grace on thee!
> And crown thy good, with brotherhood, from *sea* to shining *sea!*

They had emphasized the word "sea" and the initiative was tabled indefinitely.

Later that same night, Mr. Chase had gone out to Posey's Oyster Bar in St. Marks, a twenty minute drive from Panacea, and was two sheets to the wind on draft beer when he was approached by a strange man in a lightweight barn jacket. "He looked like city," Delaney remembered her father saying. He had asked Mr. Chase if this was the kind of behavior he planned on maintaining the rest of his life, or if he would turn to reason and support an opportunity for the great expansion of his hometown and fellow residents of the panhandle.

Drunk as he was, Pally Chase had his wits about him and told the man, "As long as I'm eatin' oysters and gettin' my cock hard, you'd might as well know what I think. Tonight, I'm goin' home to make love to my wife and tomorrow and the next day and the day after that I'm going fishin'. And if any fool son of a bitch tries to get in my way or the way of the good people of this village, I'll shove a lobster trap so far up his ass he'll need a pitchfork and a tractor pull to sit on the toilet again. And that particularly includes government snobs who wear barn jackets into the Florida Panhandle!"

Apparently, the man had never been talked to like that, except perhaps on Capitol Hill by superior lawmakers and lobbyists. The man looked around nervously, then collected what dignity he could and left the bar. The police never bothered to follow-up on who the man was as they merely wrote him off as someone sent by the government to check things out.

After Delaney and Rick had consumed their share of beer and tropical shooters at Tycoon's Tavern, they decided to end their night. Fighting their way through the now crowded bar, Rick led the way and reached back for Delaney's hand. She accepted and Rick felt a numbness run up his spine. When they got outside, they embraced the night air walking side-by- side. It was a warm 72 degrees and the night was beautiful. Rick started the conversation.

"Well, it's about ten o'clock, should we call it a night?" Rick asked.

"I guess we probably should," Delaney said, with disappointment in her voice which matched Rick's. Rick knew the relationship could be pursued at that moment, but instead he pulled back and walked Delaney to her car. She felt the same electricity between the two as Rick did, but only proffered him a kiss on the cheek before getting into her white Jeep Wrangler. With the top and windows down, Delaney started her car and asked Rick if he wanted to have lunch the next day.

"Well, it would be my pleasure to collect you and treat you to lunch, my fair Delaney," Rick said with some Civil War accent akin to Rhett Butler and quoting the name of Pally's favorite fishing boat. "May I gather you from your homestead tomorrow around noon?" he finished, embarrassing himself.

"Why certainly, Sir, you are, indeed, a gentleman of measure," Delaney said in her best Scarlett O'hara, which was far better than Rick's impression of Rhett. Delaney gave Rick directions and they parted ways for the evening.

9

The next morning, Rick woke-up without a hangover and questioned whether he was still drunk because he felt numb. He hopped into his rented convertible around 11 a.m. and headed from downtown Tallahassee to Panacea. Following Route 98 to Bottoms Road just a mile outside of Panacea, Rick traveled east to Plantation road where Delaney had instructed him to turn up the hill. As he traveled further into the rural area, the roadside convenience stores and wood-framed houses gave way to a bosky landscape replete with woodlands and grasslands as far as the eye could see.

"Plantation Road," Rick mused out loud. He wondered if Delaney did, in fact, live on a plantation. He was curious to find out whether the abode of his interest was a trailer home or perhaps just a normal house on a regal sounding road.

As he crested the hill of Plantation Road, he was greeted with a broken stone gate entrance to a brick drive which offered the only direction he could continue. There was no mistake about Delaney's upbringing when Rick saw the only house in sight for miles. About an eighth of a mile up the brick driveway was a large antebellum home and Delaney's version of Scarlett was quite easy to believe now. Rick stopped his car. At first he felt trepidation at the thought of courting a southern belle, though Delaney didn't act like one. Rick had never been too impressed with high society and vice versa, but his experience with Delaney taught him that she couldn't be any different from what she had led him to believe.

The house stood behind two gigantic Spanish Moss trees. The home was magnificent with six columns running along the front veranda. The meadows beyond the house were full of unadulterated fields of grass and trees, mostly Spanish Moss and pines, replete with birds chirping and flying on the warm wind. The rest of the property was void of other buildings or man made structures. As Rick began the final ascent up the drive, he realized the mansion was run down, with the white paint on the side of the home chipping and the yard poorly manicured. Rick was feeling a little more at ease, considering the present state of the home. Certainly it was worth a lot of money, but it seemed to Rick that there was no money to restore the home to its original grace.

Rick parked the car out in front of the porch and was quickly greeted by a black Labrador Retriever, with a friendly bark, wagging tail, and childlike curiosity toward its newest visitor. Rick loved dogs, but never owned one of his own. He greeted the young dog and wrestled with it as though they had been college roommates. Delaney, hearing the commotion, emerged from the house and watched from her veranda the two mammals frolicking in the front yard. By the time Rick looked up, he saw Delaney sitting on a porch rocker with a glass of sweetened iced tea, simply smiling.

"Hey," Rick said.

"Hey," Came her soft, smiling reply. "I should warn you, he smells awful."

"Are you referring to me or the dog?" Rick asked.

"Oh, sorry about that. I'm talking about that smelly thing you're befriending. He's been outside all day."

"So, this is your dog?" Rick asked, still playing with the Labrador.

"Yes, and my roommate, boyfriend and best friend," Delaney replied. "So don't go getting any ideas about winning his loyalty."

"Well, actually, ma'am, the law out in these here unpopulated parts says that finder's keepers, and it's obvious this dog is mine for a day," Rick said. Delaney laughed. "What's his name?"

"Southpaw," Delaney said.

"That's fitting, he a southern dog and he has paws, I assume that's where you got it," Rick said.

"Good try Yankee," Delaney said. "You know what 'assume' does, don't you?"

"Yea, yea," Rick said. "It makes an ass out of you and me. So, we're both asses. How do you like that." Delaney raised both her eyebrows, smiled and tilted her head in response. Rick continued. "My next guess is that he's left handed."

"Actually, you're getting warmer. My father named his fishing boat after me, '*My Fair Delaney*,' as you know, and he named his ketch rig after himself, sort of. It was a beautiful twenty-eight foot sailboat my dad owned when I was a child. Dad called it '*Southpaw*' because dad was left handed, much like you as I observed from your eating style when you came into the restaurant. And, of course, dad was my 'Paw.'"

Rick was impressed by Delaney's observation that he was left-handed and flattered that she was noticing things about him so early in what he now considered a southern form of spooning, or courtship.

"So, when I got him four years ago, I named him 'Southpaw,'" she concluded.

"I think that's a nice tribute," Rick said.

"He's a great dog. Always thinks he's on a squirrel hunt, looking everywhere from under the house to under the trees," Delaney said. "You know when he finds something though, 'cause he barks like crazy until I come out, rub his belly, and tell him what a good boy he is."

"Can't blame him there," Rick said.

Delaney offered Rick some tea and an invitation to the porch chair next to her. She was wearing a white cotton sun dress and, as she stood, Rick noticed the translucence of the dress as the sun from behind the home penetrated the fabric in the areas her body didn't fill. The gentle breeze from behind Delaney further accented the sun's discovery. Her physique was modest and beautiful. To Rick, she was breathtakingly beautiful, though she was dressed so plainly. Rick approached the porch and told her how attractive she looked, especially in the sunlight.

"What do you mean, do I need to rely on this light to impress your eye?" Delaney flirted. "Hardly, you're quite the vision in most surroundings. You probably wake up looking like this and piss off the rest of the female population," Rick said. Delaney laughed and thanked Rick while she blushed. Delaney excused herself and went inside to get some iced tea. They sat on the front porch for twenty minutes and reminisced about the old days in which their parents were reared and how life had become a little more complicated for their own generation. They didn't bother discussing the fact that Rick's age group started generation 'X' while Delaney's was one of the last to be admitted. They were over ten years apart yet related on a personal level that did not acknowledge or even recognize time.

Without offering to show Rick the house, Delaney said she was hungry and ready for a big lunch. Rick escorted her to his car and they left the house and dog behind.

Delaney had Rick drive by some of the sights of Panacea and the surrounding villages and it was one thirty in the afternoon when they pulled into Posey's Topless Oyster Bar off Route 363 near St. Marks. Rick had been there as a college student and knew that the only thing topless there was the oysters. Posey's was an entirely unassuming dive for a bar, which served great seafood and offered live music all day Friday and Saturday. When they walked into the restaurant/oyster bar, the familiar sound of Jimmy Buffett was being played by a fairly talented young black man on an acoustic guitar without accompaniment.

"He's pretty good," Rick whispered to Delaney, as if the bar were a library.

"Sam? Yea, he's played here for two years," Delaney said out loud, and loud enough for Sam to hear and nod to Delaney with a smile.

"You must be a regular," Rick said.

"Well, sort of; my father had brought me in here first when I was six years old, then my grandfather took me after my father died, so, if fifteen years makes someone a regular, I'm her," Delaney said with a smile and a confidence of belonging.

Posey's reminded Rick of Vince Planet's bar only to the extent that ties were definitely not allowed in here; as evidenced by the fact that hundreds of them lined the upper walls of Posey's entry area where violators of the "no ties" policy were greeted with a pair of scissors and a thumb tack for their ties. Clearly, if a patron wasn't here to drink beer and suck oysters, he could just high tail it north back to Tallahassee. Other than this philosophical similarity, Posey's was nothing like Vince Planet's. At Posey's, the decor was fishing, neon beer signs, and car racing. The entire building was surrounded with tens of thousands of empty oyster shells, serving both to promote the aesthetics and as gravel for the parking lot. Hell, it beat the cost of throwing out hundreds of pounds of trash each day and, somehow, it made Rick feel comfortable.

There was no hostess to seat patrons at the oyster bar, and the two went straight for the only open seating in the place. Seating at Posey's consisted of bar stools and unstained wooden picnic tables. Rick and Delaney chose an empty table near the stage. After sitting down, Rick commented that it was perfect, and Delaney agreed.

The waitress brought a bucket of five Coronas and took the couple's order. "A pile of oysters on the half shell and some fried crab claws," Delaney ordered. "That should be enough for starters, don't you think?" she said. Rick nodded with a smile. He opened their beers and the two drank straight from the bottles.

"When I used to come here in college, the guy who played guitar would sometimes make me sing Buffett songs with him because I would be singing so loudly from my bar stool. I was crazy about Buffett then, one of the first parrotheads," Rick said.

"Was? You don't like Buffett anymore?" Delaney asked, sounding disappointed.

"Well, I love the music still, just the image and the thought of losing the innocence of discovering his music only to lose it to millions of other fans has kind of left me disillusioned," Rick said. "So, I quit going to concerts and decided just to listen to the music from my CD player. I still think it's some of the best," Rick completed his defense.

Delaney responded, "You know what? Me, too. The concerts, I mean. Actually, I was still enjoying the party atmosphere of the concerts, but it was beginning to take 45 minutes in line just to get a beer, so I've moved on. Hey, you ought to do a song with Sam, he always has people come up on stage with him and embarrass themselves," Delaney said.

"What do you mean, 'embarrass themselves,' don't you think I can sing?" Rick asked.

"Of course I think you can," she lied. "I was just kidding." Delaney was about laughing now and she hollered to Sam, who was on a break with a beer at the bar, "Hey Sam, we got another sucke... uh, singer!"

"No, we don't, Sam, thanks though, you're doing just fine," Rick interrupted, embarrassed.

Sam Chesterfield walked over to the couple with a smile on his face. He appeared to be in his mid to late twenties. He was scrawny, yet handsome. His big, white toothed smile emitting from his dark caramel-colored skin was contagious. As he began to introduce himself to Rick, he stopped cold, recognizing the face from years ago. "Say, aren't you a Delta Omega from Florida State?" Sam asked.

"How'd you know?" Rick was surprised.

"My cousin is Eddie Chesterfield." Sam was animated. "You sang with his band at your frat house parties. I was the 16 year old pussy who couldn't keep his drinks down," he said.

"No kidding?" Rick paused. "Oh, yea, I remember," Rick said, remembering the scrawny black kid who vomited in Eddie Chesterfield's room seemingly every Friday night during Rick's senior year. "How's your cousin?"

"Oh, he's quit the music business and decided to be vice-president of a bank in Apopka," Sam said.

"Well, I didn't know you could just decide to be a bank vice-president. If I'd have known that, I be one myself." Rick humored Sam.

"Shit man, it's nice to see a blast from the past. Man, I remember my cousin telling me you got lai. . ." he paused embarrassed, and corrected himself, "laughs from all the girls."

Delaney noticed the slight of words. Rick looked at Sam hoping for a smooth transition out of his college years.

"Shit, man, what are you doing now?" Sam inquired.

"Just enjoying the panhandle of Florida, and your friend Delaney Chase," Rick said, looking to Delaney for her response, which appeared to be a perfunctory smile.

"Can't blame you there, on either count, they're both attractive pieces of real estate," Sam said.

"Sam!, you're terrible." Delaney slapped him playfully and turned her attention to Rick. "So, you're holding out on me, you can sing?" she asked Rick.

"Yes and no. I sing, but not pleasingly for other's ears," Rick said. "Unless I'm in the car singing with the CD player turned up full blast. Then, for some reason I can't explain, I sound just like the guy singing."

Delaney laughed. "I think we all sound great when the radio is loud. Come on, Rick, for me, will you do just one song?" Delaney pleaded with a playful expression.

Rick thought to himself and then said out loud, "Well, this could just be the biggest embarrassment for me in front of you, so if you'll promise to continue lunch with me afterward, I guess I can do it for you." Rick thought that if she accepted his singing, she just might be the most fantastic girl he'd ever met. Delaney raised one eyebrow, nodded and smiled.

"Great, I'm ready now, Rick," Sam said. "But I'm tired of my Buffett medley, and I think the crowd is too. You can only take so many versions of 'Margaritaville' before you have a hang-over without drinking a drop of alcohol. How about Van Morrison?"

"Is this guy reading my mind, or what?" Rick said to Delaney. Delaney continued to smile and Rick headed up to the small, makeshift stage. Sam started picking and introduced "Ragin' Rick" from FSU to the 20 or so people in the bar, mostly FSU fans, which comforted Rick. "He's a ragin' 'Nole!" Sam said into the mike. Sam leaned toward Rick and asked if he knew "Brown Eyed Girl." Rick did, and grabbed Sam's back-up microphone.

Rick sang the song with Sam's back-up vocals and three of the couples from the bar got up and danced on the restaurant floor before them. Rick was flush through the whole number but he retained some dignity by remembering all of the words to the song. He was almost beside himself as he hit nearly every high note and stayed in tune, with Sam's help, for most of the song. He only looked at Delaney once, which was during the line "our hearts were thumping, with you, my brown eyed girl." Their eye contact was electric, and Delaney's own brown eyes were smiling with her. The song finished with a guitar solo by Sam and the crowd of 20 cheered like 200. Rick thought they were merely patronizing him, or humoring Sam, but he didn't care. At the song's end, Rick leaned forward into the microphone and said in his best Elvis Presley, "Uh, thank you, thank you very mucccch." The crowd cheered and laughed and Rick headed back to his seat with Delaney. She was all smiles and Rick felt a happy moisture welling in his eyes, but warded off the elation. He proffered a funny face with a sunken lower lip and sat down across from Delaney.

"That was fun!" Delaney said. "You're a blast, what other songs can you sing?" Delaney was genuinely curious.

"That's the only one, but I wasn't really singing, Sam put the compact disc on the speakers and I was just lip synching," Rick said.

"You sounded so good, I could almost believe it." Delaney continued to compliment. Rick thought for a moment about Sam's cousin, Eddie Chesterfield. Eddie was the first black pledge at Delta Omega who wasn't ousted by the members before his turn at brotherhood initiation. Rick recalled with melancholy the speech he had made on behalf of Eddie to keep him in the fraternity when many of the white brothers didn't want a black man in the house, other than the chef. It was Rick's first stand in life where he chose the unpopular position because it was the right one. He had single-handedly convinced the membership to keep a kind and sincere black man included in an all-white fraternity purely by the power of persuasive oral rhetoric. It was after that speech that Rick had first been encouraged to pursue law or some form of public speaking as a career. He never regretted the speech, but had oftentimes rued the occupation that sprung from it.

The atmosphere of Posey's bar never settled down after the Van Morrison number; and Delaney and Rick shared a lively conversation over beer, oysters, fried Gulf crab claws, and hot boiled shrimp as more customers came into the bar.

"Wow, I haven't felt so good in here since my dad used to bring me with his fishing buddies. They were a riot. Thank you, Rick," Delaney said. "I really enjoy being with you." Delaney was sincere, and Rick was pleased by her sentiment.

"I enjoy you, Delaney," Rick responded.

After eating seafood and drinking beer for two and a half hours, Delaney and Rick left Posey's and headed for Delaney's house. They'd had a terrific lunch together and enjoyed the sun drenched twenty minute ride back to Delaney's. They were both a little buzzed from the beer and the company they were sharing with one another. The conversation on the way home never ceased. They were realizing how much they each had in common. Naturally, music was an easy topic. Delaney liked just about everything, including some rap music.

"Oh, you like crap, I mean rap music?" Rick teased as Delaney punched him softly in the shoulder. Rick told her some of his favorites. "I like most everything, too. Old and new stuff, like Van Morrison, Buffett's old tunes, of course, then Neil Diamond, Pink Floyd, Dean Martin on occasions, and basically any song you can sing along to. Then of course, there's album rock of the late seventies, the eighties, then the current stuff like Dave Matthews Band, Train, and then there's country music, Dixie Chicks. . ."

Rick was droning on like a broken record himself when Delaney interjected, "Oh, I love Christmas music."

Rick stopped delineating his play list. "I do, too!" he exclaimed.

"Even in July!" Delaney continued.

"Me, too!" Rick said. They were confidently buzzed. "How

do you get into liking winter songs in the Sunshine State?"

"It's easy, we probably miss the snow more than you yankees who get too much of it." Delaney said. "Besides, our beaches are so white, it looks like snow."

"Ah, yes," Rick said. "I get it. It's like, 'Dashing through the sand, trying hard to get a tan, wondering where I am, singing a song without a plan!" Rick paused. Delaney laughed. "Damn, I suck at writing songs," Rick said.

"You're funny," Delaney said. "In fact, I like all the artists you named except I haven't heard Dean Martin," Delaney said. Rick looked at Delaney mischievously, and said, "Sure you have. You know," and he began to bellow, "Whennnn the. . . moon hits your eye like a big pizza pie, that's Amoré!"

Laughing at Rick's rendition, or maybe just laughing at Rick, Delaney agreed that she had heard that one. "That's a great song," she said.

"Oh, there are plenty others that he sings. How about Elvis?" Rick asked.

"I like the 50's songs; he was awesome then," Delaney said. "You probably never heard of the man, but I like a guy named John Prine," Delaney said, trying to stump Rick.

"Never heard of him?" Rick retorted. "He's from Chicago. I know his music. He's a great writer." Rick could hear himself slurring. He put in a CD of Prine he had in the car with about ten other favorite CD's. They started singing together,

| PANACEA |

Please don't bury me,
Down in the cold, cold ground,
Nah, I'd rather have 'em cut me up,
And pass me all around.
Throw my brain in a hurricane,
And the blind can have my eyes,
And the deaf can take both of my ears,
If they don't mind the size.

By the time "Don't bury me" finished and the next Prine song began, they were at the front of Delaney's house.

"So, have you lived here all your life, Delaney?" Rick inquired.

"Nearly, we moved here when I was seven. It was my grandpa and grandma's home, but they gave it to my mom when the nursing home came calling. Papa died a couple years ago, but my grandmother is in a life-care nursing home in Atlanta with Alzheimer's. She still knows who I am though, and let's me know it every time I see her, which isn't often enough." Delaney paused. "You know, Rick, I don't have to work tonight, would you like to come in and I'll show you around?"

"Sure, I'd like that," Rick said.

As they got out of the car, Southpaw came running up and jumped on Rick.

"You just may be the rightful owner, Rick," Delaney acknowledged. Just then, Southpaw took off after a gray squirrel that had made its way under Delaney's front porch. "Well, I take that back. Provided my dog isn't chasing animals, which he does incessantly, you may just be the rightful owner. He'll be under that porch for hours until

I come out and pat him on the head and rub his stomach. The usual rewards."

"You know, Delaney, a friend of mine from school, Barry Bossanova, the one I told you tried surfing with me in the hurricane, sells boats down here. I bet I can get him to lend us one for a cruise next week, if you're interested. It probably wouldn't be as big as your dad's sailboat, but it could be fun," Rick said, wondering if his buzz was now giving too much away.

"I would like that, let me know," Delaney said.

"I will," Rick said. "It's just that, could you take a day or two off school?" he asked.

"Of course," Delaney said with flip confidence. "I'm sure my professors wouldn't mind." They both laughed together. Delaney took him inside, growing more and more impressed with the boy who would be a man.

During their conversation Rick contemplated the sailboat trip he had now planned. Rick had taken a course in sailing at FSU and had joined the sailing club, but he thought he might be in over his head if the weather wasn't just right or if the boat was too big. His only blue water excursions were in a bay or along the gulf shoreline, and never out on the open sea. He prayed silently for the best when the day came for their mini-voyage.

The two entered Delaney's home still talking. The foyer to her house was large and opened to a center staircase leading to the second floor. It was modestly decorated with real life pictures on the wall and no obscure art or paintings which Rick would expect in a home this regal. Most of the pictures were of family and life on the Gulf of Mexico. There were fishing boat pictures, pictures of Delaney as a child holding her father's catch of the day, bottle-nosed dolphin pictures, and some water colors of Panacea and the panhandle, ostensibly done by a local artist.

"I really like the water colors of the beaches and the Gulf," Rick said. "They remind me of pictures I have back home."

"My mom did all of these." Delaney stared at a picture of the shoreline on St. George Island. She pointed at it. "This was her favorite place to paint. It's on St. George Island. We spent many weekends there."

Rick noticed that Delaney seemed wistful, but he didn't want to press her. "She's got a talent I wish I had," he said. "She's very good."

Delaney led Rick left of the stairs into the large kitchen. She opened the refrigerator and offered him a beer, which he gladly accepted. She led Rick around the downstairs and revealed the intimacies of the living quarters of her home. Throughout the tour Rick thought it to be tastefully modest; mostly bright colors and lots of windows in the back, showcasing the beautiful meadows and trees. There was a deck in the back and Delaney commented that Rick should come over some time and cook on the charcoal grill. They both agreed that gas grills were no comparison and that charcoal grilling was always worth the effort and the wait.

Delaney politely omitted the upstairs and led Rick out to the back porch where they sat on chaise lounges arranged tetę-a-tetę and talked incessantly. The weather was a pleasant and sunny 75 degrees and the light sea breeze blew at 3 to 5 knots. Though it was usually taboo to talk politics without knowing each other very well, Rick threw the dice and figured if she didn't like his politics, he'd better find out sooner than later.

Ultimately they agreed on most issues and became delighted in one another's philosophies and thoughts on politics. They laughed about the lunch and began to plan what they would do that night.

Delaney wasn't too embarrassed to admit that the beer had rendered her a little tired and that she wouldn't mind a nap. Normally, Rick would have fought the idea of sleep, for fear that the moment would be gone when he awoke. But Delaney spoke for Rick, as he was a little sleepy himself.

"You know, at the side of the house is an oversized hammock, would you like to lie down outside and take a power nap?" Delaney inquired.

Though Rick had hoped he'd never hear the phrase power nap again, being an expression used in legal circles in Chicago with lawyers who worked 18 hours a day, including Rick, this time it sounded perfect and he responded, "You lead the way, Delaney."

They left their half-full beers behind and Delaney grabbed Rick's hand and took him playfully to the two Spanish Moss trees at the side of the house that held the hammock. Delaney jumped into the hammock as if it were a trampoline and Rick tried to follow suit. The hammock flipped immediately under Rick's added weight and the two tumbled to the ground, Delaney on top of Rick, both laughing. Delaney's laughter turned to a gentle smile and Rick put his hand on her cheek. Delaney's face grew more beautiful and serious as Rick's lips neared hers. They came together as Delaney's arms wrapped softly around Rick. The kiss lasted only seconds, and when they pulled away slowly, Delaney's eyes were sparkling. Rick's face showing only bewilderment.

"Want to try again?" Rick asked.

"The kiss or the hammock?" Delaney responded, smiling.

"I'm pretty sure we got the kiss right," Rick said, "but I'm willing to try both again." They got up from the ground and managed to fit comfortably snug in the hammock. They kissed again, just as gently as before, and Delaney buried her head on Rick's chest. The idea of sleep had left them both but they each seemed to know that the romance shouldn't be rushed. In time, they rested comfortably in each other's arms and slept for three hours.

10

Rick woke up first to a gentle breeze and the panhandle sun that was just beginning to set over the meadows. The moon was now appearing on the opposite horizon and the two discs appeared to be dancing slowly in both apposition and concordance with the other in a gentle and beautiful promenade. Rick softly rolled out of the hammock and stood up to stretch and embrace the end of the day. As he turned to observed Delaney's recumbent figure, he couldn't help noticing her peaceful and happy disposition, even with her eyes closed.

After a minute, Delaney's eyes opened. "How you doing?" she asked.

"Good. How about you?" Rick said.

"Terrific," came her soft response.

"You know, at my hotel I saw an ad for the FSU symphony playing tonight. Would you be interested in going?" Rick said.

"I've never been to a symphony before, that sounds interesting," Delaney said. The two talked for a few more minutes, taking in the end of the day and reminiscing over their now celebrated lunch date. She rose from the hammock and kissed Rick on the lips. Rick smiled at her and watched as she went inside to change clothes. He waited restlessly and thoughtfully in the hammock for Delaney to return.

| PANACEA |

They drove into Tallahassee and stopped at the Radisson hotel where Rick quickly changed into the only suit he brought down from Chicago. The symphony began at eight o'clock and they arrived minutes before it began. Rick felt at home in the Ruby Diamond Auditorium on FSU's main campus where he'd seen several operas and symphonies and even made a speech to entering freshmen when he was a senior. Tonight's theme was Gershwin and the symphony began with Rhapsody in Blue. Rick held Delaney's hand throughout the performance and felt childlike as the couple's two palms began to sweat lightly into the other. The nervous sweat between their palms reminded Rick of moonlight roller skating from his childhood, which had been his first public encouragement for holding hands with a girl in a roller skating dance. Rick glanced at Delaney frequently during the instrumental rhapsody and noticed her soft smile and eyes glistening. She was enjoying the music and Rick was pleased.

During the symphony, all Rick could think about was the woman next to him. Career didn't matter. Money didn't matter. Life didn't matter. He was falling for Delaney and the world outside held no significance. Rick knew she liked him too, but what did she expect, he wondered. Of course, it was too soon to think about spending the rest of his life with this beautiful person, but, being human, the thought entered his mind and all he could produce was a blank image. Rick's melancholy vanished at the end of the instrumental's first movement. Symphonic music always had a way of mesmerizing Rick, sometimes to the point of being uncomfortable. In a way, he loved it, but sometimes it made him think too much on issues he always hoped to avoid. Delaney squeezed his hand tightly and looked to him with an open smile. "This is wonderful,

Rick," she said.

"Isn't it?" he replied.

When the symphony ended, both were hungry again and Rick took Delaney to a seafood restaurant where he'd worked in college. They arrived within minutes at First Mate's Seafood where the owner and the manager recognized Rick and offered the couple a chair in the Sandbar Lounge. With a complimentary round of drinks the conversation became more lively and they each ordered shrimp and scallops Alfredo.

"Let's go dancing," Delaney said. "I know this great place that plays awesome music. Kind of a weird spot though."

"What's it called?" Rick said.

"The Oynx Club," Delaney said.

"Oh, I know that place, good music, but most of its customers are gay or transsexual. Isn't there a drag queen parade nightly?" Rick said with sarcasm, remembering the joint from years ago and its clientele of which he spoke. In fact, the Onyx did have a lot of cross dressers among the regular heterosexual dance crowd, but it was a great place because nobody cared who you were or what you did. Though Delaney and Rick were dressed for the symphony, their attire would not be out of the ordinary for the Onyx club as all manner of dress was accepted, if not simply ignored.

After eating they drove to downtown Tallahassee and the Onyx Club. They waited in the block-long line of people for two minutes before Rick took Delaney's hand and walked to the front of the line.

"What are we doing?" Delaney asked.

"Well, I hope you don't mind, but I'm going to get us in a little early. I never waited in line in college so I hope times haven't changed much," Rick said as they approached the front door and the three hundred pound bouncer. "We could stand out here for hours if we don't do what the bouncers expect us to do," Rick said.

"And what is that, might I ask?" Delaney said.

"You've got to duke 'em," Rick said.

"Okay, smarty, what does 'duke 'em' mean?" Delaney asked.

"Finally, a term you're not familiar with," Rick smiled.

"It's probably just some dork northerner term, anyhow," Delaney replied.

"Well, we're here, so I'll let this nice man explain what duking is," Rick said in front of the bouncer so he could hear. The bouncer looked at the smiling couple and took Rick's lead.

"We need identification. How old are you two?" he asked, proffering his hand for Rick and Delaney's I.D.

"We're fifty," Rick said, as he placed a fifty dollar bill in the bouncer's hand. The bouncer accepted the "duke" and waved the couple inside the decadent dance bar.

"Rick, are you sure that's okay?" Delaney asked.

"Normally, no. But we're anxious to dance and I'm pretty sure we're thirsty. So, let's just consider it an act of necessity," Rick said. Delaney laughed and grabbed his hand as Rick led them to the bar and the dance floor. It was retro night and "Come on Eileen" by Dexy's Midnight Runners was being played. Rick ordered two Bud Lights and found Delaney, entirely within herself, dancing happily on the dance floor. Rick joined her as the song changed to a slower rock beat. In one song they danced far apart and together, and even did an amateur's version of the Tennessee Waltz. Rick had learned the basics from his aunt who had danced country style with her husband since they courted in high school fifty years earlier. Rick and Delaney danced and sang out loud for over an hour and left the bar.

It was a little cool for a Tallahassee night in October, and they hopped into Rick's convertible rental. Despite the cool wind, they left the top down and turned the heat on for the half hour ride to Panacea. The stars were out and Delaney, without anything to cover her exposed arms, accepted Rick's offer to wear his suit coat and she snuggled up to Rick as he drove. They said nothing after they got outside Tallahassee's city limits. Rick hadn't considered that he'd have to drive back to Tallahassee after he dropped Delaney off. He was just enjoying the night drive and the smell of the honeysuckles that bloomed along the side of the road. It was a fragrance he'd never matched to any other wonder of nature, and one which no Parisian perfume factory could imitate.

Delaney was asleep when Rick pulled onto Plantation Road. As he entered, Rick saw a dark colored stretch Lincoln Continental drive by them, coming from the direction of Delaney's house.

"Delaney, are you awake?" Rick asked, rousing Delaney.

"You bet," she mumbled. Her eyes were still closed.

"I just saw a fat car coming from your house. Did you expect any company tonight?" Rick asked.

Delaney sat up. "No, nobody has a reason to be coming up here. Our house is the only one on this road. Maybe they were just lost," she contemplated.

When they pulled up to Delaney's house, Southpaw was barking hysterically and Delaney told Rick there must be something wrong. Delaney jumped out of the car before Rick got it into park.

"What's the matter boy?" Delaney said, rubbing Southpaw on his ears.

"Let's take him inside," Rick said. When they got to the front door, they noticed blood on the door handle and Delaney exclaimed softly, "Oh, my God." They opened the door to find a young black man covered with blood lying face down.

"Sam!" Delaney screamed. Sam Chesterfield was lying face down on the floor of Delaney's home.

"Sam, are you all right!?" Delaney rushed to his side as Rick closed the door and looked around the house for any other visitors.

Sam stirred and sat up. He spoke weakly. "Some fat ass with a team of honchos beat the livin' shit out of me, Delaney," Sam said, exasperated. "I guess they didn't care much for my singin'," he said, trying to make light of the moment. "They brought me here and said you'd know what to make of the situation. They said you're the reason I was getting a good southern beating."

"Delaney, how is he?" Rick re-entered the room. "The rest of the downstairs is clear. It must have been those people we passed on the driveway."

"I'm beat up pretty good, Rick. Can you take me to the doctor?" Sam asked.

"Of course. Let's go. Lock-up Delaney," Rick ordered.

They got to the hospital in Crawfordville and Sam was stitched-up and released. He'd been beaten bloody, but his permanent damage would consist only of scarring above the right eyebrow and his upper lip. Delaney called the police who came to the hospital and took statements from Sam and the other two. Rick and Delaney both knew that cops in north Florida's panhandle towns didn't care much to investigate "nigger beatin's." As a result, the police weren't expected to make much of their investigation. Delaney invited Rick and Sam back to her house to spend the night.

They arrived at Delaney's just after four in the morning and they were all exhausted. Delaney prepared a pallet for both men in the living room and Rick started a fire.

"Does anybody want some wine or something?" Delaney asked.

"Bourbon, if you've got it," Sam said.

"Make that two," Rick said. Delaney made the drinks and brought them into the now warmed living room.

"What do you make of this, Delaney?" Sam asked. "What were you supposed to know?"

"Sam, I don't know. I can't think of any enemies of me or my family since my daddy died, and those guys were just politicians. They were harmless anyhow, and that was over ten years ago," Delaney said.

"Sam, can you describe any of the men?" Rick asked.

"Not really, I was just getting off work at Posey's. I was on my way out the door and not even twenty feet from my car when they came up from behind me in the parking lot and threw me into their car. They all had white pillow cases on their heads. I don't know if they were in the bar or not." Sam paused. "Shit, I'm sure this isn't Klan related, though."

"Why?" Rick asked.

"I've seen the asshole Klan before and these pillow cases were a pretty shitty imitation of a Klan hood," Sam said. "I think they might have wanted me to think it was Klan, or maybe they were just operating on a low budget." Sam's humor went unnoticed by Delaney and Rick who feared the truth.

"Did they say anything to you, Sam?" Rick asked.

"Naw, not much of anything," Sam replied. "Although, one guy said something I thought was kind of odd."

"What was that?" Delaney asked.

"Well, I was yelling for them to let me out of the damned car and one of the fellas said, 'fuck you, negro,'"

"What's odd about that?" Delaney asked.

"Well, to the Klan, I'm a nigger not a negro. Years ago, negro was a polite way of saying nigger. Now we're just called black. . .or nigger if you're prejudiced," Sam said. "You know, if I hadn't been scared half to death, I mighta' laughed," Sam continued.

"Why? What's funny about that?" Delaney asked.

"Well, nothing really. Except he was trying to be a polite KKK member and he stuttered so bad that I thought he'd never get the word 'nigger' out and then it turned out he was trying to say 'negro.'" Sam looked at Rick and Delaney's blank faces. "I guess you had to be there," he said.

Delaney was worried. "This is about the scariest thing I've ever witnessed. I don't know what's going on Rick," she said.

"Delaney, did your dad ever piss off Billy Barute?" Rick asked.

"Constantly. They were political enemies. You know Barute; he's a jackass and as conservative as they come. He hated dad's politics and desire to protect the coastline from oil drilling, but Billy's a professional man. I don't think he's capable of harming someone and jeopardizing his own career. Besides what would he have to do with Sam?"

"I don't know. Maybe he's that stupid," Rick said. "Did they say anything else, Sam?" Rick asked.

"They told me they know where my mother lives and that I'd better not cross them," Sam said. "And I asked them how could I cross them if I don't know why they're telling me that."

"What did they say?" Delaney asked.

"They just told me not to fuck with anything that isn't my business if I knew what was good for you, my mom, and me," Sam said.

"I don't know what to think, Sam," Rick said. "Anything else?"

"Not that I remember. It was just weird," Sam said.

Rick paused and looked at Sam. "Well, we'll just have to sort this out later. We need some rest," Rick said. Though exhausted, the three went over Sam's story several more times before they grew too tired to stay awake. They all fell asleep in the living room with Delaney and Rick sharing the couch as Sam slept on the pallet in front of the fire.

11

Rick woke up at daybreak Sunday morning and went to the kitchen to make some coffee. He thought about Delaney, how everything was perfect and, as fate would throw him a curve, how there had to be a catch. Rick tried to understand the sudden attack on Sam. He knew he could handle some complications in a relationship, but he questioned whether he was prepared for issues like the previous night. Sam and Delaney were good friends and the attackers chose Delaney's home to deposit Sam. Rick was concerned for both Delaney's and Sam's safety. Fleetingly, he wondered about his own.

Rick had a cup of coffee and his thoughts to himself and then woke the other two.

"I've made some coffee. Delaney, I've got to head into Tally. Your favorite lobbyist and mine wants me to meet Winston Skroggsdad to talk about some legislation. You did say Skroggsdad was a plaintiff's lawyer didn't you?"

"Yes, he's a Democrat, Rick," Delaney replied. "But be careful, anyhow. He's also a lobbyist, and they can be a little too faced, depending upon whose paying the bills."

Barute had offered to help Rick find some work with yellow dog Democrats and Skroggsdad was a former District Attorney who now concentrated on labor issues - union side, and he was a Plaintiff's lawyer, which usually meant he was a Democrat. Driving to Tallahassee, Rick thought that Barute couldn't be a thug if he was willing to help Rick find work on the other side of the Republican party.

Rick drove by himself to Skroggsdad's and hoped the man was nothing like Barute. Skroggsdad had arranged their meeting at his residence this Sunday morning and he greeted Rick at the door of his ranch style home in Killearn, an upper-class subdivision of Tallahassee.

"Hey, ya, Morrissey, right?" Skroggsdad said.

"Right," Rick said, "nice to meet you, Winston."

"Come on in, my wife has bacon, sausage and grits. Can I interest you in some breakfast?" Winston said.

"No, thank you, but I wouldn't mind a cup of coffee," Rick responded.

The two men sat down with coffee in Winston's den, replete with pictures of the former D.A. with big time Florida politicians. One picture that looked out of place was of Winston and Marshall Rodriguez, former governor of Florida and, later, the national Drug Czar thanks to a presidential appointment after Rodriguez lost his gubernatorial reelection bid. Rick remembered that the former Governor Rodriguez had commissioned the spot checking of the Gulf for oil in the late 1980's.

"Rick, Billy said you'd be of help to the labor workers in the GOP's latest campaign to eliminate the workers' compensation system here in Florida," Winston initiated his intent for the meeting. "I'm convinced the House of Reps has a strangle hold on this issue and unions and working folks are gonna lose. But the victory will not be as complete as they want it. We're likely to see a modified version of the comp act passed, instead of its all out repeal. I'll pay you, on behalf of several union lobbyists to draft a proposed law that protects union workers under the reformed comp act. Give those in the G.O.P. a fight. How's $7,500 for re-drafting a proposal of the amended workers' compensation act?" Winston offered.

"That sounds reasonable," Rick said. "Apparently you know I've done comp in Illinois."

"Not really," Winston said. "You're a lawyer and I'm offering this job as a favor to Billy. I'm sure you're capable. I would have done the work myself but I've chosen to take a vacation to the West Indies instead."

"How much were you to be paid?" Rick inquired without embarrassment. Rick knew most lawyers loved to brag about their fees anyhow.

"Fifteen thousand. I'm still getting it. You're just doing the work for me," Winston said.

"I guess I'm lucky to have the work. Thank you, Winston," Rick said and looked around the room. "I can't help but notice the pictures on your wall. They're impressive and consistent with your politics, except for you and Governor Rodriguez. What's up there?" Rick asked.

"Oh, Marshall and I worked together when I was D.A. and he was governor. That's how I met Billy, actually. Billy got him in the governor's chair, or so Billy contends," Winston said.

"What do you mean, you worked together?" Rick inquired.

"We had to. I was in charge of prosecuting the criminals and Rodriguez was big into cutting crime as part of his platform," Winston responded. "So we worked together. Come on, Rick, don't be so naive; it's all politics."

Though Rick knew from his college years that Rodriguez had proposed drilling off the Florida coastline, he didn't want to question his new employer about the present drilling proposals off the panhandle.

"Here's a copy of the GOP's proposed changes. Change them to protect my union men and give me your ideas in writing in 21 days." Winston gave Rick the proposed legislation, with its proposals.

"Thank you," Rick said.

"For what? You're making me the money, son." Skroggsdad said, without affect.

"Well, it's something to do." Rick responded.

"If you're looking for something to do, I've got a gardener who's on disability. You can take his job, if you'd like."

"Thanks, but no thanks." Rick said.

"Well, that's it for now. I don't mean to rush you out, but the Mrs. and I need to get to the First Baptist Church. See you soon, Rick." Winston escorted Rick to the door.

Rick drove back to his hotel and realized he didn't even have Delaney's phone number. He tried directory assistance and found she had an unpublished number. He tried for a listing for Sam Chesterfield or any Chesterfield in Wakulla County and learned that no listing existed. Rick made a few other phone calls and took a nap. He woke up in the middle of the afternoon, feeling troubled with heartache and apprehension for Delaney. He didn't feel like driving back to Panacea right away and decided to go for a run through his old stomping grounds at the university. Rick put on his running shoes and took off from the Radisson toward the university about a half mile away. As Rick ran down College Avenue toward the front entrance of The Florida State University, he felt energized - not unlike the way he had felt as a younger man in undergrad here. The gothic spires of the main buildings were inspiring and picturesque as they were silhouetted by the sun in the autumn sky behind them. He ran around the perimeter of the university and had gone about two and a half miles to the student union. He began walking through the mall area and observed the bulletin boards showcasing what were the major interests of young students of the day. Most of the bulletins spoke of safe sex, responsible drinking, date rape and AIDS. Not much had changed, Rick thought to himself.

Rick noticed a bulletin placed by a student group called Save Our Shorelines, or S.O.S. He didn't know Delaney was a member, but he had always believed in coastal preservation, and he read the bulletin with interest as it announced a meeting to discuss the off-shore drilling proposals in the Gulf. At the bottom, the bulletin read the group's mission statement against Copperhead Oil Company and announced a protest at an upcoming political event to be held at the Capitol Building. Rick glanced back at the bulletin, remembering he had heard Delaney speak of Copperhead the night they threw darts together, and how Copperhead had been vying for drilling rights in the Gulf when Pally Chase was alive.

He continued running through the union and down Copeland Street back toward the hotel. He stopped at Tycoon's Tavern on the way and sat at a table under dried palm fronds. He ordered a club soda and thought about the events he'd experienced over the past week. Though he was falling for Delaney, he was uncertain for the days to come and the prospect that maybe she had some family or personal dilemmas that she didn't feel comfortable discussing. Nevertheless, he wanted to be with her. The relationship had been too good to let fade without the old college try, he thought to himself.

When he got back to the hotel, he noticed Billy Barute sitting in the hotel lounge with a couple of white shirt and red tie fellows whose apparel glared of politics. Rick knew he wasn't quite dressed for the occasion, but he figured that now was as good a time as ever to thank Barute and maybe find out more about him. He went into the lounge, sweating, with his hair windblown back and announced himself to Barute and his colleagues.

"Billy, sorry to interrupt you, I just wanted to tell you thanks for your help with Mr. Skroggsdad," Rick said.

"Hey, boy, how ya been? Are you feeling okay? You look a little winded, or out of shape as the case may be," Billy said in a hollow loud voice that reverberated throughout the bar. Rick knew Barute was on his way to being drunk and took exception to the fat man's saying that Rick was out of shape.

"Feeling great," Rick said. "Drinking on a Sunday, Mr. Barute? Maybe you should try a lap or two yourself. Want to come with me for the cool down?" The men with Barute chuckled at the remark.

"You're all right, my boy. These are a few friends of mine down from Washington. Bill Wallace, Ray Nieson, and Ned Carson." Barute gestured to each man.

"How do you do, gentlemen, I'd shake your hands but I've been jogging and sweating up a storm," Rick said.

"This humidity can really get rid of last night's alcohol. Detoxification, they call it," Billy said. The men all offered a perfunctory laugh and Rick felt accepted.

"Tied one on last night, did ya son?" Wallace said.

"Where'd you go, any good piece of ass in this college town?" said Nieson.

"Well, you are in Florida. All you have to do is look around. Tallahassee has never suffered for want of beautiful girls," Rick said, as he noticed the wedding band on Nieson's hand, but knew it didn't mean a goddamned thing to him. "So what do you boys do besides chase the good life?"

"Nieson, Carson, and me hold down lobbying jobs in D.C.," Wallace said. "We're working for Copperhead Drilling now for about a month. Maybe we'll need some legal work, you interested?"

"Working for Copperhead?" Barute said to Wallace. Barute turned toward Rick. "Hell, Rick, these guys will own the fuckin' company when they're through. The low-life bastards," Barute said, laughing at himself.

"Don't worry, Billy. Someday, maybe you'll aspire to be like us," Ray Nieson said, taunting Barute.

"I couldn't afford to live that well," Barute said, slapping Ned Carson on the back. "Could you, Ned?" He asked.

"I-I-I w-w-wouldn't mind it," Carson said. All of the men laughed. Rick couldn't tell if they were laughing at Carson's statement, or at his stutter.

"Say, Rick, you been seein' Delaney? She's a fine piece of ass, hey boy?" Billy said, slurring now. Rick wanted to give him a verbal punch, and knew he could land it on Billy's brain, but he held back.

"I see her now and then, Billy. I've been pretty busy, though."

Rick thought he'd try to catch Barute's curiosity.

"Doin?" Billy said. "It can't be that job for Skroggy, he just hired ya."

"Naw, I've been doing some biological research in the Gulf," Rick said, speaking way out of his academic league, but hoping Barute and his buddies were similarly ignorant.

"Really? I thought you were just a lawyer, too good for laboring work. What are you studying?" Barute said, taking the bait Rick offered.

"Snake Oil," Rick said. "You know, the oil that's supposed to cure all, for little to no cost? Gypsies used to peddle it."

Barute's smile left his face and his look was now somewhat bewildered. "I think you've lost your noggin with this heat and humidity. Ain't no snake oil in the Gulf," Barute said. "If there's any oil out there, it's crude or natural gas, but thanks to Delaney's father, nobody knows just yet. No good liberal," Barute continued, looking for approval from his company.

"Besides," Barute continued, "that was a pipe dream from years ago, no pun intended, and it's long past. Chase beat us fair and square. He was a damned fine man. Wasn't he fellas?" Barute was straightening up, as the men around him nodded agreeably, though appearing confused. Rick noticed the other men seemed to be following the conversation pretty well and they weren't questioning Barute at all. If anything, they looked concerned, red faced, and drunk.

"You guys all knew Pally?" Rick asked.

"Actually, I meant Pally beat me fair and square." Barute said, now straightening his posture. "These guys were screwing sorority girls back then."

"Wow." Rick said, with feigned surprise. "You all look to be the same age. No offense."

"None taken. I'm sure." Ray Wallace said. "But I'm pretty sure we've been out of college for more than ten years."

"T-t-t-try th-th-thirty." Ned Carson said.

"Ricky, let us buy you a drink, and get to know the crackerjack from Chicago," Barute said, patronizing Rick and using "Ricky" now as an endearment. Rick didn't like the nickname, Ricky, being used by a stranger for whom Rick held no esteem, and he became a little nervous with the crackerjack line, wondering what kind of homework Barute had been doing. He also didn't miss the immediate change of conversation by the obese lobbyist.

"Crackerjack? What do you mean by that?" Rick said, smiling, and then thinking to himself that it was a far too familiar and ugly line.

"It means damned good," Barute interrupted Rick's thought. "It's a southern expression we use for lawyers, legislators, and lobbyists. The 'triple L's!,' eh, boys?!" Barute started laughing and the others did as well. The men with Barute appeared to be servile and self-seeking flatterers, praising Barute's every utterance. Rick was unimpressed.

"Say, sit down, Ricky," Barute said. "Join us for a drink."

"Well, how long you guys here? I'd like to shower and would be glad to join ya for a round," Rick said, feeling a little more comfortable that Barute's own ego was the only thing Barute had done homework on.

"Aw, we'll be here for at least an hour, right guys?" Wallace said.

"Yea, uh, yea, B-B-B, Billy's here's, he's l-l-lined up some d-d-dates, huh, B-Billy?" Carson had spoken, sort of.

"You got that right, Ned." Barute was acting drunk again, and slapped Carson on the back as if he were helping him swallow his last sentence. Carson gulped visibly to confirm the gesture.

"Sounds fine, guys; I'll be back in twenty minutes. Save some of the booze would ya?" Rick said. The men were all chuckling again and Rick left the bar feeling as though he'd either dodged a bullet or opened a wound.

Back in his hotel room, Rick noticed the message light blinking. He called the hotel operator and she put through the voice mail message. "Hi, Rick, it's Delaney. I realized that you probably don't have my number, so I'm calling." She left her phone number at home and the number at Captano's, which Rick wrote down. "Sam's doing fine and so am I. If you have a chance, call me at work tonight or stop in. I know it's a school night and everything, but I wouldn't mind hanging out a little tonight. Hope to see you. Bye." Her voice was soft and Rick was back in a trance.

"Fuck those bastards downstairs," he said out loud. "I'm going to the coast!" Rick showered and put on blue jeans and a t-shirt. He had planned on having one drink with the men at the bar, but they had already left when he got there. The bartender recognized Rick from before and told him that Barute left a message for him to meet the men at Sharpe's Café for a late dinner. Rick was relieved with the message and hopped into the convertible for a sunset drive to Captano's in Panacea.

When Rick arrived at the restaurant, he was greeted by the same hostess as he'd been a week before, and he took a seat next to the bay windows overlooking the water. Delaney's expression was bright as she approached Rick. "How'd you know what section I'd have, sailor?" she smiled and said.

"I think the hostess knows I have a crush on you; that's how I got here," Rick replied. Delaney smiled. "And speaking of sailors, I talked to my friend, Barry Bossanova."

"The guy who sells boats?" Delaney asked. "And is that his real name?"

"Yes and yes," Rick said. "He's got a 28' foot ketch he sold to a guy in Key West, and if I run it down for him, he'll pay my air fare back. So, if you've got nothing else to do, I'd like you to come along and I'll cover your airfare back. Do you think we're capable of enjoying each other's company for four or five days on a boat?" Rick said.

"Really!?" Delaney was excited. "Capable we are. That's sounds great; when can we do it?" Delaney was surprisingly enthusiastic for a girl who must've grown up on the water and become used to its allure by now.

"Two weeks," Rick said. "It's got a fresh water hose and berthing space for two. Not that we couldn't nap together like we did in the hammock, but I just don't think two people can fit into one berthing space on this rig." Rick was trying to play on the platonic theme, but he knew he wanted to sleep next to her, and with her for that matter, but he wasn't fool enough to rush the idea.

"Rick, that'll be terrific. I haven't been on a boat in three years. I'll be right back." Delaney left to work at other tables and sent a Heineken beer to Rick's table.

As Rick watched her work, his heart ached to have the hammock scene all over again. "Hey, Rick!" came a familiar excited voice from behind Rick's chair. It was Sam.

"Hey, hey. How ya doin Sam?" Rick asked.

Sam sat down across from Rick. "Better. Haven't heard back from those asswipes," Sam said.

"Any idea?" Rick asked.

"Well, Delaney and I started talking it out. You know, we've been pretty good friends for the past few years or so; I mean, we've been to football games together, parties, stuff like that. We never dated or anything, but at some of the college parties we went to, Delaney would have to pretend she was with me to keep the boys away when all she wanted to do was dance. Well, we remembered one night at a Pi Lambda house party this last August when these two assholes started calling Delaney names because she shattered the ego of one of the guys by not going out with him a second time. Apparently this asshole tried to force her to have sex with him on their only date and she slapped him and walked home from Tallahassee. Anyhow, they used to come into Posey's and ask me about her, and, you know me, I got a little lippy and voila!, we think they're the assholes who kicked the shit out of me."

"That's quite the detective work, Sam. Are you doing anything about it?" Rick asked.

"Yea, gonna kick their ass next time I see 'em, that's what," Sam replied. "Say, want a beer?" he continued.

"Yes, and I've got all of yours tonight, Sam. Don't hesitate to look me up if you need any help, okay, I mean it." Rick was sincere, and hopeful that all of this was just college punks and not some vision of his imagination with G-men and dark suited knee-breakers.

"Thanks, Rick," Sam said.

Delaney finished her last tables and joined them. As gracefully as possible, Sam left the two love-birds, as he called them upon exiting, to themselves, saying he had to go to work. Delaney never sat down, and invited Rick out onto the veranda overlooking the bay. As they sat down with two Heinekens, Delaney stared out at the open blue bay and put her arms between her legs while leaning forward and sighing. "This is one place I wouldn't mind staying forever. I love the view from here," Delaney said.

"Delaney, what's on your mind?" Rick said.

"Am I that obvious?" she said.

"No, but that's a question I've asked myself many times when I'm with you. 'Am I that obvious?'" Rick said, trying to make her feel better. Delaney gave him a broad smile.

"Rick, my mom isn't coming back from Atlanta for some time and, considering what happened to Sam, well, she wouldn't mind, in fact, she'd probably appreciate. . . well,..." Rick interrupted, not knowing where she was leading but trying to help her through humor.

"What, she wouldn't mind if we have a beer outside on the porch at this restaurant," Rick said.

"No, I mean, yes, I mean, she wouldn't mind that at all. In fact, she'd probably think you're one of the more charismatic men to visit Panacea in a long time," Delaney said. "No, what I mean is," Delaney continued, unfazed by Rick's interlude, "she, or I, I mean, I would like you to not have to ride back and forth to Tallahassee every day. You could stay with me, platonically of course. There, I said it."

She was charming. Rick was impressed to have the platonic card played on him. In fact, coming from Delaney, it was the best invitation he'd ever received.

"Delaney, that'd be. . ." he was interrupted.

"I mean, you can use our computer for your job with Skroggsdad and you really don't need to be in Tallahassee for that. Besides, why waste money on a room you've spent about an eighth of your time in?" Delaney continued to persuade, as though she needed to.

"As I was saying," Rick was smiling, "I'd like that very much," Rick finished. "How did you know what I'd be doing for Skroggsdad?" he asked.

"Oh, Billy told me about it when I. . .," she hesitated. Rick jumped in,

"You got me the job, huh? Pretty sneaky, sister," he said in his best John Wayne.

"I hope you don't mind," Delaney said, sounding truly apprehensive of disappointing Rick.

"Not at all," Rick said. "Thank you. You're a good friend." The endearment seemed pleasing to her ears.

"You know, I should've offered to stay. I don't want you harassed by any more college punks," Rick said, offering his own inside info on Delaney.

"How'd you. . ., oh, Sam. Well, we just figured. . .I mean he told you the story?" she asked.

"Well, I understand," Rick said.

"I just don't know why people behave they way they do. Prejudiced bunch of jerks," Delaney said.

"Prejudiced and chauvinistic," Rick offered. "Don't worry, Delaney. Everything will even out. What goes around, comes around." His comforting cliché seemed to put Delaney a little more at ease.

"That's funny. My dad used to say that," Delaney said. She was becoming wistful, but then perked up. "What do you say we go watch Sam sing? Maybe you can do another duet for me?!" she smiled at Rick and held his hand.

"Well, the first part sounds great. I'll need about ten more of these to do the latter," Rick said, as he raised his beer bottle. They clicked their bottles together and got up laughing, arm and arm, and headed for Rick's car.

They returned to Posey's for some soft Sam music, replete with medleys of Jim Croce, Jimmy Buffett, John Prine, and Van Morrison, and went back to Delaney's after picking up her car at Captano's. They arrived home exhausted, and fell asleep on the couch in the living room wrapped in each other's arms.

PART TWO
- Diagnosis -

12

For the next two weeks, Rick worked diligently on his project for Skroggsdad, having had to make only one trip to Tallahassee to check out of the hotel and visit FSU's law library for research on case law and legislative histories in labor law and workers' compensation. Delaney was busy throughout the daytime with school and occasional lunch shifts at Captano's. She worked dinners on Tuesday and Wednesday nights and Rick thought it proper not to eat there then, as if he were keeping too close a watch over her. His was not a suffocating personality and he knew too well from prior experience, with girlfriends who followed him everywhere, that failing to give someone his or her space often resulted in that person's gaining all the space in the world.

Working at Delaney's house in the downstairs den, Rick had still not seen the upstairs and, yet, his natural curiosity to explore the house never got the best of him. Rick thought she'd show him around when she was good and ready. Though, on occasion, Rick wondered where they were headed intimately, since they hadn't had sex. He knew there was a time for everything, and trying to create the perfect mood for anything wasn't the best approach. Perfection wasn't something that could be created. Perfection created itself. For the first time in his life, Rick recognized that he wasn't creating a relationship, but that a relationship was creating him. He hadn't thought this clearly about the opposite sex in years and appreciated himself for respecting another human being. Throughout the two weeks, they talked, Rick cooked, Delaney cooked, and they slept together on the couch, fully clothed. It seemed better than sex in many ways. They were contented, and their expectations completely fulfilled. Sex, on the other hand, could have destroyed the chemistry, as odd as that seemed to Rick.

On Thursday night, November 2nd, they shared a toast to their sailing voyage to the Keys the next morning with a bottle of Merlot and filet mignons prepared by Rick on the charcoal grill. Delaney made broccoli with Hollandaise sauce, spinach salad, her mother's recipe for thrice baked potatoes and boiled shrimp cocktail for dessert.

They awoke at five in the morning on Friday and headed for the boat which was anchored in a slip at Lanark Village on the gulf waters of St. George Sound. For forty-five minutes, they loaded the provisions for the next four days into the boat. Rick packed two large coolers with food, beer, ice, sodas, milk, orange juice, and fresh fruit. Delaney had made cold cut sandwiches the night before and put those in the cooler. They had also brought along plenty of wine, cheese, and Carr's table water crackers and fresh baked French bread. The boat was equipped with a fresh water tank and Rick packed ten more gallons of drinking water in the storage areas. They were prepared to set sail.

Excitement filled the air as the boat left the slip with a full mainsail at seven-thirty in the morning. It was a bright and beautiful warm day for early November in the panhandle, and the seas were friendly as the sun inched farther up the sky from the eastern side of the planet. The wind was steady at fifteen knots from the west and Rick knew they could travel at three to five knots with the steady blow, kicking on the power motor whenever necessary. Rick called in for the weather forecast from his cell phone, not wanting to attempt nautical terminology on the boat radio, since he didn't speak the language. The weather service predicted smooth seas for the weekend. He was relieved, as he had never been blue water sailing with this big a boat, this far from shore. He planned to trace the coastline of Florida, staying within fifteen miles of the shoreline, all the way to the keys as he feared his inexperience with the instruments could land him in Cuba or even Costa Rica if he weren't careful. Though Delaney probably knew more about sailing, Rick was too proud to ask, and naturally, he wanted to impress her. Rick knew himself to be a show-off in front of Delaney, yet she was humored by it, if not flattered.

Delaney didn't seem the slightest bit concerned with her surroundings as she sat down at the bow. With the mainsail up, Rick released the jib to catch the additional wind and they sailed for an hour with the only conversation being that of the waves gently tossing against the boat, and Rick offering Delaney coffee.

"It's another great day in paradise," Delaney offered as she took the coffee. "This was a great idea, Rick. I've longed to come out on the ocean, but wasn't sure how I'd feel once I got here. Now I know. It's the best," she said.

Rick smiled at her as he steered the boat deep into Apalachicola Bay and out into the Gulf of Mexico. By 9 a.m., the air began to warm and Rick took off his t-shirt. Delaney followed suit around 9:45, still sitting at the bow, now reading a book in her bikini. She smiled at Rick as she took off her t-shirt, revealing her already tanned skin and modest, attractive figure. He studied her while she read, trying to concentrate on her eyes as they peeled the pages away, occasionally looking at him, but he was naturally distracted by her entire physique. To Rick, she remained a vision.

Delaney got up and made sandwiches about 11:30 and Rick tied off the steering while he enjoyed lunch with her. Something about the ocean and the day at sea kept them from much open conversation as they smiled at each other while eating and glancing out to the sea in awe of its beauty.

"A masterpiece, just as I'd expected, Delaney," Rick said, as he licked his fingers clean of the excess dijon mustard from the sandwich. "Would you like to throw a line out in a few hours and catch whatever fish is silly enough to have skipped lunch at the proper time of day?" he asked.

"Sounds good, captain," Delaney responded with a salute and a smile as she went down to the cabin area to clean up from lunch.

Rick opened a beer and turned the boat into the headwind, putting her in irons, letting the main sheet and jib fluff aimlessly in the wind. He took off his sandals and dived into the clear blue water. Opening his eyes underwater, Rick was reminded of the final scene from the book "Jaws" by Peter Benchley. In the book, the lead character, Brody, had opened his eyes underwater to watch his friend fade away to the sea bottom clenched in the shark's mouth, until the salt water burned his eyes so badly he had to surface. Rick thought about how Benchley must have never opened his eyes in the salt water before, because the only time it stung was when one came out of it and salt water dripped into the eyes. It was the same principle with sweat dripping into one's eyes. The drops of sweat stung even though natural tears in the eye had the same salt proportion as perspiration. Underwater in the Gulf, Rick realized that the saltiness merely numbed his eyes and it was very comfortable.

Rick swam under the boat and touched the bed of the continental shelf, just fifteen feet below. While underwater, he heard a splash, and then thought of Benchley's book again, this time for its namesake. He surfaced quickly and found Delaney treading water five feet away.

"Didn't your mother teach you not to go swimming right after lunch?" she said, smiling.

"Well, she did say something about that, but I thought it was just fresh water swimming," Rick replied. "But, oh, uh, uh-oh, I think it was for salt water too!" Rick said as he submerged and headed for Delaney's legs. Delaney screamed out loud while Rick pulled her underwater. As he pulled her down, he pulled himself up to meet her face-to-face under the clear blue. Both of their eyes were opened when they met, and Rick went for her lips like a Barracuda chasing a fluorescent tube lure. She wrapped her arms and legs around him as they slowly sank, lip-locked. Rick released first, nearly out of breath, and grabbed Delaney's hand as he swam them both to the surface. For a few minutes they continued the mating ritual as though they were bottlenose dolphins, kissing and frolicking in the water before re-boarding the boat.

Rick helped Delaney aboard at the stern and put a reef in the main sheet and they were off again, riding the wind. Neither of them sprayed down with fresh water, and the salt air dried the salt water on their bodies making their skin feel tight as it tanned in the early November sun. They sailed until dinner time having lost all ambition to want to know what time it was. On the Gulf, there were only four times in a day, morning, daytime, dinner time and nighttime. About an hour before sunset, Rick dropped the main sheet and jib and baited frozen squid on two poles. Delaney got each of them a beer and they sat with their feet over the edge of the boat, next to one another, facing the westbound sun and hoping no fish would bite and cause them to leave their comfortable position.

In twenty minutes, Rick got a bite on his line and it was a small fighter. From his past experience fishing, he figured it was either a dolphin fish or a grouper. He exchanged poles with Delaney and offered her the game. She was as proficient with a rod and reel as Rick had expected and she brought the animal to the surface in no time. It was a small grey shark, and they were both surprised with the catch. Delaney seemed squeamish over the catch and the idea that, hours ago, she was swimming in the same waters with this animal.

"I won't be lipping *this* grouper for you," Delaney said.

Rick confided that it was harmless, as if Delaney didn't know it already, and he netted the shark while Delaney got her camera. She offered the 35 millimeter camera to Rick and he pulled Delaney and the shark within his chest and, with an extended arm, took a self-portrait of the happy twosome and their exasperated friend. Rick released the shark, commenting how nice it would've been to have a grill handy. He was only half serious, because, while he loved shark, he didn't want to kill one. Killing any animal was difficult for Rick, though he had no trouble eating the delicacies that someone else had killed for human consumption.

Rick cranked the engine and motored the boat for half an hour. When he thought they were somewhere off the coast of Horseshoe point and about one quarter of the way down the Florida peninsula, he dropped anchor for the evening. They had a small dinner and several drinks and talked about the day as the remains of the sun stretched across the horizon in brilliant red, orange and purple. Down below, Rick had found a makeshift hammock and tied it to the mast and starboard rail. It was built for one, but they both managed to lie in it, with Delaney comfortably half on top of Rick. They fell asleep early, contented with the day.

Within a few hours the moon had emerged across the southern sky and Rick woke up to find Delaney sitting on the edge of the bow with a glass of wine and her feet dangling off the edge. He got up, grabbed a beer, and sat next to her.

"Guess we hit it too early?" Rick said.

"Yes, but I didn't mind," Delaney said. "Besides, I enjoyed watching you sleeping."

"You mean enjoyed because I was drooling all over myself and it was funny?" Rick responded.

"No, you're a pretty clean sleeper. You just looked like a child lying there. Comfortable, peaceful, and innocent," Delaney said.

"Well, two out of three ain't bad," Rick said, and they laughed.

By now, the sky was overwhelmed with stars, a vision that beat any the mind could imagine unless one had seen this beauty before, without lights from the mainland to remove some of the stars glistening wonder.

"I've seen stars, seemingly millions of stars, from the beach at night, but I've never witnessed something so humbling and astonishing as the sky is tonight," Rick said, still looking upward. "Look, there's Orion," he said, pointing at the constellation which was halfway up in the sky.

"Where?" Delaney said. Rick put his left arm around her and guided her right arm with his, while he pressed his cheek against hers as if they were lining up their sights on a rifle.

"Right there, the southern constellation of Orion," Rick said.

"How do you know stars?" Delaney asked.

"I had to take an astronomy class at a junior college because I failed normal science in high school," Rick said, without apology for his stupidity in science.

"Okay, college boy, what about 'Orion?'" she asked.

"Well, I tell you what I think I remember, bearing in mind I may have to embellish the story where my memory fails me," Rick continued. "Now, Orion, as you probably know, was a Greek god, 'done too soon,' as the Neil Diamond song goes. He died in the prime of his life. It's been a long time since college, but if I remember the story right, Orion was the son of Poseidon," Rick said.

"God of the seas," Delaney interjected.

"Right," Rick said. "Poseidon gave Orion the gift of walking under water, along with his famous talent of being a great marksman and hunter," Rick continued. "As luck would have it, Orion was handsome and strong but he was always getting into trouble over women."

"Is this autobiographical of Rick Morrissey?" Delaney laughed.

"You'd better hope not when you hear about Orion's fate," Rick said, smiling. "Orion was asked by King Oenopion of Chios to kill all the wild animals on the king's island. My guess is Orion didn't like killing anything, so instead of following orders, Orion fell for the king's daughter, Princess Merope." Rick was now becoming animated with the telling of the Greek myth. "The king was very, very mad at Orion for this because he didn't want Orion to hook-up with Merope and he wanted those damned animals killed," Rick said as he furled his eyebrows and tensed his upper lip.

"I can see the king's point," Delaney said, nodding with a sarcastic look.

"So the king invites Orion over to his place and gets him drunk and places some hocus-pocus spell on him that blinds Orion."

"Poor bastard never saw it coming," Delaney chimed in.

"Funny," Rick said. "Do you want to hear this story or what?" he asked.

"Go on, please. I just couldn't resist the pun," Delaney said as she slapped Rick on the leg.

"Okay. So to get his eyesight back, Orion sought the help of an Oracle, or a wise man know-it-all," Rick continued. "The Oracle told Orion that to regain his sight he would need to journey east allowing the sun to strike his eyes until he could see again."

"To think mom was wrong about staring at the sun all these years," Delaney said.

"Okay, smarty, I'm gonna make this long story short," Rick said. "So, next thing you know, your mom is proven wrong and Orion gets his sight back and falls in love with Apollo's twin sister, Artemis, who was goddess of the moon. Artemis was an expert marksman in her own right. Pardon my lack of neutered English, but that's the way history was written," Rick said.

"Soon to be rewritten," Delaney said, smiling.

"I suppose I could have said 'marksperson' but that sounds pretty dumb," Rick said.

"Go on," Delaney offered.

"Orion was deeply in love with this beautiful goddess, and Apollo couldn't stand Orion, because Orion was an expert marksman and overshadowed Apollo's skills and those of Artemis. Furthermore, Artemis loved Orion and this made Apollo jealous, for some odd reason, but you know those Greeks, the rules are different." Rick was now enjoying the storytelling as if teaching a classroom full of interested students as he continued. "So, one day, of course this is a very long time ago," Delaney sarcastically nodded her understanding of the time frame, "Orion was walking in a long pond with only his head bobbing up out of the water. Apollo approached Artemis and challenged her to spear the animal in the pond, which was indistinguishable as a man. Artemis accepted the challenge and shot her arrow straight and true, through the head of Orion," Rick continued, noticing Delaney to look almost sad over the lovers' fate. "When Artemis found out what had happened she was so distraught that Apollo offered her any wish she had. She chose to have Orion placed in the skies forever, as a testament of her love for Orion. And poor Apollo never regained his sister's love," Rick concluded.

"Are you sure you flunked a science course?" Delaney asked.

"Two of them actually," Rick said.

"Well, you sure remembered Astronomy well," she said.

"Only because it was science with a good story," Rick said. They both laughed.

"There look," Rick pointed her arm along the constellation. "There is Orion's sword, and the little stars, barely twinkling, are the diamonds on the handle, and up here," he moved her arm up, "is his bow with arrows," Rick paused. "Sad, story, but true. Well, as true as mythology goes.

"That's awesome, Rick. What a sad tale," Delaney said, touched by the Greek legend. Delaney paused and stared upward. Moisture filled her eyes but she was smiling. "You know, Rick, when I look up there, I see my father. I see other people I love, and I see God," Delaney said.

Rick was pleasantly surprised that she brought religion into it as they had not yet discussed religion and Rick considered the topic an important one.

"Do you see anything other than Greek gods, Rick?" she asked him.

"You mean people?" Rick asked.

"I mean, what do you think of it all. It's so amazing. So beautiful. So meaningful, yet so meaningless because we just don't know what to think," she said.

Delaney was truly philosophical, Rick thought, though alcohol may have had a part in bringing about a sentimental conversation. There was a moment of silence. "Do you believe in God?" Delaney asked.

"Of course, I do," Rick said. He did believe. He continued. "I don't know what's out there. I just know what I feel, and that there must be a Creator. It's just too damned vast and beautiful to attribute to nothing other than circumstance," Rick said, recognizing himself to be opening up on a personal issue. The wonders of alcohol, he thought to himself.

"I agree," Delaney said, and paused. "Are you a Christian, Rick? I mean, for whatever that's worth in today's definition?" Delaney was more bold and convicted than Rick. "I like to think I am, Delaney. If what I believe in is true, then I am. I mean, I've been to southern Baptist churches and can't say I agree with the whole credo, but I just may be too human," Rick said.

ɔ you mean?" Delaney asked.

..., ɪ believe in the immaculate conception. I believe in prophecy and the prophecy fulfilled in Mary's having the baby Jesus in Bethlehem. I believe in the boy who grew up to be the man who healed, did miracles, and really lived his life as an example of love for everyone. I think any man like that should be believed in, no matter what your religion, or lack thereof. Here was this amazing, gifted man, saying he was the Son of God, and backing up his words. Even if the miracles weren't true, which I believe most were, still this guy is a wonder," Rick continued without a pause, "He cared, he was compassionate, he gave of himself for the betterment of others, and he was tortured and killed on behalf of those he said he loved. I mean, this was one amazing personality to walk the earth, and he's the reason for this overwhelming movement called Christianity. He's the best role model any of us could have, I think, yet we're accepted for what shortcomings we have. We're just people subject to emotions and feelings, and sometimes we just lose our minds, but that's okay with Christianity." Rick thought he'd gone on too long and wasn't making sense, but he was happy with himself to disclose the thoughts he did, though they ran a little deeper. "All I know is, I'm happier believing in him, than having nothing to believe in." Rick paused. "I don't want that to sound like a cop-out. I mean, there's plenty to believe in, if you're willing, I just choose this. It's beautiful, it's romantic, really, and it's fulfilling, so it makes sense to me. If anything, the one indisputable example of Christianity is that it teaches selflessness." Rick finished.

Delaney looked at Rick and smiled. She was glowing as she said, "I like you, Rick."

Rick put his right hand on her left knee, looked into her eyes and said playfully, but seriously, "I love you, Delaney."

Delaney's eyes, serious as never before, stared at Rick's face and then she laid her head onto his shoulder, looking out into the Gulf, "I love you, Rick." Rick turned into her and they kissed softly.

Rick pulled away with a smile. "Not to mention, I really love Christmas," he said, as an afterthought to their discussion on Christianity. They both started laughing as Delaney wrapped her arms around him and they rocked with the gentle waves.

"Me, too," she said. "Me, too."

That night, they fell asleep in the arms of each other, comfortably situated in the hammock built for one.

13

Their second day on the water was much like the first, as they suntanned, fished, and swam. They had fallen for one another, never growing tired of the company, and always talking. Delaney made most of the daytime meals and they showered for the first time since the trip began. The fresh water hose was to be used conservatively at sea, and showers were rare, taken only when necessary.

That evening, Rick set-up the Coleman mini-camper's grill and prepared grilled chicken breasts and baked potatoes for dinner. Delaney watched Rick work diligently in the galley as the sun was setting.

"What, no seafood tonight?" Delaney asked, pouring a glass of wine for herself and making a Maker's Mark bourbon and coke for Rick.

"I thought you might like a little land-lubber's delight," Rick said. "We don't want to take all of the fish from the Gulf, the next generation may want to try seafood, too."

"Okay, you convinced me. Chicken it will be," she said. "You're way of thinking is not all that bad, you know?"

"What do you mean?" Rick asked.

"Well, you're thoughtful. I mean, I know we can eat all the fish we want and there'll be plenty left for the next guy, but you're still thinking about the future, about the people who will be here long after we are," Delaney said.

"Wow, that's pretty deep. Are you getting sentimental on me? Can I pour you another glass of wine?" Rick said.

"I'm serious. The environment, the marine life; it's all very important to me and I'm glad it is to you, too," she said.

"I know," Rick said. "I was only kidding. I think you and I feel the same way. Although my appreciation for nature is self-taught, since all I had to appreciate as a child was cornfields and black ants. It wasn't until I saw the ocean that I first realized how beautiful the world outside of the midwest can be. But you had your dad to show you the wonders of a sunset over the Gulf of Mexico and the enjoyment of sea creatures and the shoreline. You were lucky."

"I know I am. But you got to see lots of awesome things, like snow falling and . . . well," she paused with a blank expression, "I'm sure there's a lot of neat stuff happening up where you're from." They both laughed.

"So, do you intend to follow in your dad's footsteps at all?" Rick asked.

"Philosophically, yes, but I have my heart set on teaching. I am involved in a student-based group that works to protect the gulf waters, though. I think that's something I'll always be active in, even after I'm in the real world."

"That's great, Delaney. What's the name of your group?"

"Well, it's kinda queer, but it's called, 'S.O.S.'" she said.

"Save our ship?" Rick kidded.

"No, Save Our Shorelines." Delaney responded.

Immediately, Rick remembered the poster he read at the FSU student union during his run through the university before being introduced to Barute's buddies at the Radisson. "I saw a poster of yours at the student union." Rick said. "Something about a protest against drilling in the Gulf. Is that still going on? I mean the drilling proposals and everything. I thought it ended years ago."

"It did. But now it's back." Delaney said. "You remember that night we played darts at Tycoon's and I told you about the proposals my dad fought?" she asked.

"Sure." Rick said.

"Well, the company my dad fought, and beat, mind you, Copperhead Oil, received permission to drill off St. Augustine about six years ago and now they are back under the federal government's lease area 181, which is an area designated for oil drilling in the Gulf of Mexico off the Florida coastline."

"Damn, some things never change." Rick said. "So what is S.O.S. doing about it?"

"Oh, the usual stuff. Letting people know the facts about oil drilling, spills and disasters." Delaney said.

"Such as?" Rick said. "Remember, I'm a yankee and a little out of the loop."

"Okay, you gave me Orion, I'll give you oil." Delaney said.

"I'm listening," Rick said.

"Well oil and natural gas exploration and drilling in the sea is not as safe as the corporate giants want the world to believe. The oil conglomerates want to pursue an energy solution and the almighty dollar that takes years to implement, and, ultimately, results in just months of oil supply," Delaney continued, "I'm sure you've heard of the Exxon Valdez disaster in Alaska, but that's just the tip of the iceberg, if you'll pardon the expression. There have been documented and undocumented oil spills all over the world that have ruined marine life and shorelines for generations." Delaney was animated.

"Just ten minutes after a spill of one ton of oil, the oil disperses over a radius of nearly 100 yards, forming a slick that is as thick as an inch. Remember though, that most spills are much more than a ton."

"I've never been that good at math, so I appreciate your keeping this simple," Rick said.

"This oil or natural gas can immediately penetrate the gills of the marine life and cause respiratory, circulatory and nervous system breakdowns. Obviously, these breakdowns lead to death for the fish and other life."

"Obviously," Rick said. "If it would kill us, it would kill them."

"Right. Now, many people may not care so much about the marine world, but these disasters affect humans due to our consumption of sea food and the damage done to our shorelines. So, if you like shrimp or sandy shorelines, either way you're in trouble if there is a gas or oil spill. The poisons in the fish we eat, such as carbon monoxide, can cause serious illness in us," Delaney concluded. Rick was impressed.

"Are you sure you're not in the oceanography department at FSU?" he asked.

"Yes, I'm sure I'm not that smart," she continued, "But, we have to realize that it's not just the ships running aground that cause the disasters, like with Exxon. The most common causes of gas and oil accidents include equipment failure in the pump stations, personnel mistakes, and natural conditions, like seismic activities and hurricanes. The closer to shore the accident, the more likely the disaster will be irreversible for hundreds of years. In fact, routine hydrocarbon spills and blowouts occur during any drilling operation, but that news doesn't make the papers, because the companies are good at hiding it. Our job at S.O.S. is to let our neighbors know about it," she concluded.

"Well, I'm convinced, but I was before you started talking," Rick said. Delaney smiled, almost embarrassed at her winded diatribe against the oil companies. Rick saw her blush and made the best of the moment. "Okay, Senator Chase, what's your best platform statement for this year's re-election?"

Delaney straightened up and smiled with her hands folded before her. She spoke in solemn voice, "The Gulf of Mexico is a unique ecological treasure and, unlike land drilling, the mistakes, blowouts and spills in the salt water spread further and have a much larger impact on our precious marine environment and mankind alike. That's why I believe the oil companies should be forced to stay away from the Gulf of Mexico!" she held out her hands with bilateral peace signs and Rick applauded as he laughed.

"Tell you what, Delaney. Once I'm through with Mr. Winston Skroggsdad I think I'd like to be the free legal counsel to Save Our Shorelines," Rick said. "God knows I should use my talents toward something worthwhile."

"Rick, really? That would be awesome," Delaney said.

"Just tell me when and where and I'll be there," he said.

Rick and Delaney ate their dinner and sat around the deck singing songs and laughing at Rick's horrible Elvis impersonations. The night air had grown a little windy and they slept below, managing somehow to fit together snugly into a single berthing space.

14

They woke to a glistening sunrise on their third day at sail and the waters had a medium chop. Rick was concerned about the waves, though he tried not to show it. He called in for a weather report and was told the seas should be one to three feet that day due to a tropical storm out in the Gulf Stream waters near the Antilles. The storm was expected to die out in a matter of hours due to the cooler sea temperatures further north, or, at worst, make landfall on one of the Caribbean Islands before ever reaching Florida waters. It was rare for the Gulf of Mexico to experience any tropical storm activity in early November.

The wind was thirty knots from the southeast now and Rick had to lower the main sail and run the motor to continue making headway through the strong wind. They were somewhere off the coast of Nokomis Beach, just a day and a half from the Keys, Rick thought. There was no swimming this day and Delaney spent much of her time reading a book down below, out of the weather. It had started raining by dinnertime and the winds were steady at thirty-five knots. Rick secured the main sheet and jib and ran the motor for another hour before dropping anchor. Delaney had made a shrimp cocktail and cold chicken breast sandwiches with dijon mustard. They were both concerned about the weather, but kept their thoughts about it to themselves as they spent most of their time in the cabin with the hatches closing out the elements of nature while they played game after game of gin rummy.

With worry came more beers and glasses of wine. Drinking in a storm like this was not the mark of an experienced sailor. Rick had called into the coast on his cell phone for a weather report to learn that there was a small craft advisory out. He thought he should head in toward shore, but he ignored the impulse. No immediate danger from the storm, even though it had been upgraded to a hurricane with 70 mile per hour winds down in the Caribbean. It was still three hundred miles away and the experts didn't expect it to run through the Gulf Stream up into the Gulf of Mexico. Rick took comfort in the fact that the coastline was only ten to twelve miles away if they needed to pull out of the water. Neither of them talked about heading closer to shore, though they both thought about it fleetingly.

With each new drink, Rick and Delaney became irreverent of the storm and sat around the dinner table playing compact discs of Van Morrison, Joni Mitchell, and Bob Marley on the boom box and singing at the top of their lungs. Delaney had found a set of maracas and a tambourine and they beat the instruments on every hard surface in the cabin and on their legs. They danced and sang until around ten o'clock and, comfortably buzzed, but not drunk, fell asleep in the love seat around the dinner table as the waves gently rolled the sailboat.

About four hours later Rick woke up to a rocking boat and the sound of thunder and lightning crashing outside. The lights that were left on in the cabin were now darkened and Rick knew they had drained the battery. He jumped out of bed, feeling a little hungover, and ran up to the deck. He saw the boom swaying to and fro with the waves of the Gulf, and the jib had come loose and was now flapping violently in the wind.

He tied a rope to the halyard to hold the yard arm down and then secured the jib. By now, Delaney awoke and came up on deck.

"Rick are we okay?" she hollered. "I can't get the radio to work."

On his hands and knees at the bow of the boat trying to secure all the lines, Rick hollered back, "I think we drained the battery. We'll need to run the engine to charge it up. The storm must have turned north. We'll have to ride it out until we get the radio back." He had no idea what he was doing, but tried to appear in control, though death by drowning embraced him. "Put a life jacket on!" he hollered back.

Delaney was frantic. "Where are they?" she yelled back.

They both searched the boat and couldn't find any life preservers. Rick found his cell phone and tried to call the mainland, but couldn't get a signal. The waves now had swells of over six feet and Rick tried to maneuver the boat so that it faced the waves head-on. There was water flying everywhere and now Rick knew what Benchley was talking about with the stinging salt water in the eyes. Delaney was on deck with him, trying to batten down everything that could fly away or float off the boat. Rick came to stern and tried to help Delaney. They were fastening a line to the beam when a huge gust of wind hit them in the back and a large wave crashed over the starboard side of the boat, violently throwing them both to the deck. Rick landed on top of Delaney and he tried to shield her from the storm.

"Rick, I'm scared," Delaney said, almost sobbing, but retaining her composure.

"Don't worry, Delaney, there are worse storms than this. We can ride as fast as the waves can take us. We'll be all right," Rick said, hoping he sounded comforting, and more so that he was right.

As they arose to head down into the cabin, another burst of water smashed into the boat, spraying water copiously on the couple and nearly turning the boat sideways as Rick and Delaney were thrown down the steps to the cabin. Rick shut the cabin door to the world outside and tried the radio again.

"Still no response, Delaney, we'll need to ride it out," Rick said.

Immediately, Delaney threw herself into Rick's arms and he held her tightly. She looked up and smiled with her eyes welling with moisture.

"This is unbelievable, Rick," she said.

"Yea, but think of the stories we can tell when we come through this," he said, and smiled.

Delaney lunged at Rick and kissed him on the lips. The boat was rocking slower now, keeping pace with the waning wind and the waves. Delaney's second kiss grew more passionate. Rick wrapped his arms around her so tightly that he thought she'd need to gasp for air, but she only reciprocated and they were locked in a passionate and fervent embrace. Their kiss grew even more sensual and Delaney pulled off Rick's water-drenched shirt with a primal fervor. She put her hands on his face and pressed her breasts against him. For the first time, as far back as he could remember, Rick didn't know what to do with a woman in the middle of a passionate moment. Releasing his mind and inhibitions, Rick lifted Delaney's shirt from under her shorts and pulled it up over her head, throwing it onto the floor. They kissed and their satisfaction with one another grew as they disregarded the storm outside.

Delaney pulled her right knee up along Rick's side and he held her thigh from underneath as their clothes fell off as if they were too big for the wearer. Rick gently took Delaney to the floor of the cabin. Now lying side-by-side, they never said a word as she felt him and he caressed her. Irreverent to the storm, they were electrified experiencing one another. Their intensity increased to match the storm as Rick rolled over to Delaney. With their hands wrapped around each other's heads and the waves controlling their sexual rhythm, they made love and became one with the storm. A reflection of nature itself, they remained connected in an intimate endeavor that lasted through the hour-long storm. The weather seemed to power their passion for one another and the world outside no longer mattered. In the most terminable moment of humanity and the thought of losing one's body and spirit, they became one, losing self to partner and exposing their souls to the unpredictability of love.

They slept in spurts and awoke together on the floor of the cabin, to the gentle roll of the tide. They'd made it through the storm, and it didn't seem to matter to either that they had. They'd revealed themselves to each other in a matter of hours since the beginning of their journey, and they were contented, at last.

"Good morning," Rick said.

"Good morning," Delaney smiled.

"That was some storm," Rick said.

"It sure was. The one outside was a pretty good one, too," she said, and smiled. "What did you really think about our chances of making it through?"

Rick replied, "To be honest, I wasn't really thinking about the storm as much as I was wondering who built this boat?" Delaney laughed. "I mean, he must have had us in mind, because here we are," he said.

"It seems like the weather is past," Delaney said.

"I think so," Rick said. "I'll call the weather service." Rick got up, wrapping his nude figure in a blanket and called the coast from his cell phone. The weather service reported that the hurricane made landfall on Rum Cay in the Caribbean. "We went through a squaw line of thunder storms which spun off the hurricane," Rick said.

"Those were magnificent thunder boomers," Delaney said.

"I'll say," Rick said. "I'm gonna check up top real quick. Don't move."

"I don't plan to," Delaney said. Rick kissed her, went on deck and was greeted by a cool wind and a sunrise that took his breath away.

"Delaney, would you care to join me on deck ? It's beautiful out here," Rick said as he leaned into the cabin.

"I would, of course," she said. "But it's not so bad down here either," Delaney smiled and invited him back. Rick joined Delaney and they made love again, softly and slowly this time, conforming to the roll of the sea once again.

"I've never met anyone like you, Rick," Delaney said as they looked into each other's eyes. "But I always thought it was possible."

The stunning compliment moved Rick toward Delaney and they remained in one another's arms for most of the morning. Rick was in love, and actually knew it for the first time.

Flush with energy, Delaney made some coffee and invited Rick onto the deck. They watched the late morning sun and talked favorably about the storm and all of its circumstances. The seas became entirely calm and a gingerly wind was blowing steady at five knots from the southwest. Rick hoisted the mainsail and they tacked south as a seagull landed on the bow of the boat.

15

It was past sunset on the fourth day, and Rick anchored the boat, believing he'd brought them firmly inside the northern part of Florida Bay. Florida Bay had always been a fisher's paradise as it was replete with yellow tail, dolphin fish, grouper, shark, and flounder. Though the bay didn't offer much for deep sea fishing or large game fishing, there were plenty of games played by its most beloved visitors, the Atlantic Bottlenosed Dolphin. Here they would come to frolic, mate, and abundantly eat. Fishers knew that when a school of dolphins was around, there would be fishing galore.

Rick and Delaney ate, drank, and sang songs together again on this night and their sleeping ritual in each other's arms while spooning didn't change, except for the fact that they hardly slept.

Now programmed with nature, Rick woke up with the sun on the fifth and final day, even though the sun's brilliance never pierced through the cabin walls. He let Delaney continue sleeping and was surprisingly wide awake and energetic for not having much sleep. He came on deck and observed the day for fifteen minutes. Land to the east was not in sight and the sun rose over the water with an imposing majesty. He didn't put on his sunglasses, but chose to watch the soft light of the sun grow to its full low-horizon intensity until it nearly blinded him. Rick thought of

Orion, and smiled. He was oblivious to pain or discomfort, and felt good about his life, right then, right there. He knew the euphoria he felt couldn't possibly be a constant, yet he realized that any successful relationship has to face challenges to be happy. At last, he thought, he could relate to what happiness was. Rick said a soft prayer of thanks while looking over the Gulf, feeling as though the past few days were inspired by Providence.

Rick stood up and surveyed the ocean around him. With a wide grin and the need for an emotional release, he took off his boxer shorts and plunged into the water head first. He swam nearly thirty yards from the boat, mostly underwater, surveying what was possible with his clouded salt-water vision. When he surfaced for air, far away from the boat, he heard a human-like, but hollow, exhalation. He turned quickly while treading water to see three dolphins swimming between him and the boat. He took a deep breath and swam toward them. Each time he surfaced, he noticed the dolphins had continued on their course, keeping an equal distance from him. He stopped swimming and watch their magical pass through the bay. He felt invigorated enough to swim to the Keys from there, and he swam through the water imagining himself to be with the dolphins at play.

When he got back to the boat, he put a reef in the mainsail and figured this would be the last leg of the enchanted trip. He woke Delaney when the sun was in full bloom and they had coffee on the deck. They suntanned until past noon and Rick kept the boat on course.

From her spot on the bow, Delaney watched Rick sail. "Wow, Rick," Delaney said as she threw her head back to look up to the sky, "this is the best week!"

"Maybe I should go into the business of sailing for a living. Then we can have this all the time," Rick said.

"That would be nice," Delaney said. She rolled over to read her book and, as she looked out over the bow, she yelled with excitement, "Rick! Dolphins!"

Two dolphins were at play on the waves created by the sailboat which was traveling at only three to four knots. Rick tied the wheel and joined Delaney.

"I wish we could go faster," Rick said. "We're probably boring them."

"Maybe they're older dolphins and they enjoy the leisurely pace," Delaney said.

"Where was that optimism during the storm, Delaney?" Rick kidded her. As they watched the dolphins, they noticed over a dozen flying fish shoot out from the bow and land twenty yards in front of the boat. "My friends back home don't believe flying fish are real," Rick said.

"You're kidding? I've seen 'em hundreds of times with my dad," Delaney said. "Of course, I've only seen snow twice and I'm beginning to wonder if I was just imagining it. Does snow exist, Rick?"

"If it didn't, we'd of never met, Delaney."

"Aw, damn, then it doesn't exist, because this is just a dream," Delaney said. She kissed Rick and they watched the boat make its progress through the bay.

Delaney studied Rick for a moment and said, "My dad would have approved. Though he might be a little jealous. . .I wish he could see me now." She looked up, beaming.

"He can, Delaney, he can," Rick said.

Delaney took a nap in the sun and Rick checked in on the radio. He expected to dock the boat near Mallory Square in Key West around six o'clock. Just in time for the sunset, he thought as he looked ahead over the water.

They had a glass of wine for lunch and both admitted they'd drunk quite a bit on this trip. "One more night on the town!" Rick exclaimed, as they toasted one another. "I never asked you, Delaney, have you been to the Keys before?"

"No, in fact, I bet more northern yankees like yourself have been there than Panaceans," she said.

In his lifetime, Rick had been to the Keys over a dozen times and was constantly surprised to talk to Florida Natives, as they liked to be called, and learn it was their first trip to the Keys. To them, it was another state, and they never thought to visit it.

"Put on your crazy suit, Delaney," Rick said. "The Keys are not for the weak-at-heart. 'The rules are different here,'" he quoted a Keys advertisement. "Come to the Keys and have a fling with your wife, uh, life. I mean. . .," the embarrassing pause followed with just laughter from Delaney and then Rick.

A few hours later, the southernmost part of the continental United States was in sight. As they came within a hundred yards of the shoreline, Rick could see the street performers and the crowds gathering about Mallory Square. Delaney saw fire flashes coming from the pier and asked Rick what it was.

"Every night in the Keys, people, well, eccentrics, but people all the same, come to the pier to celebrate the sunset and perform street shows for their friends and the tourists. I'm sure the fire is a juggler and a fire-eating, fearless S.O.B.," Rick said.

Most of the street performers were transplanted middle Americans, expatriots, or simply loners running from the IRS to the seclusion of anonymity in Key West. Here, people were accepted for who they were, regardless of their eccentricities, politics, religion, or sexual preferences. They wove clothing and accessories, made jewelry, read palms and tarot cards, and relied on their creativity for sustenance. Ten years ago, the shows at sunset were more genuine, but now that tourism had taken hold in the Keys, it had become more Barnum & Bailey. Street performers who used to starve could now earn five hundred dollars cash per week performing nightly at the pier and in local establishments, not to mention their day jobs, which were usually in the service industry or t-shirt shops.

Rick brought the boat into a slip in front of the Hyatt Hotel and they walked from the long dock to the shore. A black man with long dreadlocks dressed in a pseudo tuxedo greeted them and asked if they were staying at the hotel. "We are if you've got room," Rick said.

"Oh, yea, mon. Come, come, I take you to the front clerk," their host replied. Rick duked him twenty dollars and told him they'd be back and to hold a room for Morrissey.

"Morrison, like Jim, mon?" the man answered.

"Yes," Rick said, not wanting to explain. "We're going to the pier for the sunset."

"Ah, very good, mon, I see you later. You and the lovely lady enjoy," the man bid them a fun evening.

"Thank you," Delaney said, as she and Rick walked hand-in-hand toward the pier.

"Are we staying at the Hyatt?" Delaney asked on the way.

"Sure. You know Hyatt is one of the few hotel chains that have union workers. My dad would be proud. Besides, I've got to be loyal to my employer, Skroggsdad." They both laughed. Just as the sun was burying its head into the horizon they made it to the edge of the pier. Early November wasn't a huge tourism period for the Keys, and the absence of thronging crowds made Rick feel like a native. A street performer took a picture of them and Rick gave the man five dollars for the polaroid. They watched with childlike enthusiasm the jugglers, fire-eaters, acrobats, and musicians who were eliciting smiles from anyone who was willing to watch them. Each performer was animated and loved the appreciation offered from the crowd in the form of applause and tips.

Delaney was invited to dance the meringué with one of the singers and Rick watched her enjoying the music and having the time of her life. Her sun dress floated in the wind as the sea breeze wrapped it around her body with every turn. The crowd was cheering her and she seemed to have found her element. The three-man Caribbean band played on as Delaney danced and Rick watched with unharnessed pleasure. When she finished, she grabbed Rick and they danced down the pier, appearing drunk to others, but they hadn't even begun to drink.

Before it was dark, they'd had their palms read by a self-proclaimed psychic who told them nothing that they didn't already know; that they were in love. Rick bought Delaney a bracelet and Delaney posed for a charcoal caricature of herself at Rick's request. They went back to the hotel and checked in to drop off their souvenirs and clean up. They lit the room candles, turned down the lights, and showered together.

They enjoyed each other as they made love. The "jolly mon," as Rick called their first greeter, had taken their bags up to the room and Rick dressed in bermuda shorts and a t-shirt. Delaney wore a sunshine yellow, knee-length cotton dress and they went out on the little town, tanned, dressed, and ready.

Rick took Delaney to all of the famous bars, including Captain Tony's, Sloppy Joe's, and The Bull. They took in the island music played by the bar room singers and sang along to a lot of their favorites. They had their first hot meal at The Pelican restaurant on Caroline Street and they told some of the local servers of their adventure in the storm. They felt like hometown sailors, and the world seemed to revolve around them.

The waiter at The Pelican came up at the end of the meal and offered two shooters of snowshoes, the same drinks Rick and Delaney had on their first date at Tycoon's Tavern in Tallahassee.

"On the man at the bar," the waiter said, and gestured toward a man in a straw hat.

Rick looked and noticed Ned Carson, tipping his cheap straw hat at him. "Tell him to join us, won't you?" Rick said, as he looked at Delaney.

"Who is that, Rick?" Delaney asked.

"Ned Carson. He's a friend of Barute's. You've never met him?" Rick asked.

"I don't think so," Delaney said.

"Well, you'd know if you did. Try not to laugh," Rick said. Delaney looked perplexed. Carson made his way over to the couple.

"Hi, Mr. Carson, what in the world brings you to this world?" Rick asked.

"Heh, hey, R-R-R-Rick. I-I-I'm down here f-f-f-fishin' with some Con-Con-, uh, clout, from D.C.," Carson said.

"Well, Ned, I'd like you to meet Delaney. She's a friend of mine. Billy knows her." Rick introduced Delaney. Delaney extended her hand to shake Carson's.

"Nice to meet you, Mr. Carson," Delaney said, as they shook hands.

"N-N-N, Ned, uh, C-C-C. . .," Ned tried to speak.

"CARSON," Rick finished for him, enunciating slowly. Rick thought Carson was either overcome by meeting a woman as beautiful as Delaney or he just hadn't worked on his name long enough.

"Sit down, Ned," Rick said.

Ned sat down and they tried to carry on a conversation for fifteen minutes. Ned said that he was down fishing with some colleagues, but they hit the sack early. Between sputtering syllables, Ned asked about the couple and about Rick's work for Skroggsdad. His questions seemed innocuous enough, but Rick was questioning the coincidence of their meeting. Rick wondered to himself if the man was spying on them. He remembered that a man in a cheap straw hat was not at the bar when he ordered their first round of drinks and wondered why Carson would want to follow them. He had no clue, really, and he and Delaney looked at each other over their shooters, trying not to laugh at Carson. It wouldn't have been funny if Carson were just another person from the street, but this powerful man was a lobbyist in D.C., and, by the way he communicated, Rick took comfort in knowing Carson worked for the G.O.P. and not the Democrats. "Lobbying must not be all that hard," Rick thought, as he looked and listened to Carson.

"S-s so are you kids here on b-b-b-,business, or p-p-p-pleasure?" Carson asked. Rick had a feeling that Carson knew the answer and offered him a lie.

"We flew down yesterday. Delaney wanted to check out some real estate down here for a little change of venue. Naturally, I'm here as her attorney and advisor, and quasi-tour guide." Delaney's eyes widened as she looked at Rick, innocently stunned by his remark.

"H-h-home? H-here? D-D-D, Delaney, you're leavin' your d-d-daddy's place?" Carson seemed genuinely surprised, and almost pleased.

"Naw," Rick butted in, "just vacation property. You know, even North Floridians get cabin fever. Besides, might work out to be a good investment considering the way this place has developed, unfortunately," Rick concluded wistfully, remembering the island from ten years earlier and hundreds of buildings fewer. Delaney appeared relieved she didn't have to join the charade.

"Oh, I s-s-see," Carson said. They talked for a few more minutes and Rick, out of perfunctory custom, offered to buy Carson a drink as they left, which Carson declined.

Walking hand-in-hand back out on Duval Street, Rick and Delaney looked at each other and laughed. "Does his appearance here seem suspicious to you at all, Delaney?" Rick asked.

"Not at all, I'd never met him before," she said.

"I know, but didn't he seem nervous?" Rick asked.

"Well, I think that's how he always appears," Delaney laughed. "He was pretty lucky in the choice of shooters he bought us, though. Snowshoes. You bought my first one in Tallahassee."

Rick looked at her with a smile on his face that turned to

contemplation. "That *was* a pretty lucky guess. He probably drinks 'em in D.C." Rick said, dismissing the coincidence.

Rick hailed a bicycle-taxi service and they were carted off to the south beach where they rented a small catamaran for fifty dollars to enjoy a moonlight sail. There was an occasional light breeze, but the main sail mostly fluffed with the rocking of the boat in the small waves. The night air over the water was cool, but comfortable, and the moon close to the southern horizon reflected off the water and gave a remarkable light upon Delaney and Rick's faces. As Rick managed the tiller, they headed out to meet the moon ever slowly, with Delaney resting the back of her body against Rick's chest.

"You know we're only 89 miles from Cuba right now, don't you?" Rick asked Delaney.

"Oh, Rick, we are not."

"Yes, we are. We really are!" Rick paused. "I mean, I was trying to startle you a little, we're certainly not going to Cuba. But it is 90 miles from the south beach and we're about a mile out," Rick said.

"Right," Delaney giggled.

"I'll show it to you on a map. You know, Havana, Cuba used to be a heavy tourist area, and it probably will be again someday," Rick said. "Soon as we castrate Castro."

"Maybe you can take me there." Delaney turned to Rick.

"I can think of nothing better," Rick offered.

Delaney kissed him on the lips and smiled at him. Running her fingers through his hair, Delaney stared at Rick quizzically.

"What?" Rick said.

"It just occurred to me, and I can't believe I never thought about it before, but, you know, you don't look 31. I guess I've never considered your age because you seem so young," she paused. "Or maybe it's because you act so young," Delaney said.

"You mean I'm immature?" Rick said smiling.

"Hardly," Delaney said. "However, I would venture to say you're childlike, as opposed to childish. And that's probably what keeps you so young."

Rick accepted the compliment. "Well, you know, I was cryogenized for three years," he said.

"What's that? Cryogenized?" Delaney asked.

"Delaney Chase stumped on a word? Wow." Rick kidded her.

"Okay, smart guy. Enough sarcasm. What's it mean?" Delaney asked.

Well, you remember when the rumor was going around that Walt Disney was locked up and frozen in a tank right before he died so he could be unfrozen when they found a cure for dying?" Rick asked.

"Yea, I do remember that. Is that for real?" Delaney inquired.

"Not for Walt, he's actually cremated, but it is a real technique. Scientists have frozen animals for short periods and brought them back to life. The purpose behind it is to freeze people with terminal illnesses and bring them out when there's a cure or some other remedy. Or for those rich eccentrics who are about to die and want to be frozen for a hundred years so they can see the future. That's cryogenics. I'm pretty sure I made up the word 'cryogenized.'"

"So, when were you in a tank? Like I believe that," Delaney said.

"Well, I wasn't frozen, as you've so wisely guessed, but I was in law school for three years." Delaney laughed. "So," Rick continued, "in law school you don't really live, you merely exist. The only thing that registered time was my pulse, but I was so consumed by the academia that I didn't really live. Time sort of stood still. Therefore, I am truly three years younger. Or four or five years younger," Rick said. "Maybe even six."

"Feeling a little self-conscious about your age, Rick?" Delaney kidded him.

"Maybe just a tad," Rick said, smiling.

"I've never heard that one before, Rick," Delaney said. "You do have quite an imagination."

"I try," Rick said.

Rick brought the boat about and they headed back to shore. After tying the catamaran off on the beach, they strolled quietly along the esplanade next to the sea holding hands, and, then returned to downtown Key West amidst the carnival lights and party atmosphere. They had conversations with the beggars and the street musicians and sang along with one of them to "Do Wah Diddy." Nursing frozen daiquiris at a couple of bars, they shared comfortable minutes of silence enjoying each other's company. They retired to the Hyatt around two in the morning, content and well-pleased with their journey.

At 5:45 the next morning they caught a flight to Miami on Windstream Airlines, then planned to catch a jet to Tallahassee. As the plane left the runway of Key West International Airport, Rick stared out the window, enamored with the science of defying gravity. For the first time in his life, Rick wasn't worried flying in a plane. The plane rose above the scattered cumulus clouds blown over the island by the sea breeze effect and Rick's face was greeted with the gentle rising sun, resplendent in its display of multicolored beams of light. Rick considered the beautiful trip and the propitious setting in which it was ending.

16

Rick and Delaney spent the next two days working and going to school, respectively. After coming home from her classes on Thursday, Delaney announced that her mother wanted her to come and visit in Atlanta for a long weekend. Rick was surprised with the announcement. "What about class, Delaney, you've already taken a few days off from the sailing trip? Can you handle it?" Rick asked.

"Has it been that long, Rick?" she asked. Rick knew what she meant.

"I guess you're right. I think I might have attended a third of my classes at Florida State," Rick said.

"Then you don't need to worry about me. You northerners have snow days and the kids get out of school, and, since we don't have snow, we southerners get sun days," Delaney explained. "The only difference is the amount of days off we have and the fact that we go to the beach while the poor students up north stay inside."

"Boy, I really missed this part of the country. I'd almost forgotten how simple life really is," Rick replied.

Rick took Delaney to Tallahassee International Airport around noon on Friday and saw her off safely, after joining her for pre-nerves, pre-flight maneuvers of gin and tonic with lime. Rick didn't learn until later that Delaney's need to calm her nerves wasn't for fear of flight, but for anxiety of spending time with her mother.

Instead of returning to Panacea to work on his legislation drafting, Rick decided to try his luck at the dog track in nearby Monticello. He'd figured he'd been pretty unlucky in love in the past, and now that things seemed to be turning around, he might just strike a winner with the dogs. He also wanted to make contact with a judge who sat on the Jefferson County Circuit Court in Monticello to try to learn more about Barute and his company of thugs. Rick didn't feel comfortable with the situation surrounding Delaney and Sam, and thought, only fleetingly, that Delaney might not be sharing everything about her father's past and her own present life. Whatever it could be though, Rick knew that Delaney must not want him involved for his own safety or because of her own embarrassment. Lack of trust never entered his mind.

17

Judge Parson Tilly was an amiable man of sixty years who was raised right in the Southern way. He had a noble bearing, yet he liked the racin' dogs, his sour mash whiskey straight up, and a good political battle. Rick had first met Judge Tilly through his son, William Tilly. Rick and "Willy" Tilly, (for obvious reasons, Willy preferred "Bill"), were roommates in college during Rick's junior and senior years. Willy was two years younger than "Old man Rick" as he called him, and he looked up to Rick, though Rick never understood why, and he felt uncomfortable with it. Willy was proud and enthusiastic about introducing Rick to his father after Rick and Willy had first begun rooming together at FSU.

One Saturday afternoon in the fall of 1990, during Rick's senior year at FSU, Willy invited Rick to meet Judge Tilly and play golf with Willy and his dad for a round at the country club in Monticello. Monticello was a small town ensconced in the Florida panhandle just thirty miles east of Tallahassee, boasting only a golf course, a dog track, and a bar as its recreational attractions.

The two planned to meet Judge Tilly at the country club a little after one o'clock in the afternoon. As usual with the judge, a "round" was not what one meant when one wanted to play some golf. A round meant you wanted to drink.

Willy drove them out to the club and Rick was excited to meet a judge and talk to one on a personal basis, which was something he had never contemplated being possible at the time. Judges were held in high esteem where Rick came from, and they were to be revered and not bothered by the lower middle class. Rick wouldn't realize until he had become a lawyer and gone around the block a couple of times that judges could actually exist at the bottom of society if one got to know them well enough. Judge Tilly was one of the few judges respected by colleagues and laymen alike because of his impartiality, honesty, and compassion, notwithstanding his propensity to drink. Tilly was one of the few judges Rick would ever admire.

The country club was not so regal as Rick had expected. In fact, the public courses back in his hometown made this place look like a depressed neighborhood yard mowed with a weed eater. Of course there were tall pine trees lining some of the fairways, which enhanced the aesthetics only slightly, but the grass didn't flourish in the southern clay as it did in the rich, black soil of the midwest.

Rick wasn't a very good golfer at the time, and was apprehensive of making a fool of himself before Judge Tilly. He didn't worry for long as the only swings he took were at the practice range. After parking his Lincoln Town Car next to the clubhouse, Judge Tilly approached the two boys practicing and introduced himself to Rick in a loud and confident voice. "Pahrs'n Tilly," he extended his hand.

"Nice to meet you, Sir. Your son speaks of you often," Rick said. This was actually true and Rick hoped he wouldn't have to explain further. Willy talked of his father incessantly, but it usually was about his drinking and gambling.

| PANACEA |

"Ya 'kin call me Pahrs'n, son. We ain't in court," the judge replied in a deep, slow, southern drawl. Parson only half-smiled at his son, doubtlessly knowing of his son's derogatory reflections on his father.

Rick thought the judge to be a pretty handsome man who was in fair physical shape for his age. He was medium in build and only had a slight poosh belly. Rick thought the judge resembled the spit-and-image of John F. Kennedy, if the president had lived that long, and he carried his title of "judge" with pride. Judge Tilly's face looked tan and glowing, but Rick was pretty sure it was just flush from all the booze that he drank. Rick took notice, however, that the judge's nose wasn't swollen or purplish, which is a trait he was told signified a man who drank too much.

The judge was peeling and eating pistachios which he held in his left hand and he appeared happy as a man could be when he announced, "Ya'll, I'm starved, ain't had a bite all day. Let's grab some grub and wait to see if this storm approchin' is gonna blow on over." He began walking toward the clubhouse, and turned back to the disappointed son and his bewildered friend. "Ya'll boys come along."

Now, there may have been one cloud in the sky that afternoon, and Rick wondered what in the world his Honor was talking about. Had he heard a weather report in the last ten minutes that suggested thunderstorms? Rick knew that they could come up in a hurry along the panhandle, but there were usually a couple more clouds in the sky beforehand.

They never golfed that day, and Rick got drunk with a real life judge. Willy didn't seem as impressed with his father, but he didn't seem too concerned either. After all, a cold beer tasted pretty good on a hot afternoon. For nearly four hours the boys drank and listened to the judge tell jokes and stories. Rick was a good listener and Judge Tilly seemed to appreciate him.

Almost as abruptly as he'd introduced himself, the judge washed down the last of his liquid lunch and said he'd see everyone next time. Rick blinked and raised his eyebrows as the judge paced carefully out of the clubhouse.

"Wow, did he forget about a trial or something?" Rick asked.

"Naw, man," Willy said. "My stepmom knows how long a round of golf takes; he's supposed to be home for dinner after he finishes. If he's late, it's no night at the track for him and no sex, if he's still having it." Rick was amused that a woman was dictating the judge's schedule. The boys left the club with an alcohol buzz and Willy drove them back to Tallahassee, "keepin' it between the lines" as his dad so often warned him.

Though neither of them considered law as a career, Willy and Rick both ended up big town lawyers. Willy was now in Atlanta working for Basin & Powers, Ltd., a medium sized firm with just over twenty lawyers concentrating in criminal defense.   Rick had gone on to one of the largest firms in the world only to pound out legal briefs and do personal injury and labor litigation while becoming bored as hell with his job.

Over the years, Rick had kept up with the judge and his son on an annual basis, usually through a phone call around Christmas time, and Rick knew the judge would be pleased to hear from him. Rick got hold of the judge's chambers by telephone Friday afternoon around three thirty and was informed that he was "in court." Rick knew from past experience that this response from a judge's secretary meant one of two things. Either the judge was drinking for the rest of the afternoon at the club, or he was taking a nap in his posh leather office chair with his shoes off and feet propped upon his desk. The one thing the judge definitely was not, was in court. For if he had been in court, his secretary would have to be with him, as she did all of his paperwork and was also his stenographer. Rick knew from Willy that the judge didn't function without his secretary.

"Would you please leave him a message?" Rick said, without response. He continued, "Please tell Parson that Rick Morrissey called and that I'll be at the dog track tonight at seven if he'd like to join me." Because Rick thought the secretary wasn't really paying attention, he addressed the judge by his first name, hoping the secretary would perk up and actually take down a message from someone who knew the judge personally. Other than this one time, Rick had never referred to the judge by his first name, he'd always called him "Judge."

Rick got to the track around quarter to seven and bought some popcorn, coke and a dollar program. The dog track was built with two distinct classes in mind. The downstairs, outside area, was for those who couldn't afford to sit in the air-conditioned restaurant track club, but could afford to piss away their paychecks on a night at the track. The upstairs club was for those people who paid the downstairs people their puny wages and also for some of the older money. Though there were mixed groups present in both places, this was the general scheme of things. Rick preferred the downstairs area because it was outdoors and he felt much more a part of the action vis-a-vis watching it all take place on a television monitor placed at every table in the club's restaurant. He didn't feel sorry for the people who wasted their paychecks on a game of chance, but he did feel angered at the ones who he thought must've had a family with kids who weren't eating dinner several nights a week because their daddies thought more of the greyhounds.

Rick had studied his program for only three minutes when a hand landed on his left shoulder. Pleasantly startled, Rick smiled and leaned back to find the judge smiling. Rick turned and rose to meet his glance.

"Judge, glad you could make it," Rick said.

The judge responded with a deep drawl, "Nehver a prob'm, son. Gotch'r message 'bout five o'clock." Rick presumed that meant the judge had been at the club drinking when he talked to his secretary. The judge's voice was much deeper than Rick remembered. "What brings ya down here, ya din't lose your license to practice lawh in Illinoiz, did ya?" the judge laughed out loud.

Rick wasn't sure if the judge's accent was deeper southern than years ago, or if the judge was just drunk and slurring. "Naw, Judge, just thought I'd come down and clear my mind. . .," Rick was interrupted.

"Lawh kin do that t'ya, son. Let's grab a drank and pick a dawg." The judge was lively spirited and they walked upstairs to the restaurant's teller windows and chose their races.

Rick always liked playing the quinella. He would pick his four favorite dogs, one of them always a long shot, and box them for a twenty-four dollar bet. That meant that if any of the dogs he picked came in first or second, he would win. Usually, the winning combination only covered his bet, but if the long shot came in first or second, the payoff was pretty good, usually over a hundred dollars, and sometimes as high as three hundred. Of course the payout was larger with a higher bet. The judge, on the other hand, was a real gambler. He played only trifectas and he wouldn't box them, he'd just pick the exact order of the first three dogs as he saw them coming in and let the bet ride. Oddly enough, the judge was more successful at this against odds technique than Rick was with his much safer bet, or so it seemed.

The two men sat down at a table next to a window overlooking the track. The judge ordered a Jack Daniels straight up in a brandy snifter and Rick had a Maker's Mark and water.   "What's on your mind, son?" the judge asked. "Have you seen my boy lately? Grown into a full fledged man, don' cha know."

"No, but I spoke with him on the phone several months ago," Rick said. "The reason I called you is because you're the only person I know down here who enjoys a good night out with the dogs."

"Like hell, you fraternity boys always had a hunger for gambling. 'Sides, I'm just an old man, couldn't keep up with you if I tried," the judge said, pretending modesty, but actually believing a little of what he said. "Really, boy, yah're a piece a work. What're ya doing down here, workin'?"

"Actually, I am, Judge. Ever heard of Winston Skroggsdad?" Rick asked.

"The lobbyist? Sure have. Tells everyone he's a Dem'crat. What'cha doin' for him?" the judge asked.

"Rewriting the law on workers' comp reform, democratic enough?" Rick replied.

"Depends on who's askin'." the judge said. "I don't think the man has a backbone and I never cared much for the son-of-a bitch who has him in his back pocket," the judge said.

"Who's the s.o.b.?" Rick asked.

"Fat ass suit named Barute, Billy," Tilly said.

"Guess how I got the job, Judge?" Rick said.

"You don't say? Hell, don't surprise me a bit. Barute pretty good at schmoozin' people into liking him. Skroggsdad's just a venal bastard who changes his politics every time someone slips him a little money. Ya know your politics are different than Barute's don't cha?" the judge replied.

"Not only are our politics different, I can't stand the asshole, either. It's just that this girl I'm seeing introduced me to him to help me find some work. Other than that, I try to stay as far from him as possible."

"Who's the girl?" the judge inquired.

"Delaney Chase," Rick said.

"Ah, Pally Chase's girl. Isn't she in high school?" the judge asked, seriously, but amused. "Maybe three or four years ago, she's twenty-one now," Rick said.

"Good for you, son. Bring 'em up right," the judge said.

Rick never liked the male domineering society of the south, but, naturally, reserved comment in front of the judge and he nodded agreeingly.

"Is Pally his real name?" Rick asked.

"That's his name since I've known him. Apparently he had a god-awful given name and he used to beat the tar out of ev'rone who used it, in his presence or not. Other than that, he was ever'bodys' pal. So, I reckon, 'Pally' emerged," the judge explained. "I haven't seen his girl since Pally got killed in that storm. She sure was a pretty one."

"Still is, Judge, still is," Rick said.

The race announcer's voice came over the closed circuit television monitor. "Five minutes to post time, ladies and gentlemen. Five minutes to post," the announcer's voice reverberated outside the windows as the same message was proclaimed simultaneously on the loud speakers.

"Sure you got the right one in, Judge?" Rick kidded him.

"I'll never tell until it's over. But I'll give you a hint, that number six dawg took a dump right before being led out to the post," the judge said.

This strategy always baffled Rick. Ostensibly, southerners thought it propitious if a dog defecates or even urinates before a race. Rick thought it must be due to the excess weight now resting on the track that made the dog much lighter for the task. Whether they run faster has yet to be proven scientifically. Or maybe, it was just that they were so relieved and happy that they could tear wildly around the track chasing Rusty, the stuffed mechanical rabbit. Rick glanced down at his ticket. He had boxed dogs one, three, seven, and eight. Six was a ten to one shot. Rick felt the gamblers' nervousness and indecision in his stomach about whether to change or add to his bet. He decided he'd made good choices and continued talking with Judge Tilly.

"What do ya need to know 'bout Barute?" the judge asked, reading Rick's mind as those well-trained in jurisprudence were wont to do.

"Well, since you asked, what's his story, not from the beginning of time, but from the beginning of his relationship with Pally Chase?"

Rick inquired.

"Barute, I don't know, I guess he's about fifty years old, but he met Pally when he was just a junior in college at the University of Florida," the judge said.

"A Gator, huh? That figures," Rick mumbled.

"Pally and a man named Buddy Bear were good friends," the judge continued, "and since Buddy was a Gator, he introduced Barute to Pally when Barute was looking for some work during the summer break."

"I met Buddy at the Capitol," Rick said.

"Don't hold his alma mater against him, son," the judge said. "His daddy made him go there. He's a good fella."

"I guess I won't judge; he seemed like a pretty decent man. Besides, Delaney likes him. Go on," Rick said.

"Well, Barute was a real piece of shit to Delaney's father. He'd sit around the boat all day, supps'd to be workin', and loaf his ass off 'til it was time to go in," the judge started laughing. "Damn sure pissed off Pally. I guess they came to blows late in July that summer long ago and Pally sent Barute swimming for shore. At least that's what Pally told me years later." Rick stared at the judge with anticipation. "Before you knew it, Barute got his political science degree at hogtown and started up the lobbying ladder for the conservative-minded in the State of Florida. As you probably guessed, he wasn't much for environmental issues like fishin.'"

"I guessed," Rick said.

The judge continued, "So, somewhere 'bout late 1986, Pally had gotten involved with other commercial fishermen down there in Panacea to try and stop all the barge and shipping activities that were polluting the bay and gulf sound waters along the panhandle. To make a short story long, Barute won the battle. Barute stymied Pally by gaining legislative support and got laws passed providing for free access shipping and no serious controls on the dumping or pollution going on in the bay. The fishing industry was dealt a pretty good blow."

"I remember being down here as a student when the oysters were all of a sudden not so good to eat," Rick said.

"Well it all started before then and just got worse. The two men exchanged victories several times in the war of commercial fishing, and, in the interim, lots o' Pally's brethren lost their livelihood. Pally was making some progress to reclaim the waters and he had won a battle against the Copperhead Oil Company by delaying the company's spot checking, but he died around a year and a half later. Since his death, Copperhead has become an oil drilling juggernaut here in Florida. They've drilled off the Atlantic coastline at will, apparently, and they've tried to claim the northern Gulf waters as their own too. I believe the fight's still goin' on between them and the Emerald Coast residents, but I'm afraid Copperhead is leading the way," Judge Tilly said. "And guess who's spearheading the charge?" the judge asked.

"Do I have to guess? I think I know," Rick said. "Barute."

"Don't have to be Sherlock Holmes to figure that one out, eh?" the judge replied.

"Hell, Judge, Larry Holmes could've guessed that," Rick said, as both men laughed.

The announcer came on for fair warning, "One minute to post, ladies and gentlemen. One minute to post."

"Do you know how Pally died, Judge?" Rick asked,

sympathetically.

"Just what I heard, Rick. Hurricane." They both looked off to the post and waited for the race to begin. Rick glanced back at Judge Tilly, noticing what he thought to be a little sadness in his normally ebullient face.

"Did you know him well?" Rick asked.

"Good 'nuff to know he shunt've died like that," the judge replied. "To good o'va sailor. Then to be cut in half and in quarters by a forensic scientist. The coroner was supposed to have had problems arriving at the cause of death but when he testified at the inquest he said it was just a simple drowning."

Just then the race buzzer went off and all bets were closed as a new announcer came on, this time a woman. "Everyone ready to race, the dogs have reached their post. . .and here comes Rusty!" The mechanical rabbit came screaming around the far bend nearing the post. The gates lifted. "And they're off!" The dogs emerged from the gate like bulging waters released from a restraining wall that crumbled from the sheer tonnage of liquid. They were immediately in a straight and single file line and the number six dog was leading the way, followed by seven, two, three, and eight.

The judge was now smiling and, without looking at Rick, shouted at his dog. "Look at 'em go! Hot damn! Go, Crackerjack, go!" the judge was now laughing.

Rick looked at his program. Indeed, the dog's name was "Crackerjack." "Bound to lose," Rick thought, as he remembered the first night of the rest of his life in Chicago when he decided to forsake his career for the more simple life in the Florida panhandle. He had still not determined what that life was about, but he had begun to realize he was here for good reason, and not as a crackerjack lawyer.

Crackerjack led the pack around the first turn and into the straightaway which was directly in front of the restaurant sky box and the judge and Rick. Just then, Crackerjack went to the right hand, outside lane of the track and headed straight for the outside rail. The dog was now wagging his tail, which had been pointed straight the whole race, and he stopped cold along the rail. The judge looked on in disbelief as he watched Crackerjack sniffing dog shit on the track turf while the other dogs made their way to the finish line.

The judge's cigar dropped from his mouth and he didn't say a word, but only stared at the dog. One of Rick's other picks, number seven (he never looked at the names), came in second to the favorite, number three. Rick had hit a good payoff. As the rabbit stopped and the dogs surrounded it, barking in a shrill melee that could be heard through the windows of the restaurant, the trainers grabbed their dogs and headed for the stable.

Rick watched his winner, number seven, with childlike pleasure and, just before the dog and its trainer got to the stable door, Rick noticed the dog spread its legs and squat. Rick was beside himself as he noticed the judge's reaction to the winning dog's relieving himself after the race instead of beforehand.

Over the course of the evening the two men won a total of about a hundred dollars each and Rick learned about Delaney and her family. As an only child, Delaney was lavished with attention from her parents. Like Delaney, her mother, Meredith, aspired to be a school teacher but dropped out of FSU in 1974. Meredith Chase was of rich southern blood and tradition, and the house Delaney now lived in was built by Mrs. Chase's great-grandfather in 1912. Meredith had been a debutante and was raised under the most strict and proper southern rules and traditions. This meant that she had the proper balance of religion and southern etiquette. She and Pally never even slept together until after they were properly married, and they only slept together afterward for the religious purpose of creating a child.

They had a traditional southern marriage in 1975, with Pally as the leader of the family and Meredith comfortably partaking in husband worship and being active in junior league, garden clubs, and auxiliary organizations. Although most of the money came from Meredith's side of the family, it was understood that Pally would make the financial decisions around the house and would decide which income was discretionary for the use of Mrs. Chase.

Pally was from a fishing family and had begun work on his father's boat when he was just ten years old. He was a natural leader and had tremendous skills with people and getting them to do things they didn't want to. Pally's fishing business eventually became a commercial success and, after his death, left his family financially secure. As far as the judge knew, Delaney was the heir to her father's estate, with Ms. Chase taking her widow's mite under Florida probate law. The judge wasn't sure what the estate was worth, but he had heard that a trust was established that would take care of Delaney for her lifetime. Delaney wouldn't get the money until she was 22 years old.

Rick thanked the judge for his time and for the informative evening. The two men parted company promising to do it again sometime.

18

Rick spent the next several days working on his legislation job and longing to see Delaney again. He knew he already drank too much socially, but with Delaney gone, he was bored and went out each day beginning around six o'clock in the afternoon on the front porch of Delaney's with a bourbon and continuing into the night at Posey's where he had become accepted as a friendly face and a regular. As each day passed, he grew more excited to see Delaney. Finally, Tuesday night, November 14th, arrived and Rick went to pick her up at the airport.

Delaney came off the plane trying to smile, but crying sadly. Rick was at the bar, which still permitted smoking, trying to appear nonchalant when he saw her. Quickly he dropped his cigarette in the ashtray and darted toward Delaney.

"Delaney, what's the matter," Rick said, trying to hide his joy of seeing her for fear this wasn't the best time to act playfully.

"Nothing. I'm okay Rick. I'm glad to be back. It's good to see you," Delaney said reassuringly. "I want to talk about it, but I can't right now. I am glad you're here though," Delaney said, reading Rick's need for reassurance that he wasn't the cause for her tears.

They got into Delaney's Jeep and drove to Panacea in silence.

Rick was usually very uncomfortable with silence around a woman, and this experience was misery.

When they arrived at Delaney's house, Delaney jumped out of the Jeep and ran into the house with her duffle bag, greeting Southpaw at the door. Oddly, Rick noticed at that time that he admired her for her ability to travel light. Erasing the odd moment, Rick followed Delaney inside. He found her in the pantry area where she was loading her clothes in the laundry. She didn't say a word and, as she put the lid down on the washer, she looked down toward the floor and took two steps into Rick's arms. She kept her arms at her side as she looked up at Rick's lips and, without making eye contact, kissed him. Rick could taste her tears as they rolled from her eyes down into the corner of their mouths. Rick thought her tears had the taste of honeysuckle drops, which had a density and sweetness that, until now, Rick could never quite compare.

The kiss and Rick's embrace lasted only seconds. Delaney looked up into Rick's eyes and stared seriously, then smiled.

"Come with me," she said, as she led Rick to the foyer and up the center staircase to the mysterious upstairs. Rick was confused as he passed by family portraits on the staircase walls and beyond several doors which must have been bedrooms. Delaney led Rick into a corner room in the rear of the house. The gibbous sun offered a less than complete disk of light as it faded into the earth and the horizon while gently lighting the room Delaney and Rick had entered.

Delaney took Rick by the waist and pulled him close as they embraced once again. Delaney's tears were now gone and she struggled to kiss Rick. Without a word, Delaney left the embraced and turned toward the bed where she threw her head into a pillow and began to sob.

It was an odd moment for Rick, and he felt as if it were the last time they would be together. Delaney's mood was different, almost disapproving. Delaney turned away from Rick and fell asleep while Rick tried to spoon her from the back. He rested next to her with his eyes open, staring out her westward window. He attempted a conversation, but Delaney only returned soft, disinterested noises that weren't even words. Rick's stomach began to hurt. He felt a distance had come between the two, but he couldn't explain to his mind or his heart just why or how it happened.

"Passions make us feel, but never see clearly," Rick said softly to Delaney, trying to analyze his own feelings.

"Hmmm," came Delaney's disinterested sound of acknowledgment.

Rick and Delaney spent the next two days in uncomfortable silence, aside from the usual perfunctory greetings. Delaney would attend her classes and Rick was wrapping up his legislative project. By Friday morning, Rick offered to cook out on the grill that night.

"How about some boiled shrimp and some filets this evening, hon?" Rick knew too late that adding "hon" to the end of his invite sounded desperate. He was about to make light of the situation, but Delaney was quick on the draw.

"Can't, Rick, I'm working late tonight with a study group." Rick was confused by Delaney's lack of a "thanks anyhow" or "how about tomorrow." For the first time since they met, Rick felt his affections were not mutually reciprocated by Delaney. He felt his throat tighten.

Delaney said goodbye and bade Rick a nice day. "Well, that's a start," Rick said to himself. He moped around Delaney's house for the better part of the morning. His mind was consumed with just what in the hell was happening. He wasn't angry, but confused, and found himself sickly humored by the gut-wrenching he was enduring. After all, his life in Chicago delivered many gut-wrenching moments to his female encounters with Rick's never having a moment of lost confusion as he had now. He tried to smile and quickly went to get some work done to take his mind off his personal life. Rick tried to work for an hour and realized he had read the same proposed legislation over ten times and still couldn't recall what it was about. He sat back in his chair, mentally exhausted. "I'm whipped," he said.

Rick had not been "pussy-whipped," as his friends called it, for as far back as he could remember. At one point during his formative years in college he'd been burned for wearing his heart on his sleeve. By becoming whipped, Rick felt he made himself vulnerable and, consequently, he vowed not to let it happen again, and he hadn't. Up until his chance meeting with Delaney in Panacea, Rick had been taught through his peer group, including other women, that no two people were meant to be together. Fate had nothing to do with it. Togetherness was simply a matter of convenience. He was led to believe that there was no such thing as love at first sight. Consequently, long dating relationships were hard for him to come by and, if he happened into the prospect of one, he would cause it to self-destruct in apprehension of the word "forever."

Swearing never to wear his heart on his sleeve made Rick insensitive, he thought, and he knew he would miss the person in him who was willing to love without promise or prediction. Rick was even chagrined at succumbing to the pressure of his peers in this philosophy, but it seemed to protect his heart. But now, he was ready to forsake all that he had learned in this arena and return to the genuine and compassionate personality he had once embodied, although the risk of heartbreak intimidated him.   He always considered his previous relationships as non-inspired and, now that he found Delaney and himself melting so perfectly together, he was no longer afraid of forever, but of goodbye.

Sitting on Delaney's porch, Rick realized that he needed to give Delaney time to sort through whatever thoughts she had on Rick. He knew Delaney was fond of him, or had been, and, whatever her reason, Rick needed to be gone for at least a while. He couldn't force her to talk about what was bothering her and, eventually, he would know. The only problem was how to leave gracefully, saving Delaney the need to call and ask dutifully why he left. Rick wrote Delaney a letter stating that he had been called to put in some late hours on the legislative project before it was due and Skroggsdad would need him in Tallahassee. Rick left the number of the Radisson and he moved out.

Van Morrison's "Brown Eyed Girl" came on the radio as Rick drove north up Route 319. Rick's eyes welled with moisture. He sang out loud.

19

When Rick arrived back at the Radisson in Tallahassee to check in, it was nearly five o'clock in the afternoon and time to think about dinner. Still consumed by thoughts of Delaney and wanting answers, Rick decided that a trip back to St. Mark's and Posey's Oyster Bar would give him a chance to talk things over with Sam. If anyone knew Delaney's mind, it was her best friend. Normally, Rick wouldn't approach a girl's best friend for advice on the girl, but this situation was different since Sam liked Rick and since Sam was a male best friend of Delaney's.

Sam had just sat down after his afternoon show for a few beers when Rick arrived. Rick approached Sam's booth before Sam noticed him. "Hey, Sam, how'd it go today?" Rick said.

"Not bad, but I could've used you today. Not many of today's customers appreciated the black Jimmy Buffett sound," Sam said. "How has Delaney been since she got back from Atlanta?" Sam asked, apparently knowing what had been on her mind.

Rick was surprised he didn't know the answer and nodded, "Well, she's back all right. At least her body is, but I'm not so sure her spirit made the trip," Rick said solemnly.

Sam took a drink of his beer. "You look like a rudderless boat, Rick. What's the matter? Love got you in a fluster?" Sam seemed to read Rick's mind and make light of his wistfulness.

"You know, Sam, I'm not one to investigate a girl I like; I'd rather just take things as they come and hope fate throws me some helpful cards. But I'm damned confused. Just a week ago this girl was seemingly as crazy about me as I was her, and now she's entirely removed. Hell, I'm too old for games and, even though I think I can play them pretty well still, I don't want to." Rick paused. Feeling more insecure than he'd ever felt in his life, he asked the question, "Do you think I screwed up?"

Sam chuckled with a wide-assed grin that made Rick feel a little more comfortable as he hoped for a positive response. "Shit, man, nobody can understand a woman, not even a big time looker like you." Rick was somewhat confused by the criticism and compliment all in one sentence.

"But since I like you, I'll tell you what I can," Sam continued. "My pal, Delaney is just plain confused."

"What do you mean, Sam?" Rick asked.

"Well, we had some beers the other night and she opened up a little. You sure you want to hear this?" Sam asked.

"I don't know, am I?" Rick said.

"Well, stop me if you think you've heard this one before," Sam said. "Delaney and her mom had a heart-to-heart over you. I don't know if you know it or not, but Meredith Chase was fifteen years younger than Pally," Sam continued. "Well, Ms. Chase and Pally never got along so well. According to Delaney, her mom and dad never had sex for the five years preceding Pally's death."

"And Meredith Chase attributes that to the age difference?" Rick asked.

"I don't know. I don't think that's it at all. My mom has another theory, but you'd have to ask her," Sam said. "But, maybe Meredith Chase isn't a big fan of couples who are over a decade apart."

"Doesn't Delaney understand that we're not her mom and dad?" Rick asked, helplessly. "I mean, who knows if they even had sex at all, or even felt the same way about each other as Delaney and I do?"

"Well, for one, they did have sex, or we wouldn't be having this conversation about Delaney," Sam said.   Rick acknowledged the sarcasm.   "Second, you'll have to ask Delaney about the difference between your love for her and Pally's love for Ms. Chase."

"I never said anything about love," Rick said.

"You didn't have to," Sam said. "I know you two have already said the "L" word. Don't try to play coy with me."

"Okay, fine. I won't," Rick said. "I love her. And I guarantee you that I'll make love to her right up until the day I die at the ripe old age of one hundred," Rick said with a little more conviction than he wanted to give away.

"That's a little more than I want to know," Sam said. "By then, all your bones will be soft and limber, with the exception of one." They both laughed. "If it makes you feel any better, Rick, Delaney did tell me that her mom and dad never got along for as long as she can remember. In fact, she told me that her father never really seemed in love at all. She does believe you two are different. I think she's just a little apprehensive. Give her time," Sam said.

"Thanks, Sam," Rick said. "Please, if Delaney and I ever get together, don't tell her. . ." Rick was interrupted.

"How you were so whipped you couldn't see straight?" Sam

asked.

"Something like that," Rick admitted.

"Don't worry, she's whipped too. Women just have a different way of going about it," Sam said. "There's one more thing, Rick," Sam said.

"What now, Delaney's mom hates lawyers?" Rick asked, smiling.

"No. I'm afraid it's a little more serious than that. I didn't want to mention it, but I know you've earned an answer. I think I've straightened Delaney out, though," Sam said.

"About what?" Rick asked.

"Well, you remember Buddy Bear, don't you? He was a good friend to Pally and the Chases?" Sam asked.

"Of course, he introduced me to Barute. Don't tell me he disapproves," Rick said. "He seemed to like seeing Delaney and me together."

"Well, Buddy Bear had a conversation with Delaney's mom. He got this damned fool notion that you were some kind of drug dealer, cocaine I believe, hiding out down here until things calmed down back in Chicago," Sam said. "And he told Ms. Chase that you were wanted by the authorities in Chicago. That's why you left a great job with great money to hide from the feds, or whatever. Apparently, he showed a picture of you having lunch with a drug lord in Chicago. I guess he's in prison now."

"What?" Rick was stunned. "How the hell did that story come around?" Rick asked. "I don't know any drug lords. If I had lunch with a drug lord, I sure as hell didn't know it!" Rick said.

"It's not true, is it?" Sam asked.

"Fuck no, Sam. Do you think it's true?" Rick asked.

"No. That's what I'm trying to tell you. I think I straightened Delaney out on that one," Sam said. "I just know what I was told and Delaney remembered that you told her you were offered drugs from some clients. She probably just got a little spooked."

"I told her that because I was offered drugs, favors, whatever; and that's why I left all that shit behind. I wouldn't have mentioned it if it weren't the truth," Rick paused. "Well, how the hell did Buddy Bear come up with that story?" Rick asked.

"Delaney didn't know. Buddy had just wanted to tell her to be careful with you because a good source, whom Buddy agreed to keep confidential, told him that you were in the business," Sam continued. "Said you had a ton of money, all from drugs, and that the feds were getting close to you in Chicago so you dropped out of sight. Said that's why you're here, spending money and not really looking for any permanency, in work or in love."

"You've got to be fucking kidding," Rick said. "That's bullshit."

"I'm sure Delaney can't believe it, Rick, and I bet Buddy doesn't either. Buddy just wanted Delaney to be careful, that's all," Sam said.

"Did Barute or any of those assholes start this?" Rick asked.

"Buddy wouldn't say, Rick. So, I don't know," Sam said.

"My god." Rick ran his hands through his hair. "Sam, I hope you believe me. Somebody just doesn't want me around Delaney. Hell, I'm surprised you haven't been poisoned on me too," he paused. "Who the hell?" Rick said, trying to contemplate the origin of the unfounded aspersion.

"Rick, you're a good person. You're honest. I'm in your

corner," Sam said.

"Thank you, Sam," Rick said.

"Hey, in a hundred years it all won't matter anyhow," Sam said.

"What do you mean by that?" Rick asked.

"Nothing. I believe you," Sam said. "I just said that because it's one of your favorite sayings." Sam gently slapped Rick on the shoulder.

"I guess it is," Rick said. "And even I'm not sure what the hell it means." They both smiled.

"Hey, I've got to get to my momma's for dinner. Why don't you come along. There's a lot more to Meredith Chase than I could tell you. If anybody can explain Ms. Chase, it's my momma," Sam said. "Just bear in mind that once you get her started on Ms. Chase, she's likely to tell you everything, true or not. So brace yourself. Momma can be quite a gossip."

"Home cooked southern cuisine and gossip?" Rick said in pretended indifference. He smiled. "Sounds like a great offer. Should I bring some package to drink?" Rick said.

"Naw, my momma's got some hard liquor that should set you straight," Sam replied.

"Where's your daddy?" Rick asked, then grimaced in the thought that he might have asked the wrong question.

"Never knew him, Buddy," Sam said. Rick started to apologize. "No big deal though. Love my momma and I can't imagine life any other way." Sam paused smiling. "Let's go. Grab your car and follow me."

"Not that I'm trying to be polite or anything, but should we call first to let your mom know I'm coming?" Rick asked.

"Hell, no. She's always making too much food. Besides, Rick,

I've told her all about you. She won't mind," Sam said. "Anyways, she doesn't have a phone. She entertains a crazy notion that phones only bring bad news or good news and she'd rather have either delivered to her in person."

20

Sam's mother lived in Sopchoppy, just a twenty minute drive from the bar. Sam had given Rick detailed directions and Rick found the home without any trouble thanks to the wooden mailbox clearly marked, "Chesterfield's - Est. 1974." As Rick pulled up to the house on a gravel road off highway 319, he realized that the South still liked to keep the black and the poor in their place. The small, wood-framed home bordered the Apalachicola National Forest. From the looks of the kids playing in the adjacent yards, Rick knew that this was a black neighborhood as there were no signs of white inhabitancy. Each of the five homes along the gravel road looked nearly the same. The house that Sam grew up in was a beaten down wooden shack. The Chesterfields' neighbors delineated the property line with a dismantled 1979 Chevy van in their side yard hoisted up on blocks, as if someone put it there just to remove the tires and sell them for scrap change. Additional scrap along the side yard included more car parts and an outdoor washing machine. "Shit," Rick said as he pulled into the gravel driveway. "This is terrible," he thought, looking around and feeling pity for the area's inhabitants.

As Rick exited his car, three young boys and one girl approached him screaming in delight over the new convertible being in their neighborhood.

"Hey, Mister, can I sit in your car?" One of the young boys

asked, while the other children looked on with interest.

Rick paused and looked at each of the children, noticing their clothing was covered in dirt and their hands were muddy. Rick laughed and smiled at the young boy, "Sure. In fact, you can all get in."

The kids cheered and jumped into the car.

Just then, Rick noticed an elderly black woman take to her feet off the rocking chair she was occupying on her front porch next to the Chesterfield's house. Rick left the kids in the convertible and walked toward the elderly woman.

"Hello, ma'am. I'm a friend of Sam Chesterfield's," Rick said. "The kids were begging to jump in the car; I hope you don't mind." Rick was apologizing for not having asked the woman's permission. "My name is Rick Morrissey."

She responded with a soft, southern voice, "Oh, child, that's okay. I was just a little alarmed at such a nice car being in our neighborhood. Thought maybe you were lost," she said, without indicating that she was concerned for the children's safety. "Looks like the children are having a good time."

Rick was amazed by her lack of suspicion of a strange man allowing strange children to jump into his car. Just then, the kids starting honking the horn on Rick's convertible. Rick turned around and then back to the elderly woman, who was now laughing at the children.

"I think they want a ride," Rick said.

"Child, if you've got the time, they've got the inclination," the woman said.

"But you don't know me," Rick said.

"But I know people, child," she said. "Besides, you can't spend your whole life not trusting other people.   You know Havana Chesterfield, I know Havana Chesterfield. I trust her, so I trust you."

"Actually, ma'am, I only know Sam," Rick said. "I'm here to meet Ms. Chesterfield and have dinner with her and Sam."

As Rick was talking, Sam pulled into the driveway and parked his car. He noticed Rick talking to the woman. As he stepped out of his car he said, "Hey, Rick. This is my house over here. It says 'Chesterfield' on the mailbox." Sam pointed to his house. "How long were you in college?" he kidded Rick.

"Hey, Sam. Just met this nice lady and those children out there in my car," Rick said. "Thought I might drive the kids down the lane and back."

"It's your car," Sam said. "And there's not a car wash around for miles," he smiled at Rick and the woman. "I'll see you inside my house. Just knock and come on in."

"Okay, it'll just be a couple minutes," Rick said. He turned to the woman, "You sure it's okay?"

"Oh, go on, now." she said. "I only wish there was room for me."

Rick paused, looked at her and said, "there is, ma'am," and he held out his keys.

"Oh, my heavens!" the woman was shocked. "No way can I drive your car," she said.

"Do you know how to drive?" Rick asked.

"Well, yes, but it's been a couple a years."

"Then you can drive it. It's an automatic transmission, so you don't need to shift. Just take it slow until you feel comfortable. There's plenty of gas and I'll be here for a while. Enjoy yourself and the kids," Rick said. "I'd love to take them, but I'm sure Ms. Chesterfield has some good food waiting."

"Really, child. I can't take your car," the woman said.

"Look, you trusted me first. Now, I'm trusting you," Rick said. "Only, I don't know your name yet."

"It's LaVonne. LaVonne Colton."

"Ms. Colton," Rick took her hand and placed the keys in it, "Enjoy yourself. Just let the wind blow through your hair." Rick smiled and left the woman with the car keys.

Sam met Rick on the front steps of his porch as Ms. Chesterfield opened the door with a gleaming smile. Judging by appearance, Sam was definitely his mother's child.

"Lawd have mercy, aren't you an attractive young man?" Ms. Chesterfield said as she looked toward Rick.

Rick observed the matriarch as discreetly as possible. She must have weighed only one hundred thirty pounds and she was very attractive, looking about 35 years old, but she must've been at least in her late forties since Sam Chesterfield was in his late twenties. Her skin was light black and oily, but Rick couldn't tell if it was genetic or from her working over the hot stove, assuming they had one.

"Hello, Ms. Chesterfield, I'm Rick Morrissey, actually an old friend of Sam's cousin, Eddie. We went to FSU together. But I've got to admit that your son is more interesting," Rick said, confident and secure in his surroundings, and drawing a laugh from Sam's mother.

"Havana Chesterfield, Rick, I'm glad to have you here. We've got plenty of food and I'm sure that's why Sammy brought you." Just then Rick thought her "lawd have mercy" line with the thick southern accent must have been feigned. She had a true speech and sounded somewhat refined in her invitation to dinner.

Sam made a couple of drinks and led Rick to the dinner table which was waiting with appetizers of fried Gulf crab claws ready to eat. Ms. Chesterfield was in the kitchen working on the final touches to dinner while the men were in conversation. Rick was just excusing himself from Sam to use the restroom when Ms. Chesterfield entered the room. Rick had just stood up when Ms. Chesterfield walked in and said, "My, my, you are quite the gentleman, Rick. Please sit down, no need to stand for me; I'm just a mom. It's nice to see such manners though. You payin' attention to that, Sammy?" Knowing Ms. Chesterfield thought Rick had taken to his feet because she entered the room; and, not wanting to spoil the moment, Rick took his seat and held his bladder for the entire dinner, to the intense delight of Sam, who knew better, but kept his silence despite his uncontrollable grin.

The three enjoyed a true southern meal, complete with boiled shrimp, asparagus with Hollandaise sauce, pistachio salad (or Watergate salad as they called it in the South), barbequed ribs, and homemade whiskey. Ms. Chesterfield certainly could not have been used to eating with the wealthy, but her manners and table etiquette would put many country clubbers to shame, Rick thought. She was a delicate black woman with a soft style and she was genteel in her conversation. Mostly she just listened to the boys talk, but, as mother's go, she had the normal amount of curious questions for Rick. Rick never minded being interrogated by mothers. In fact, he enjoyed being questioned.

"Rick, honey, what's a nice young man like you doing without a girl under his arms? I do hope you're not gay. You're not gay, are ya' honey? What a tragedy that'd be." Ms. Chesterfield was playfully blunt and chuckling.

"No ma'am, Ms. Chesterfield, I'm not gay. I appreciate the compliment, though. . . about the tragedy and all that, not the gay part," Rick replied. The whole table was laughing.

"Mama, Rick has taken a likin' to Ms. Delaney." Sam's southern drawl was now more accented in the home of his mother. Ostensibly, Sam didn't want to sound like the educated black man he had become.

"You know, Delaney's had a difficult life, don't cha son?" Ms. Chesterfield confided.

"Yes, ma'am, she told me about her father," Rick said.

"Oh, that ain't the half of it child," Ms. Chesterfield said. Rick looked on with curious interest. "Oh, child, Delaney has had a heck'uva time in her life," Ms. Chesterfield continued.

"Mama, don't be goin' a gossip'n now," Sam said, only encouraging his mother to continue.

"Honey, you just take it easy. Rick's a big boy. Any man oughta know the truth about the girl he loves," Ms. Chesterfield said, surprising Rick that she used the word "loves." "Besides, Rick seems like he's got a good head on his shoulders. He'll understand," Ms. Chesterfield continued.

Rick was no longer curious, but scared. He wondered to himself what in the world Ms. Chesterfield could be referring to. Posing indifference, Rick replied, "So what's her story, ma'am?"

"My boy, Delaney went through one hellacious childhood with her mama. Her mama is a strange woman," Ms. Chesterfield confided. "You know, she's in the nuthouse?"

"Nuthouse, ma'am?" Rick replied.

"She started going a little crazy four or five years before Pally perished in that hurricane," Ms. Chesterfield said. "Delaney, oh, the sweet child, never really knew her mama," she continued. Delaney was only five years old when Ms. Chase started losing it. Oh, bless Pally's soul, he stood by her though," Ms. Chesterfield said.

"What happened?" Rick said.

"Ms. Chase was a southern debutante when she married Pally and then became pregnant by him," Ms. Chesterfield said. "Four years after Delaney, their only child, was born Ms. Chase got herself one of them head shrinkers to tell her she'd been raped as a child," Ms. Chesterfield continued. "She went to the shrink to talk about life as a home-mom and as the wife of a man who spent most of his time on his career. In exchange, she learned from the shrink through some memory recall therapy that her daddy had sexual relations with her when she was a child herself." Ms. Chesterfield waited for the reaction. There was none from Rick.

"Well, Ms. Chase found herself drinking every day and taking 'dem prescription drugs and, one day, she wound up in the bathroom with her four year old Delaney and a bathtub full of warm water prepared to kill her daughter and then hang herself. Fortunately for Delaney, Pally Chase walked in on them and stopped the whole thing. He checked her into a nuthouse and she seemed to recover somewhat. At least she wasn't doing or saying anything crazy and she was invited back home for a couple years. She was balancin' out a little, but then Pally got killed about two years after that, and Meredith Chase went off the deep end and the poor thing ain't never recovered her senses.

"Momma, I'm sure Rick don't need to hear no rumors about Delaney's family," Sam said. "Rick's just out for a nice dinner, ain't 'cha Rick?" Sam was only prodding his mother to continue as he looked at Rick and winked.

"These ain't rumors, Sam, honey. And you know it," Ms. Chesterfield said. "Shall I continue?"

"Well the story is unsettling, but I am interested," Rick replied. "Sam tells me that Pally and Ms. Chase never seemed too close," Rick said. "Equally curious to me though is Pally's death. Does tragedy just follow this family wherever they go?" he inquired.

"Oh, boy, Rick, you done asked the wrong question," Sam interjected. "Mama Chesterfield here has a conspiracy theory that will rival the one from the grassy knoll in Dallas if you'll let her go ramblin' on." He continued. "Mama, I've got to get back to work. The big boss wants me to play a late set because the 'Noles got a home game tonight and the crowd will be thick."

"Are you really interested in knowing about Pally?" Havana Chesterfield said.

"Now, Mom, Rick's got things to tend to," Sam said, teasing both his mother and Rick.

"Of course I am, ma'am," Rick interjected. "I suppose I could visit with you a little longer, if you don't mind," he said. "Would that be all right, Sam?"

"Whoa, you done did yourself in, Rick. I'll see you in about three hours," Sam said. "You'll be lucky if the liquor holds up. You'll need it. Stop by the bar and see me if you have time later."

Sam left for work and Ms. Chesterfield invited Rick out onto the front porch for another drink and a hand rolled cigarette made by Ms. Chesterfield. Rick felt a little uncomfortable staying behind to listen to Havana Chesterfield, but his curiosity over Delaney's mother and Pally's demise was incurable without the right antidote. In this case, Rick was hoping for an elaboration over Judge Tilly's sketchy report about Pally's death and some explanation for Delaney's odd behavior.

On the veranda, Ms. Chesterfield began, "Smell that sweet Southern air, Rick."

"I remember the smell from years ago ma'am," Rick said. "It's honeysuckle. The one scent I know of that can't be put into a bottle of lotion or a perfume without compromising its integrity."

"You got that right, Rick," Ms. Chesterfield said. "You're pretty smart for a snowbird. You know, I'm glad you stayed back to visit with a boring, and semi-drunk, older black lady. Life can get awfully boring and a little bit lonesome out here with no one around," she said. "I like you Rick. You've been good to my boy, Sam. He speaks highly of you on account of his desire to protect the well-being of Ms. Delaney," she concluded.

"He's been a good friend to me in my short time here, Ms. Chesterfield. I'm grateful," Rick said. "So what about this theory Sam doesn't buy?" Rick inquired.

"Well, normally I'd pester you over and over to see if you really want to hear it. I like building up gossip. But, since I'm feeling the alcohol a little bit, I'll just skip right to the 'chase,' if you'll pardon the expression," Ms. Chesterfield said.

"Why don't you skip right to him?" Rick encouraged her with a smile.

"Rick, for twenty years I've wanted to tell a secret that I've harbored in my heart." Ms. Chesterfield became misty-eyed but continued talking without emotional effect, other than interest in her own story. "I just met you today, and I've drunk more tonight than in the last three years, and maybe because you're from out-of-town that I feel comfortable telling you this," she said. "Besides, you seem to care a lot about my boy and Ms. Delaney."

"Telling me what? Are you thinking that Pally wasn't killed by accident?" Rick asked.

"Mr. Chase died too early at the hands of the sea that nurtured his livelihood. That's for sure," she said. "But, what I'm trying to tell you is this," she hesitated.

"Go on, ma'am," Rick said, feeling somewhat stupid for implying that Pally was murdered.

"Do you really care about Ms. Delaney?" Ms. Chesterfield inquired.

"More than I thought possible," Rick said. "Why?"

"Do you care for my boy, Sam?" she asked.

"Yes, I do," Rick said. "He's my only friend down here if you don't count Delaney. She's just a different kind of friend."

"I understand," Havana Chesterfield said. "Rick, I don't want my boy hurt physically or emotionally." She started again, "You understand?"

"Not exactly, ma'am. But I promise you that I would never hurt him," Rick assured her.

"I know that," Ms. Chesterfield said. "You've shown your kindness in caring for people other than yourself," she continued. "So, I've chosen you to help me through the most difficult confession I've ever made." She stopped as the two stared over the porch railings listening to the crickets and the night breeze. Ms. Chesterfield looked straight ahead into the darkness, took a drink, and confided her secret.

"Rick, one of my first jobs out of high school was working for Pally Chase in 1970 as an office clerk," Ms. Chesterfield said. "As you probably know, back in those days, down here especially, people of different color didn't mix so well. 'Miscegenation' is what they called it in the courts, but country folk just called it nigger and white," she said.

"Did you and Mr. Chase date?" Rick said, trying to interpret Ms. Chesterfield's intimations.

"Date?" Havana Chesterfield replied. "You're such a gentle boy. Yes, we dated all right. In fact, if you can believe it, I was a pretty attractive dark woman," she said.

"I believe it," Rick said.

"So, date is probably too nice a word, Rick," Ms. Chesterfield said. "We were in love long before he met Ms. Chase through her debutante matchmaker mother."

"Oh, my," Rick said. "I had no idea. Delaney told Sam that Pally and Ms. Chase never really seemed in love."

"It wasn't a match made in heaven," Ms. Chesterfield said. "Pally told me a year before his death that he and Meredith rarely had sexual relations because Meredith couldn't get past what her father did to her and every time Pally touched her she felt like her father was rapin' her again." Ms. Chesterfield paused. "How sad," she said sympathetically.

What happened between you and Mr. Chase?" Rick asked.

"Nothing 'cept we weren't allowed to show our affection, or our love, for one another to the world. Pally was forced to end our relationship when we learned we were expecting," Ms. Chesterfield confided.

"Expecting, ma'am? A baby?" Rick inquired.

"My little Sambo," Ms. Chesterfield uttered through teardrops welling in her eyes. "Pally and I ended our time together in the early summer of 1974, six months before Sam was born."

Rick put his hand on hers and squeezed firmly. He tried to think of what to say, but came up empty.

"Sam is Pally's son," Ms. Chesterfield said, and paused, "and Delaney's half-brother."

Rick thought about the second part of her admission and waited a minute before speaking. "Ms. Chesterfield, if you don't mind my saying so, I think Sam is a wonderful tribute to your love with Mr. Chase." Rick hoped he said the right thing.

"God bless you, Rick," Ms. Chesterfield said. "I was hoping you would understand."

"Honestly, Ms. Chesterfield, I don't know that I understand like you said, because I don't think I've ever been in love like that before. But, at the very least, you story embraces what I hope to understand someday," Rick said.

"Maybe you're understanding it with Ms. Delaney," Ms. Chesterfield said. "From what Sam tells me about you and her, that's what I think," she said, revealing that Sam had told her more about Rick and Delaney than Ms. Chesterfield originally let on. "And that's why I'm telling you the truth about me and Mr. Chase. Nobody else knows, far as I can tell."

"Ms. Chesterfield, what you and Mr. Chase had together doesn't affect what I think about Delaney, or Sam or you," Rick said.

"Oh, honey," Ms. Chesterfield said. "I not telling you because I fear you'll be judgmental. I'm telling you because I hope you can help explain it to Sam someday." Ms. Chesterfield began to cry.

"Ms. Chesterfield, I'd love to help you out any way I can. But I think this is something that should come from you. To Sam and to Delaney," Rick said. "Believe me, they act like brother and sister anyhow. I think they will understand that they are related. If you don't believe me, watch them fight over who gets to sing first during open microphone night at the oyster bar, then you'll understand the true sibling rivalry connection." They both laughed and Ms. Chesterfield gave Rick a jovial embrace. He hugged her back.

"Maybe you're right, honey. I'll tell them soon enough, I guess," Ms. Chesterfield said. She paused and looked at Rick. "I'll be right back," she said and walked into her home returning to the porch in two minutes. "Pally gave me this," she said, extending her arm with an open palm. She was holding a gold pocket watch with a closed face.

Rick reached for the watch and took it out of her hand. "It's beautiful," he said.

"Open the cover," Ms. Chesterfield said.

Rick opened the golden plate revealing the timepiece and an inscription inside the plate. He read the inscription silently as Ms. Chesterfield stated it out loud.

"A hundred years from now, time won't matter," Ms.

Chesterfield said.

Rick looked at the inscription again, exhaled, and smiled at Ms. Chesterfield. "I say that sometimes, too," Rick said.

"I don't know what he meant by it," Ms. Chesterfield said. "I like to think it was his way of telling me that being forced to end our love won't matter at the end of our lives. That our love would always matter. I'm not too sure, Rick. But you know what? I'd like to think time does matter when you love someone," she paused and wiped a tear from her cheek.

"It does," Rick said. "It does." He smiled at Ms. Chesterfield. "It's nice that you still have his gift. I'm sure Mr. Chase would be honored that you still think so much of him. I know he must have been hurting too when your relationship had to end." Rick hoped he wasn't being too personal.

"I always thought I'd give the watch to Delaney, someday," she said.

"I think that day is fast approaching," Rick said. Havana Chesterfield smiled at Rick and hugged him. Pulling away from what must have been an awkward moment for her, Ms. Chesterfield stepped back and took the watch back into the house.

Returning to Rick, she kept the subject on Pally Chase. "Say, what's this nonsense you brought up about Mr. Chase not being in an accident?" she asked.

"Aw, nothing. I'm just a blind squirrel looking for a nut," Rick said. "I thought that there may have been some foul play that outmatched the foul weather the night Pally and his friend, Coatie Gillen, died," Rick said.

"Oh, honey, that's probably just some silly rumors that float around small towns like this," Ms. Chesterfield said. "However, like Sam said, I do have what you call a conspiracy theory. It's just that I don't know who the conspirators are."

"Go on," Rick said.

"Well, Sam don't believe my theory and I'm hesitant to bring it up outside of my close group of friends, but now you know the biggest secret I've ever had so I suppose I can tell you." Ms. Chesterfield took a deep breath. "I don't think Mr. Chase died from regular drowning," She continued. "You see, when Pally died I was a receptionist doing check-ins at the hospital emergency room at Tallahassee Community General the day they found him," she continued, "They brought him in and did an autopsy. Meredith Chase herself requested an autopsy be performed because she thought men were out to get Pally. She was still crazy and all to me and everyone else, but for once in her life I was kind of on her side." Ms. Chesterfield went on, "The county medical examiner wrote on the initial death certificate that there were two causes of death. One being drowning and the other being carbon monoxide poisoning."

"Carbon monoxide? Ma'am?" Rick inquired.

"Yes. But I don't know how it could be, though. I don't know much about boats. Maybe exhaust leaked in the boat galley or maybe there was a fire," Ms. Chesterfield said. "Anyhow, the certified death certificate only listed the primary cause of death as drowning with no second cause or contributor."

"How do you know about the other report then?" Rick inquired.

"Well, like I said, I was working at the hospital and, course I know I shouldn't have, I looked in his file the day after the autopsy. There it was, two causes of death that couldn't be distinguished one from the other as the primary cause." Ms. Chesterfield began to get wide-eyed and almost seemed to be enjoying herself as a sleuth.

"But what happened to that report?" Rick asked.

"Gone. Just gone." Ms. Chesterfield started to frown. "Nobody knows what happened to it. At the coroner's inquest hearing the coroner just gave his final report which was the one that appeared on the certified death certificate," Ms. Chesterfield continued. "Oh, I suppose Meredith Chase could've took it because she, as next of kin, had access to the file.

But, yet and still, I don't know why she would take it and not tell anybody," Ms. Chesterfield contemplated, "People say she's crazy and she's got papers to prove it. I suppose that's all the explanation you need. Hell, Ms. Chase come out after the final report sayin' there's a murder and a cover-up. Wasn't long after that she was involuntarily committed into the psych unit at Tallahassee Community General and then transferred to Atlanta to be near her own mother."

"Is she living with her mother?" Rick asked.

"No, but I understand they live close to one another. Meredith's mother is in a life-care independent type nursing home and Meredith is a block away at the Swansong Institute. Pretty name isn't it?" Ms. Chesterfield asked. "She just couldn't handle the pressure, the poor thing." Ms. Chesterfield continued thinking and then commented, "Unless, the coroner just discarded that report because it wasn't the final report, you know?"

"Interesting," Rick said. "I wish someone would have followed up on that report. Did Pally's friend get autopsied?" Rick asked.

"No, and that was a funny thing," Ms. Chesterfield said. "The coroner said since they both died together that he didn't want to disgrace the other body with an autopsy that would just show the same findings. The family never objected to that," she said. "So that's my conspiracy theory, if you can call it one. Two causes of death but only one ends up on the report. A natural cause of death prevailed over the unnatural one," she said. "Only thing is, I don't have any conspirators or motive or reason to think that Pally didn't just die by accident. Pretty thin theory, huh, honey?"

"I wouldn't call it anorexic. It has a little meat to it," Rick said. Ms. Chesterfield chuckled.

"Is the same coroner still around?" Rick asked.

"No, he moved on to higher office. State Senate, I believe. Yes, Senator Amato. Senator D.D. Amato from North Florida District," Ms. Chesterfield replied.

"Did you vote for him?" Rick asked, only half-kidding her.

"Hell, no, honey. We're all Democrats in this family," she laughed, while shaking her head.

Rick looked at her inquisitively.

"What is it honey?" Ms. Chesterfield said.

"Nothing," Rick lied. "I just was thinking how interesting it would have been to get to know him. Mr. Chase, that is." He paused and gave a reassuring smile. "Well, I'd better be going. Thank you for the great dinner and conversation," he said.

"Anytime, honey. Anytime," Ms. Chesterfield said. "And I do hope there is another time we can do this again, with Delaney too." Ms. Chesterfield gave Rick a kiss on the cheek and Rick thanked her again.

Back in his hotel room from dinner at Havana Chesterfield's, Rick poured a bourbon and water and splashed a couple of ice cubes into it. Rick always requested no smoking rooms because they smelled better, but that didn't stop him from lighting a cigarette when he felt the desire. However, out of gaining respect for the subsequent hotel guests, Rick walked through the sliding glass door and took his cigarette and drink outside near the pool.

Grassy knolls in Dallas and ten foot waves, Rick thought to himself, mixing the conspiracy theory over President Kennedy's assassination and, now, Pally's death. A black woman and a powerful white man in love, and having a baby. Oil drilling off the coastline and politics taking pot shots. Hell, that wasn't conspiracy. That was just plain life on the panhandle.

"John Grisham or not," Rick thought out loud at pool side. "I'm callin' Red." Rick put out his cigarette and walked back into his room and picked up the phone.

He dialed from memory the phone number of Jeff "Red" Wilhelm, his best friend in Chicago. Red's voice mail at the FBI picked-up and Rick left the message. "Red, this is Rick. It's late Friday night. I know you're probably busy with your regular job during work hours and shouldn't be looking into other people's lives for your buddies, but I need a little homework help," he continued. "Would you please see if there is an FBI file on any of these three men. Billy, or William Barute, he's a political lobbyist, I think out of D.C.; Ned Carson, not really sure what he's qualified to do but he's about fifty years old out of D.C.; and State Senator D.D. Amato out of Florida. You probably want social security numbers and birth dates but I'm just a lawyer, not a private detective. Is my request too sketchy? Let me know. Thanks, buddy." Rick hung up the phone, and left his untouched drink on the bedside table. He fell asleep.

21

The next day Rick woke up alone in his hotel bed to a frosty Saturday morning in Tallahassee, nursing a southern hangover from Ms. Chesterfield's homemade whiskey. He didn't, however, have any trouble remembering the events of the previous evening. It was nearly ten in the morning when he finally showered and dressed for the day. As he was leaving his hotel room, the phone rang. He picked it up.

"Hello," Rick said.

"Hey buddy, this is Red," Came the familiar voice.

"Red, how are things in the cold north?" Rick said.

"Just fine, you beach boy bastard," Red said.

"What the hell you doin' working on a Saturday?" Rick asked.

"G-men never stop to rest, buddy," Red said, and paused. "No actually, I had nothing to do socially, believe it or not, and I thought I'd try to get ahead on some of my case work. What the hell are you doing in Tallahassee?"

"You know, just chasin' women." Rick felt uncomfortable pretending he was still just one of the boys to his old friend, yet he felt compelled to be just that. "Just falling in love" would not have sounded natural coming out of Rick's mouth, though it was the truth.

"Sounds to me like you're chasin' men," Red said.

"Men? What the hell. Are you calling me gay?" Rick asked.

"No, dumbshit. I'm calling you informed," Red said.

"What do you mean?" Rick inquired.

"Those men you asked me to look up," Red said. "You're chasin' 'em. I'm calling to inform you about them. 'Red's FBI singles service' at your disposal. Now are you Pisces or Aquarius because these men are pretty particular," Red kidded him.

"Eat shit, Red," Rick said.

"Aw, c'mon, sun damage. I'm only playing with you." Red pretended to pity him.

"So, did you have a chance to find out who they are or was my information too slim?" Rick asked.

"Careful when you say 'slim' buddy, that's a gay term. But, yes, I did find them," Red replied. "Hell, this is the FBI in a modern technology world. You could've found them on the internet for all I know."

"Then what the hell do I need you for?" Rick asked, joking his best friend.

"Because I'm cute and fun to be with," Red said, "and I happen to have access to just a little more information than you can get as a layman, even if you are a lawyer."

"So what's up? Please tell me they've all been to prison for criminal felony charges," Rick asked.

"Not quite," Red replied. "Seem to be law abiding as far as political people can be. I've got a few pictures of them if you're interested."

"Doing what?" Rick asked.

"Oh, just hob-knobbing, palm-pressing, chin-wagging. Things

I'm sure these guys do best together," Red said.

"Together?" Rick inquired. "Are they all in the same picture?

"All in the same picture? Hell! They're all in the same family from what I can tell. Each one of 'em got their hands in each other's pockets," Red said. "By the way. What are you interested in these guys for? You're not thinking of becoming a lobbyist, or, worse yet, a politician, are you Rick?"

"Hell no," Rick said. "I've just had some run-ins with them and I thought knowing a little more about them would help me burn their ass if the day ever came where I was up against a wall." Rick partially lied. "Can you mail me or email me the pictures?" Rick asked.

"Well, I could, but this isn't exactly an FBI requested inquiry. I could lose this lucrative government job," Red said, kidding his friend. "I don't feel comfortable letting this file out of my sight, into the hands of strange Fed Ex carriers, and hoping the pictures will get to you," Red said. "Good news, though. I'll be in Orlando next week. Want to meet up? Chase women, et cetera? I'll be on business, but I can mix that with pleasure."

"What kind of bureaucrat are you?" Rick said.

"The normal dumb kind," Red replied. "You're near Orlando. How 'bout it?" Red inquired.

"Only if four hours by car is 'near Orlando.'" Rick said. "That sounds pretty good. When will you be in Florida?"

"Well, I've got to go to start training in Orlando this Thursday, so I'll probably get in Wednesday afternoon," Red said.

"Tell you what. Any chance you can get a stop over here in Tallahassee and spend a few days? I'll show you around the beach, the bars. A lot has changed since you were here last. And tell your boss, who is your boss anyhow, the President? Tell whoever it is that I'll pick-up the extra air fare," Rick said.

"Hey. That sounds pretty good. I'll get back to ya. God knows I need a little vacation. I mean look at me, working on the weekend!" Red paused. "Okay, wait a minute. I'm single with no kids and a government job. I don't need to get back to ya. What time you picking me up at the airport?" Red said, now excited.

"Just get your flight and leave me a message at the front desk. I'll pick you up and have a frozen margarita waiting for you," Rick said. "Oh, and Red. . ."

"Yea, buddy," Red said.

"You may want to pack some sunscreen or your FBI buddies will be calling you 'Burnt Red' for the rest of your days."

"Fuck you very much," Red said. "See you tomorrow."

22

After speaking with Red, Rick was pensive the rest of the morning. He spent much of his time before lunch considering the consequences of what he had discovered about Pally and Barute. Mostly, however, Rick was consumed with thoughts of Delaney and how a relationship that seemed surreal had become non-existent. Rick dialed Delaney's work number at Captano's, hoping she was working the lunch shift. The restaurant manager answered the phone and found Delaney, who had been wrapping silverware in napkins, and told her Rick was on the phone.

"Hello," Delaney said, as she picked up the receiver.

"Hi, Delaney, this is Rick."

"I know. I know your voice," Delaney said. "You always say who you are. Did your mother teach you to be so courteous or did you learn that in the south?" she asked.

Relieved that Delaney sounded somewhat playful, Rick responded, "I think a little of both. So, are you expecting a big lunch crowd today?" he asked.

"Hope so. Are you coming in?" Delaney said.

"Well, I don't want to bother you during your shift. Can we get together around 2:30 when you finish up?" Rick asked. He was disappointed in the insecurity of his voice and hoped Delaney hadn't noticed.

"Sure. We should probably spend some time together. It's been a while," Delaney said. "We can meet at my place. I can only visit for a little while because I'm working the dinner shift tonight, if that's okay."

"Okay. I'll see you around two-thirty," Rick said. "Bye." He hung up the phone. As Rick stared at the phone he wondered what else could be bothering Delaney other than what Sam had told him. Rick questioned whether they were still even considering themselves a couple, or in love for that matter. He tried not to think about it by changing clothes and going for a three mile run. When Rick returned, he showered and dressed in shorts, a tee shirt, and sandals and drove his car to Delaney's.

As had become customary in earlier weeks, Southpaw recognized Rick's car and ran up to greet him before Rick could get the car in park. "Hey, buddy!" Rick said while exiting his vehicle. He rubbed the excited dog's stomach as Southpaw's tail wagged happily. Delaney stepped out onto the porch still wearing her work uniform. She looked beautiful and yet, un-accessible. She invited him to the porch and offered some sweet tea, which Rick accepted. Rick was reading too much into it, he thought, when he considered that Delaney didn't invite him inside. He waited for her to return with the drinks and prepared to lay his heart on the line.

Delaney emerged from the house with the cold drinks and gave Rick his as she sat down. "Sam told me about your conversation," Delaney started. "Rick, I'm sorry I haven't been very fair to you," she said, reading Rick's mind. "You know my mom has been sick since dad died. Well, even before then. As you know, they didn't get along that great and I swore they'd of divorced if it weren't for me."

"Delaney, I hope you don't think we have the same problems as your parents," Rick said.

"No, it's not that at all, really. I've just got some things to work out," she said.

"Let me help you. Hell, I'm a doctor. I can fix anything," Rick said.

"A doctor? You're a lawyer, Rick," Delaney said, somewhat confused over Rick's comment.

"Well, my degree says Doctorate in Jurisprudence, so I figure what the hell's the difference?" Rick said, hoping for his sense of humor to cut through the tense moment.

Delaney laughed quietly. "I suppose you're right," she said.

"Then you'll let me help?" Rick asked.

"I can't Rick. I'd feel stupid if I was wrong," she said.

"Wrong about what?" Rick asked.

"It's nothing. I really don't think I should talk about it," Delaney said. Rick looked sad and perplexed. "Okay?" she asked.

"Okay. I understand," Rick said. Delaney smiled. Rick chose not to bring up the conversation Buddy Bear had with Delaney about the drugs for fear of breaking Sam's confidence and broaching a subject Delaney appeared not ready to address.

The two drank the sweet tea and made idle conversation over the sunshine that day. Rick tried to reminisce over the great moments the couple had shared over the last month but Delaney wasn't enjoying the conversation as much as Rick hoped. After an hour passed of Rick's trying in vain to get Delaney to laugh or talk like the girl he fell for on their first meeting, Rick excused himself to allow Delaney to get back to work.

"Thank you for meeting me," Rick said. "I hope everything works out." Rick rose to leave without touching Delaney.

"I'm sure it will," Delaney said. "And Rick?"

"Yes?" Rick turned to meet her glance.

"I'm sorry."

"It's okay, Delaney," Rick said and walked to his car. He hoped Delaney was watching him leave as he got into his car and drove away without looking back at her. He thought she probably was.

23

After Rick left Delaney's company he felt maudlin and painfully confused. Consequently, he was thirsty for knowledge, and equally so for a drink, when he decided to pay a visit to Barker's Tavern next to Sharpe's Café in downtown Tallahassee. It was at Sharpe's Café where he was first introduced to Buddy Bear and then Billy Barute. Barker's Tavern was next door to Sharpe's serving as the after five hang-out for the politicos, and Rick hoped to see some of his new "old buddies," especially Ned Carson. Since it was Saturday, Rick hoped the crowd would be in earlier than usual. Typically, Saturdays in Tallahassee were used in the political arena for barbeques and afternoon fund raisers. These usually followed with bar talk downtown "away from the women folk," as the politicos liked to say.

For the first time in his life Rick felt uncomfortable walking into a bar. He couldn't tell if he was nervous about a possible confrontation with Ned or Billy or if he just felt out-of-place because he was the only one not wearing a suit and tie. Rick was astounded at the display of men who must look ridiculous in casual street clothes because they were so alien to them. He wondered if anyone who was part of the political south even owned a pair of shorts, or a tan. In fact, Rick was wearing khaki shorts himself and a tee-shirt, and it was obvious to the patrons and help alike that Rick was not a regular. Most of the patrons, however, paid him no attention but one woman in particular was staring at him from a corner booth where Rick could see only her and not her companion who was seated on the opposite side. Rick looked at her three times before she made her last futile attempt to look as if she were looking at someone else and then back at her companion.

Rick walked up to the bar and ordered a glass of beer, trying to angle himself to see the whole crowd and the woman's friend in the corner booth without looking too obvious. Before he could turn around toward the corner booth, which was just ten feet away, a voice called out.

"H-h-hey, Rick. Is your suit at the d-d-d-dry cleaners?" Ned Carson said from the corner booth. Rick turned and smiled.

"Hello, Ned. Fancy seeing you here. I thought this was just a beer and shot joint," Rick said.

"Hell you d-d-did," Ned said. "You're here for the g-g- women, aren't you?"

"How'd you guess?" Rick said. "Looks like you've covered that area pretty well." Rick looked at the woman across from Carson. "How do you do? I'm Rick Morrissey." He extended his hand to the lady.

"Jodi Eastbrook. Nice to meet a gentleman," Came the soft-voiced reply. "Ned, honey, I'm gonna let you boys visit. You know us southern girls feel a little out-of-place drinking too early in the day," she said to Carson in what Rick thought sounded like a fake southern accent. "Don't forget about our meeting tonight at eight o'clock."

"I w-w-won't baby," Carson said. "See you back at the hotel."

"Sorry you have to rush off," Rick said.

"Don't be sorry," Jodi said. "Ned saw me first. But I'll be back again another time." She leaned over to Ned. "See you back at the Fairfield Inn, honey." She then looked at Rick. "You'd think he could afford a nicer place, wouldn't you?" Rick shrugged his shoulders and pursed his lips and then sat down.

"Known her long, Ned?" Rick asked slyly.

"F-f-funny," Ned said. "Want a drink?"

"Well, if you're going to be primed for tonight I better order something for you to drink too. I'll try to match you drink for drink but you've got a lot more to look forward to tonight. Don't drink me under the table, Ned," Rick said. Carson laughed.

Rick signaled for the waitress, who was also wearing a tie, to come over and take the drink order. At Barker's Tavern, mixed drinks were always two for one from five in the afternoon to seven o'clock, every day except Sunday, when they were closed. Rick wasn't sure how many drinks Carson had before Rick arrived but it was obvious that Carson was feeling the effects of alcohol. For over an hour and a half the two discussed politics, women, Ned's career aspirations and hobbies, and Florida State University football. Rick and Carson conversed while consuming four bourbon drinks each before Rick began a more substantive conversation.

"Ned, that's a fine woman you're meeting up with tonight," Rick said. "I didn't think her kind hung out at these nice places."

"She a nice g-g-girl," Ned said. "Not just your run of the mill t-t-topless d-d-dancer."

"I know she does more than dance," Rick said. They both laughed. "Say, you ever been down to the topless oyster bar in Panacea?" Rick asked, playing on the metaphor of topless oysters and trying to make light of the conversation.

"Oh, yea. Old shack of a place down by the water," Carson said. "Those girls are b-b-beautiful dancers," he continued. Carson's statement stunned Rick briefly. Rick thought about the attack on Sam Chesterfield and Sam's recall of the event. He knew Carson could not have been inside.

"Ned," Rick said, "you described the building right, but the only things topless there are the oysters. It's an oyster bar, not a strip joint."

"Oh. I must be thinking of somewhere else," Carson replied and paused awkwardly.

Rick was fascinated with Carson's excuse. Changing the tone of the conversation Rick interrupted Carson's embarrassed silence. "I'll tell you what, Ned. The South is sure a different place to be," Rick said. "The rules are definitely different down here."

"What d-d-do you mean?" Carson asked.

"Well, look around this bar. It's like the old boys' club at the brandy room on the Titanic. Not a dame around, unless, of course, she's a waitress or a muse," Rick said. Carson smiled on the comment about his muse. "I mean, you guys control the world down here. In Chicago you'd find women smoking cigars in a place like this and drinking Manhattans."

"I g-g-guess it is a g-g-good ole' b-b-boys network, here," Carson agreed. Rick appreciated the "good ole boys" reference and tried to capitalize on it.

"Hell, Ned. There ain't even a nigger in the joint. Unless they got niggers cooking some barbeque in the kitchen, or washing dishes." Rick pretended to be prejudiced. Carson noticed and tried to correct him, politically speaking.

"You may be right, Rick. N-n-not a single n-n-n-negro to speak of," Carson said. It was the only incriminating statement Rick needed to hear as he remembered the bumbling, stuttering and pretend to be KKK member who, with a couple of buddies, had beat up Sam many nights before. Rick was on to Carson. A stuttering KKK member who uses the word "negro" cannot exist in pairs. Time to press Carson, Rick thought.

"Negro, right. Sorry about that," Rick corrected himself. "My family's just so goddamned prejudiced that it's hard to stop saying the other word. But I'm not prejudice myself. Hell, I've got a lot of friends who are colored," Rick said. Carson smiled in agreement, not giving away whether he caught the joke or not. "Say, Ned. You know Senator Amato?" Rick started fishing.

"Yes. He's a g-g-good man," Carson replied.

"Spend much time with him, do ya?" Rick asked.

Carson looked at Rick with a furrowed brow and responded, "Only met him a time or two."

"So you don't know him well?" Rick asked, knowing well from his conversation with Red that Carson was prevaricating.

"No. W-w-what are you, cross-examining me?" Carson appeared unsteady, but not yet nervous.

"Senator Amato did a lot of the groundwork for the oil drillings off the east coast didn't he? Hell, he's probably involved in the one south of here that got old Barute all shook up when Pally Chase fought it." Rick pushed. "Copperhead Oil, wasn't it?"

"I think you had too much to d-d-drink," Carson said, looking for a way out of the booth for better company.

"You know, I heard he was the coroner for Pally. Wow. Talk about your coincidences. Like blood and water. Or is it oil and water? I can never get that saying right," Rick said.

"I think I got to get g-g-g-going," Carson said.

"She ain't gonna be ready 'til eight, Ned. By the way, did you know prostitution is illegal in Florida?" Rick said. "Aw, never mind. I don't give a damn." Rick paused. "Say, Ned, ever take a ride in a long black limousine?" Rick asked. "Boy those things can move. Especially if you got somebody in there with you who needs to get somewhere fast. . . or someone you want to get somewhere fast. In fact, you got to keep moving fast in those things because, as a passenger, you're sitting over the exhaust system the whole time. Hell, I bet if you were sittin' still too long with the windows rolled down you get a little carbon monoxide in your system. That sure ain't a healthy way to ride in a car."

"Rick, you're s-s-starting to ramble like a d-d-drunk. I'm gonna g-g-get going," Carson said.

"Drunk I may be, but at least I'm willing to show it. Unlike some people who just wear pillow cases over their heads because they aren't willing to show their true color. Uh, pardon the expression," Rick said. "Look Ned, let's cut the bullshit. I know you and your boss don't like me much, or Delaney or, especially, Sam Chesterfield. I also know your politics. I don't mind your politics, frankly. It's a free country and makes for lively conversation. What I don't like is some lying bastard who thinks he can pull the wool over my eyes." Rick's eyes were now menacing. "I know you were in that limousine the night Sam Chesterfield was attacked. No offense Carson, but you're just a stuttering flunky who spoke when he should've sat quiet," Rick said. "There's no mistaking you or your pitiful affliction."

"You better w-w-watch what you say, friend. You're out of your l-l-league," Carson said. "I haven't the f-f-foggiest idea what you're t-t-talking about and I'm out of here. S-sober up." Carson stood up.

"First of all, Ned. I'm not in any league. I quit team sports a long time ago. Second, meeting a guy once or twice doesn't exactly put his hand in your back pocket," Rick said.

Carson sat back down. "What are you t-t-talking about?" Carson asked, genuinely interested.

"I'm talking about you and Barute and D.D. Amato smacking lips together over oil drilling." Ned tried to look surprised. "That's not a good look for you, Ned. You're too transparent to act like something you're not," Rick said. "You've been telling me one lie after another and now you're lost in your own morass of deception. Ned, I've got pictures of you, Barute, and Amato together doing all kinds of crazy shit," Rick said, not knowing what the pictures actually showed. "So, best as I can see it, you guys been up to no good the last few years, Ned."

"I-I-I wasn't part of that. . .," Carson stopped to correct himself. "I wasn't even around when P-P-Pally died," Carson said. He'd said too much.

"You want to tell me about the autopsy, Ned?" Rick asked.

"I d-d-don't know anything about the cause of death," Carson replied.

"Who said anything about the cause of death being in question, Ned?" Rick said. "I asked about the autopsy." Carson appeared agitated. "Listen, Ned. It's all coming down. You may have a chance to come out a good guy if you really weren't around then."

"I think you read too many b-b-books," Carson said as he stood up to leave.

"I hate reading, Ned," Rick replied as he rose to meet Carson.

"Well that's your p-p-problem, then isn't it?" Carson said.

Now standing face-to-face, Rick leaned toward Carson, leveling their line of sight, and spoke slowly, "Ned, you're f-f-f-fucked."

24

Rick arrived back at the hotel around 8:30 p.m. Before heading toward the elevator the desk clerk called him over. "Sir, are you room 304?"

"Yes. Rick Morrissey," Rick said.

"You've got a message," the clerk said as Rick walked over. "A Mr. Jeff Wilhelm is arriving by Delta Airlines at 7:55 tomorrow evening."

Rick thanked the clerk and went to his room for a shower. He had been buzzed from the alcohol and still felt he was full of energy; however, after his shower he felt exhausted and fell asleep on top of the hotel bed covers without getting dressed.

The next morning Rick woke up at six and called Tallahassee International Airport to confirm Red's flight.

The Delta ticket agent was friendly but couldn't confirm or deny that Red was booked on the flight. "We do have a flight arriving at 7:55 this evening. I'm sorry we're not allowed to tell you if your friend is scheduled on that plane. However, we do show a Delta flight number 1016, Chicago to Tallahassee, via Atlanta. As you know, you can't get to heaven or hell without going through Atlanta," the attendant said.

The attendant's statement about heaven and hell made Rick think about Meredith Chase and her similar thoughts on Atlanta as told through

Delaney the first time Rick and Delaney met. Rick took her statement as a fateful sign. "Ma'am, when's the next flight out of Tallahassee?" Rick asked.

"Seven thirty-five, Sir," the attendant said politely.

"I presume it's going to Atlanta?" Rick asked.

"All of ours do," she said. "Delta's home base is Atlanta. There are seats available."

"When do you have return flights other than flight 1016?" Rick asked.

"You mean today?" the attendant inquired.

"Yes, please."

"Well, we can have you back in Tallahassee and safely on the ground at either 5:39 or the 7:55 I told you about earlier."

"Please book me leaving in an hour and returning on the five o'clock flight," Rick said.

"Okay, I'll be glad to do that for you, Sir." she paused. "The flight is a non-refundable ticket and the fare is four hundred thirty dollars."

Rick gave her his credit card number and booked the flight. He showered and dressed in his suit with the hope of earning a good first impression from Delaney's mother. He remembered his conversation with Havana Chesterfield and called directory assistance in Atlanta for the Swansong Institute. He was given the number and called for directions.

The Delta flight to Atlanta was uneventful and Rick contemplated all of the questions he hoped to ask Ms. Chase; and, with any lucidity on her part, he hoped for answers. Rick hailed a taxi from the airport and took the thirty minute ride to the Swansong Institute which was located in a southern suburb of Atlanta, just outside the city limits. Rick thanked the driver and asked him to return in two hours.

As Rick stepped from the cab, he took in the architecture of the psychiatric hospital that had played host to Meredith Chase since Pally died. The building was red brick and perfectly rectangular. Rick considered that either the architect didn't have a personality or he was hired to create a building that didn't. The trim on the windows and along the front entrance was all white and appeared freshly painted. Rick stepped in through the automatic sliding doors and greeted the receptionist who was dressed in a tight pink outfit and reading a romance novel.

"Hello, ma'am," Rick said.

The receptionist looked up at Rick as she was blowing a bubble with her chewing gum. The bubble burst and she spoke. "Yes. Are you here for a visit?" she asked.

"I am. Rick Morrissey to see Meredith Chase."

"Are you on her guest list, Sir?" the receptionist asked.

"No, ma'am. Actually, I'm a friend of her daughter's who was just up here a few days ago," Rick said.

"Delaney?" the receptionist asked.

"Yes. You have a good memory," Rick said.

"Not really. I just hear Ms. Chase talking about her all the time. I think I saw her when she was here, but I don't really know her," the receptionist said.

"She's Meredith's only child. I'm sure her mom is talking about her because Delaney is all she has left," Rick said.

"Well, if you ask me, Ms. Chase ain't got much left upstairs, either," the girl said, "unless she's on the right medication.   Then she ain't half bad."

"I know. She's had a difficult time," Rick said.

"She gives us a difficult time. Always talking about her husband being killed and she's only crazy 'cause nobody believed her," the girl said, not concerning herself with any patient confidentiality, she continued, "The nurses try to increase, then decrease her meds and nothing ever works. Of course she slows down a bit when they hit her with the good stuff."

"May I see her?" Rick asked.

"Only visitors listed on her guest list are allowed back there. That's policy," the girl said.

"Do you know why that's the policy?" Rick asked.

"I guess for safety," the girl replied.

"You're right. And I'm sure you realize that policy is not law," Rick said, smiling.

"Well, I'm not sure."

"What I mean is, policy is just procedure. Kind of a safeguard, but policy isn't something that is written in the law books. It's just policy. You know, like when you go into a McDonald's and order a double cheeseburger without onions."

"Ooh, I hate onions," the girl interjected.

"Me, too," Rick said. "But McDonald's policy is that all their cheeseburgers come with everything, including onions, unless they are willing to make a special exception. Like with you and me. We would ask for them to break policy so we wouldn't have to taste those god-awful onions."

"Okay. I think I'm getting it."

"Well, what I'm trying to ask you is, do I look like a threat to Ms. Chase's safety?" Rick asked.

"No, of course not," she replied, and giggled.

"Then I'm an exception to the policy, because you're not supposed to let people in who would harm a resident, and I'm obviously not going to harm anyone. I'm just visiting because Delaney is a good friend of mine and she'd be thrilled that I stopped by to see her mother and say 'hello.' I'll let you hold onto my license if you'd like," Rick said.

The receptionist acquiesced. "Well, if you leave me your license, I guess that would be okay. I've got to warn you though. Ms. Chase is a little flippy. You know, she has good days and bad days."

"And going half-mad days," Rick interjected. The girl laughed out loud.

"Oh, go ahead. Don't keep her long though, lunch time is her favorite."

"I won't," Rick said. "Incidentally, how do I get to her room?"

"She's in 119. Just go down the hall and turn left. Nineteen doors down is her room."

"Thank you. I won't be too long. And I'll put in a good word for you," Rick said as the girl laughed again.

Rick walked the sterile, freshly waxed linoleum hallway until he came to Meredith Chase's room. He knocked on the door.

"Come in, dear," came the voice from inside.

Rick slowly entered the room to find a frail woman who looked to be in her early forties sitting in a chair in front of a television that was turned on but without the volume. Ms. Chase appeared to be studying the picture on the screen, but she was without reaction. She was pretty, Rick thought. Her frame was petite and her face was sculpted by her protruding cheek and chin bones that reflected malnourishment, but she had a waif model's look. She was dressed in a lavender skirt and a white blouse. She was wearing heels and looked as if she were waiting for someone to pick her up for church. Her short hair was done nicely and Rick saw Delaney's resemblance in Meredith's eyes and smile as Ms. Chase greeted him.

"Hello. Is it time for lunch already?" she said, without looking away from the television.

"No, ma'am. Not yet. I'm just stopping by to say 'hello.'" Rick said. He extended his hand. "Ma'am. My name is Rick Morrissey."

"Morrissey. Morrissey. Morrissey," she kept repeating to herself. Her voice was high pitched, but soft, and Rick thought she sounded like a kitten, only instead of meowing, she was saying 'Morrissey.'

"Hmmm. Morrissey. The name is very familiar. Morrissey, huh?" she asked.

"Yes, ma'am. Rick."

"Morrissey. Are you a musician?" Meredith Chase said, still looking at the television.

"No, I'm a friend of your daughter's," Rick said.

"Ah, I thought so. I knew that," she said, and paused for several moments. "Rick from Chicago." She cast her first long look at Rick and studied him for a moment. "Delaney was right. You look very young. Very handsome."

"Thank you, ma'am," Rick said.

"Did Delaney ask you to visit her sick mother?" she asked rather lucidly.

"No, I was just in the Atlanta area and thought of you. I wanted to meet the woman who raised Delaney," Rick said.

"Well, what do you think?" Ms. Chase gestured to herself. "Do I look crazy?"

"No. You don't, ma'am. You look well," Rick said.

"Thank you, boy. I'm trying to convince my doctors that I may have issues, but I'm not crazy," she said. "Take, for instance, my memory. You and my daughter fell in love not long ago. On a sailboat. Am I right?"

"I'd like to think so, ma'am," Rick said.

"Well, you're polite enough. But stop calling me that goddamned name, would you?" Meredith said intently, but without raising her voice.

"Yes, ma'am. I mean, Ms. Chase. I'm just a little apprehensive over meeting you," Rick said.

"You shouldn't be. I'm harmless, really. Except for when they put those goddamned needles in me. Depression drugs that make you undepressed. I swear I could break down walls when I got those pills. I hate needles anyhow, but they know I won't swallow any pills. 'Forced medication,' they call it." Ms. Chase sounded very coherent, but Rick understood schizophrenia could sometimes offer lucidity to its victim. Rick hoped she could hold on for the conversation. "So you know about Delaney and me?" Rick asked.

"From your first meeting at the restaurant, to your singing, to your boat trip. I know it all. My memory is good," she said. "So, to whom do

I owe the honor of your visit?"

"Actually, your husband, Pally," Rick said, hoping Ms. Chase would not cut communication off with the mention of her husband.

"Pally? You know he's dead, don't you?" Ms. Chase said flippantly.

"I do, and I'm sorry," Rick said. "But like you said, you've got a great memory and I was hoping to explore it a little."

"Explore my memory? You want to know about my husband?" Ms. Chase said.

"I already know a lot about him. Only thing I don't understand is how he died. He was such a good sailor," Rick said.

"You're goddamned right, Rick," Ms. Chase said. "He was murdered." She was becoming animated now.

"Why do you think so?" Rick inquired.

"Why? Because those goddamned idiots wanted to drill oil and cut into my husband's livelihood. That's why." Ms. Chase paused and looked at the television again. "I tried to tell the law, but they said I was crazy. And you know what? I might be. But even crazy people know when someone is trying to pull the wool over their eyes."

"I believe you, Ms. Chase," Rick said. "What do you think happened?"

Ms. Chase paused. "It's not what I think. It's what I know, and that is the coroner's report said my husband died of carbon monoxide poisoning. That he'd inhaled smoke or something and his larynx just collapsed on him. He suffocated," she paused. "My husband don't suffocate without something burning on that boat."

Rick was stunned by Ms. Chase's clarity in thought. "Didn't

anyone investigate the cause of death?" he asked.

"Investigate, hell. The coroner took the easy way out and said my husband drowned. Drowned with a life jacket on along with his friend, Coatie," she paused. "Now tell me how two men drown with their life jackets on."

"I don't know. The waves were pretty bad though," Rick said, fearing she'd see him as a devil's advocate.

"They were bad, but there was no water in their lungs," she said.

"How do you know?" Rick asked.

"You like reading, Mr. Rick?" Ms. Chase seemed to change the subject.

"Ma'am?"

"One of my favorite books is 'Gone with the Wind,'" she said. "It's over on the shelf there." Ms. Chase pointed toward a full bookshelf. "Go and grab it. It's good reading."

"Ma'am?" Rick said.

"Of course, I like most southern novels. Ever heard of Ferrol Sams?" Ms. Chase said without waiting for a response. "I love his books. You ever read "Run With the Horsemen? Oh, it's a delightful story. You can just tell by the way Ferrol Sams writes that he's a nice man, a gentleman, surely. You know, he's a doctor, and a writer. He's an old man too. He lives near here and *still* practices medicine. He's nearly *eighty* years old," she paused as Rick looked at her in fear that her train of thought on Pally wouldn't return. "I bet you one thing, Rick," she said. "I bet if Dr. Sams came to treat me, he'd let me leave this goddamned place."

"Ma'am?" Rick said.

"Course, there are plenty of books over there to choose from," Ms. Chase continued. "I love reading, don't you? You can take a couple with you, if you like. Just bring them back!" she said. "But I won't let you take 'Gone with the Wind' because that's my favorite. You can read it here though."

"Ma'am?" Rick said again.

"And quit calling me that!" Ms. Chase erupted. She paused and looked Rick straight in the eyes as she raised both of her eyebrows while shaking her head slowly. "Just get the goddamned book," she said softly with an air of smart-ass.

Rick got up and retrieved the book from the shelf and handed it to her. She gave it back to him as he looked at her in wonder. "There's a few pages missin' on account of I had to tear them out to make room for the coroner's initial autopsy report. You read it," Ms. Chase said.

Rick's eyes narrowed and he gave away a half of smile to Ms. Chase. Rick took the book and opened it to a folded report that was twenty-six pages long. "You know anything about medicine, Mr. Rick?" Meredith asked.

"Somewhat. I used to work with doctors a lot," Rick said, as he opened the report. Rick's background had taught him to skip straight to the physical findings and impressions of medical records and he quickly found the results of the autopsy in which he was interested. He read earnestly as the findings indicated asphyxiation from throat spasms, traumatized larynx, respiratory failure, and, perhaps most importantly, clear lungs. No fluid found within the body cavity whatsoever. Rick looked up at Ms. Chase.

"Ma'am, I once knew a guy, Vince Planet was his name, and he almost died from carbon monoxide poisoning. This report is identical to my friends recount of the event and his symptoms, only my friend's life was saved at the last minute," Rick said.

"You know, fossil fuels, when burned, emit carbon monoxide, don't you?" Ms. Chase said.

"Yes, I do know that," Rick said, bewildered over what he had read. "They never found the boat, did they?" he asked.

"No, I'm afraid they didn't," Ms. Chase said. "If it burned, it sunk fast. If it didn't, I would think it would stay afloat, even if it tipped over. It was made entirely of wood. Wood floats, last I knew," she said.

"It still does," Rick said.

Rick spent another hour with Meredith Chase discussing her beliefs about Copperhead Oil and William Barute. She didn't reveal anything else new to Rick that he hadn't discovered already, but it was reassuring to hear her impression of the events that transpired a decade earlier. Their conversation eventually changed to Delaney, and she enjoyed Rick's version of how they met and how they'd courted over the previous several weeks. Eventually, Ms. Chase appeared to forget about the discussion over Pally and she began questioning Rick on his own life. She laughed often when Rick told her about his job as a lawyer, though Rick didn't think the stories would be funny to others. Ms. Chase occasionally paused to looked at the silent television before continuing her questions toward Rick. She never seemed to lose her lucidity, yet Rick couldn't help but notice that she wasn't entirely there either.

Rick enjoyed Meredith Chase's company as well and, though she had her odd moments, Rick thought she could make it just fine in the real world.   They parted company with Meredith insisting that Rick leave the coroner's report with her.   She didn't trust copy machines and, unfortunately, she didn't trust Rick either.   She did, however, tell Rick that he was a nice man and that he had her blessing to be Delaney's friend.   It was more than he could hope for.   He left her company contemplating the autopsy findings and his next move, if any.

Rick arrived back in Tallahassee at a quarter to six that evening. He took his rented convertible for a ride to get a bite to eat, to think, and then return to pick up his friend Red.

Rick was back at the airport fifteen minutes before Red's plane arrived.   He sat patiently in the bar and spoke to no one.   When Red stepped off the plane Rick had a drink for both of them in hand.   They embraced as brothers would and commenced catching up on each other as they made their way to the baggage claim.

In Rick's rent-a-car, the two headed for downtown Tallahassee and a steak & seafood dinner at The Sandbar Grill.   Obviously excited to see the FBI pictures, Rick asked Red to pull them out and show them as they drove. "Boy, you're a real piece of work," Red said. "We can't even chase some skirt before you start talking business?"

"Sorry, Red.   I'm just real interested in those photos and whatever you have on these guys," Rick said. "Besides, skirt around here doesn't wake up and get out of bed until after noon and they don't go out on the town until at least ten thirty at night.   You'll have plenty of time. This ain't St. Mary's College," Rick said.

"Nice English, college boy,"   Red said as he pulled out the pictures and explained, "This one is of that Barute fella, Carson, and the senator," Red said. "As you can see, that's an oil rig they are standing on and that big thing they're holding is a $250,000 check payable to the good citizens of St. Augustine Beach."

"What's the money for?" Rick asked.

"Dividends of some type," Red replied. "The oil drill was constructed off the shore of St. Augustine Beach about ten years ago and the reward to the town came in the form of a tax levy assessed against the drilling company. This picture with the boys giving the money was taken just a couple years ago."

"Hmm. Tit for tat, huh?" Rick said. "What are the other pictures?"

"Several of them here are from the Senator's file. The government likes to keep up on politicos. I only brought the ones down where they all appear in the same picture together. About twenty times. Otherwise, there's about five hundred of the Senator shuck and jiving with the suits of D.C. and Florida."

"Twenty times they were pictured together?" Rick asked surprised.

"About that," Red said. "Most of these are pictures taken during lobby efforts for the oil drillings that were proposed to take place in the Gulf of Mexico or Atlantic and bordering Florida. Here are two from the drilling effort off the panhandle. These are from a check presentation in Pensacola last month, October 12, I think, which is about as close to the panhandle as you can get. Here are some more from other cities along the panhandle."

Rick pulled the car over and examined the two pictures from the

Panacea lobbying effort. In both pictures there were more than the three men, most of the others looking like corporate men. However, both pictures were taken with protesters in the background. In one picture, Rick could make out the most familiar sign of the protesters which unmistakably read: "Save our Shorelines," the words extending off the bold red acronym S.O.S. painted vertically on the poster. The protesters were turned from the camera, but the men on the platform were unmistakable. There stood Barute, Carson, Wallace, and Amato, along with some big wigs apparently from Copperhead. One face, however, stunned Rick. Winston Skroggdad was barely visible behind Barute, but it was he, and it made Rick sick to his stomach. Skroggsdad, Rick's employer on the workers' compensation reform legislation, was one of Barute's henchmen. What was peculiar about Skroggsdad was that he had been one of Pally's legal advisors early in Pally's career, according to Judge Tilly. Skroggsdad had drafted Pally Chase's last will and testament, and, probably, the trust established to take care of Delaney once she reached age twenty-two.

Red showed Rick a couple of more dated photos. "This one is from 1988. Taken in Panacea. It's a protest of some type, but you can see that gas and oil exploration was a hot topic some time ago. The picture was taken in front of a commercial fishery. Though the familiar protest signs were present, there was one sign that Rick saw in the background that made his throat tighten. Rick stared at the picture which captured the protestors and a sign mounted from the top of a building which read: "Chase Commercial Fishing - Pally Chase, Proprietor." Rick looked for a face in the background that might be Pally, or even Delaney as a little girl, but the protesters faces were all too small.

"So, you gonna tell me what this is all about?" Red asked.

"You're the only one I think I can tell right now, Red," Rick replied. "Let's grab some food and beer and I'll let you know how crazy I've become."

The two went for dinner and Rick explained his hypothesis which had, by now, become more of a probability. Pally Chase was in the midst of fighting against an oil conglomerate's corporate greed which amounted to a feud with a community that wanted to protect its shorelines and local businesses. The bad guys weren't necessarily the politicians or lobbyists, but they appeared to have a hand in it. Ned Carson had buckled somewhat from the pressure of that proposition. A coroner's autopsy finding by the now Senator D.D. Amato had been thrown away for a more convenient one. Meredith Chase was put away in a nut house for having what was probably the only sane thought of her adult life. Her husband was killed, not drowned, and she couldn't do a damned thing about it. Delaney Chase was heir to her father's estate and Rick knew, by some law of descent and distribution in probate, so was Sam Chesterfield. Both Sam and Delaney had been privy to the threats and Delaney just returned from seeing her mother in Atlanta, more upset than Rick had ever seen her. Both Sam and Delaney had been handled roughly in the past, especially Sam. Barute was still in town peddling his snake oil and the only opposition that was apparent was the ghost of Pally Chase, his crazy wife, their legitimate daughter, and Pally's illegitimate son.

After eating, Rick drove Red around FSU's campus and they decided to bar hop for the rest of the evening. Rick was grateful for the opportunity to go out and get drunk while trying to forget about everything for a while. He tried to enjoy Red's company like they had in the past, but Rick was pensive throughout the evening. Red didn't seem to notice as he flirted with every woman they met. Rick avoided further discussion about Panacea and Delaney and Sam. Red was enthralled with the city and the women of Tallahassee and the two didn't discuss any further the reason Red had brought the pictures down to Tallahassee. Rick drank with his friend until 1 a.m. and they retired to Rick's hotel room.

Red teased Rick about having to sleep in the same king-size bed with him but promised to keep one foot on the floor. They both passed out, fully clothed and fully "krauzined," as Old Style Beer would term it, ten minutes after returning to the room.

25

Monday morning came and Red was the first to awaken around 8 a.m. He tried to wake his friend, but Rick only mumbled something about how the room service sucked in the hotel. Starving, Red called down to room service and inquired where the nearest fresh donut shop was. It was Krispy Kreme on North Monroe, about two miles away from the hotel. Red didn't feel conditioned enough this early in the morning to walk it so he searched for Rick's rent-a-car keys and found them in the mini-fridge next to the beer.

"You crazy bastard," Red said to Rick. "You even keep your keys chilled. I'm going to get us some breakfast of champions." Red grabbed a wad full of dollars and stuck them in his pocket. "You want a creme filled or regular donut?" Red said.

"Creme filled," Rick mumbled.

"Figures," Red said. "You fags always go for the creme-filled. I'll be back in a few," Red said.

"You're hilarious. Keep it between the lines," Rick admonished him. "You're probably still legally intoxicated."

"And what's that supposed to mean coming from the drunk who drove us home last night?" Red retorted.

"I wasn't drunk. Besides, I'm an excellent drunk driver," Rick said, and pulled the pillow over his head.

"Be right back, Dean Martin," Red said as he exited.

Down in the lobby, Red exited the elevator and greeted the morning clerk. He grabbed a complimentary chocolate chip cookie and a newspaper. On his way to the parking lot, Red embraced a brilliant Florida sunrise. The sun was bright orange and the air smelled of the same.

"Wow. No wonder we spent so much time down here," Jeff said to the sunrise, referring to his college career with his best friend. "Maybe the beach today. . .and bikinis," he smiled and headed for the car, almost skipping.

Jeff unlocked the car with the hand-held remote control as if he had supernatural, or at least, magical powers. Proudly getting into the rented convertible with its rooftop still left down from the night before, Red cleared the seat from the morning dew. Red adjusted the seat and fastened his seat belt. He looked into the rear view mirror, admiring himself as he turned the ignition. In less than a second after the ignition caught, a violent, boiling liquid and expanding vapor explosion erupted from the back of the car near the gas tank. The detonation of the car bomb thrust flames and metal shrapnel into the driver's and passenger's area of the automobile, instantly incinerating and leveling the contents resting therein, including Jeff "Red" Wilhelm.

Catapulted out of bed by the sound of the explosion, Rick ran to the window over-looking the parking lot. To his horror he saw the rent-a-car burning wildly in the morning sunshine as cars on Monroe Avenue stopped instantly to observe the terror and the drama. Rick screamed, "Red! Oh, my God! Red!" Blurred from tears welling-up in his eyes, Rick ran out the hotel room door wearing the clothes he fell asleep in the night before.

Rick was outside the hotel within sixty seconds and running toward the flaming vehicle. "Red! Red!" Rick shouted. Rick approached the body of his friend which was still held under what remained of the seat belt. He went to grab Red from the car when the horrific display of his friend's flame consumed body registered in Rick's head. The explosion had removed much of Red's lower extremities while his upper body and face were indistinguishable. The heat from the fire prohibited Rick from getting within five feet of the vehicle. Rick knew that Red had been instantly killed. He fell to his knees staring at the body.

As a crowd began to gather around the area, Rick was alerted by the sound of sirens coming from a few blocks away. It took Rick only seconds to realize for whom the car bomb was intended. Not knowing who was there watching him, Rick shook his teary eyed face at Red and ran into the hotel. He didn't know if his room was booby-trapped or not, but he risked going in one more time to grab his duffel bag, his Dictaphone, Red's suitcase, the FBI pictures and Red's FBI Identification card. Rick ran out the door taking the fire escape stairs down to the main lobby where he left the building through a back exit.

Rick's heart was pounding wildly as he ran out of the hotel looking for some way of leaving the scene faster than he could by foot without being noticed. He knew he couldn't investigate the car further.

Red was gone. Life as Rick knew it had handed him a perverse stroke of bad fortune, which, for the time being couldn't be digested or even analyzed. Rick hailed down a passing taxi cab.

Sweating now and teary-eyed, Rick instructed the driver to head toward Monticello in hopes to gain an audience with Judge Parson Tilly. The half hour car ride ended outside the Jefferson County Courthouse where Rick tipped the driver and headed for the judge's chambers. Exhausted from emotional overload over the death of his friend, Rick looked up the judge's office and found his secretary. He entered the judge's chambers.

"Hello, ma'am. I'm Rick Morrissey, a friend of Judge Tilly's. Is the judge around?" Rick asked.

"No, sweetie," the secretary said from behind her librarian spectacles. "He's called in sick today with the flu."

"Probably bottle flu," Rick thought to himself. "Is he still living over on Briar?" Rick asked.

"Yes, sweetie. He swears he'll never leave the family home," the secretary said.

"Thank you. I'll try to find him there," Rick said. He nodded to Judge Tilly's secretary and made his way by foot to the judge's home which was about a mile from the courthouse. He arrived on the judge's street by 9:30 a.m. Briar Lane was named after Judge Tilly's great-grandfather, Briar Tilly, and three generations of Tillys had lived on that street since its inception. The judge's house was a simple framed cape cod and lacked any sense of regalness. In fact, the whole town of Monticello was somewhat modest and nobody appeared to be rich. As Rick approached the judge's front door he noticed the patches of natural mistletoe hanging from the big trees in the front yard. He remembered how he and the judge had years ago shot the mistletoe out of the tree with a .20 gauge shotgun the judge kept on hand for protection and occasional target practice. Rick knocked on the door and was greeted by a casually dressed Parson Tilly who had a drink in his hand that could have been apple juice from its appearance, but the smell emanating from it was indistinguishably bourbon.

"Rick, howdy son," the judge said with a smile.

"Hey, Judge. Sorry to bother you. I heard you weren't feeling so hot," Rick offered.

"It's okay, son. I'm just taking the day off to get some work done around here," the judge said. "How ya been? Come on in? Can I get you something to drink?"

"Sure, Judge. Whatever you're having is fine," Rick said. The judge made his way to the liquor cabinet and poured a bourbon on the rocks. Rick studied the judge's steady hand as he poured and contemplated how to explain the events that transpired since their last meeting at the dog track.

"Sit down, Rick. Tell me what brings you here without a car," the judge said.

"Were you looking out your window or what?" Rick said.

"Naw, I saw you coming down the lane. What's the matter? Broke down?" the judge asked.

"Not exactly judge. How much time you got for an explanation?" Rick asked.

"'Til you're finished, or this bottle of bourbon is," the judge said.

Rick told the judge about his conversation with Havana

Chesterfield, his run-in with Ned Carson the night before, and his friend in the FBI who was no longer a part of this world. Tilly listened without showing emotion or reaction. He'd heard more bizarre facts stemming from court cases and, by now Rick imagined, the judge could not be surprised by anything that is part of the human element. When Rick finished explaining what he believed happened and who might be responsible for the car bomb, the judge sat silent for a minute and took a drink of his bourbon.

"Ya don't say?" the judge said. "I won't put that one past Barute. He a real piece of change."

"Am I crazy, Judge, or is this really happening?" Rick asked, looking for reassurance.

"Hell, son. Nothing crazy about greed. That's just a fact of life and some people take it further than others," the judge said. The judge continued where he had left off the night he and Rick were at the dog track in Monticello. "What you didn't hear last time we spoke is how Ms. Chase went off the deep end after Pally's death," the judge said.

"I've since learned, Judge," Rick said.

"Well then you probably know she was committed for accusing someone, anyone, of killing Pally. Only person she left out of the accusations was mother nature," the judge said. "Until hearing what you've had to say today I agreed with everyone else that Meredith Chase was off her rocker," the judge said.

"And now?" Rick asked.

"Now, I'm not so sure, Rick," the judge said. "Barute obviously didn't get along well with Pally, but that's not a reason to kill him and I don't think Barute has the balls to do something like that," the judge thought to himself. "Has to be somebody else involved. Like you said, maybe Senator Amato, this Carson fella, or one of the other henchmen. Hell, money makes us crazy."

"Now, Rick," the judge continued. "One other thing I didn't mention at the dog track was Pally's will. Terms of certain contents of the will are to remain confidential until Delaney turns twenty-two. Obviously, I could get in big trouble with the Florida Bar for divulging contents of a confidential document that I wouldn't otherwise know if it weren't for my job as a judge. I trust you'll exercise discretion with what I'm about to tell you."

"I will, Judge. Please go on," Rick said.

"Well, I knew Pally Chase for a long time prior to his death, though we weren't close. However, after his death, a colleague of mine, Judge James Peterson told me about the estate. Judge Peterson was the probate judge who sat in on the execution of Pally's estate. The judge and I were having some drinks out at my cabin on Lake Augustus about a year after Pally died, and Peterson told me that Pally left much of his estate to the preservation of the coastline and the commercial fishing industry."

"He cut Delaney out?" Rick asked.

"Don't get ahead of me, now," the judge said. "Pally set up a revocable trust with a three and a half million dollar corpus. The purpose of the trust was for the trustee to use the earnings from the interest to fight any group, political or corporate, targeting the shoreline along the Emerald Coast. The trust was to be in effect until Delaney reached twenty-two years old and then she is directed to continue her father's efforts or lose one half of the trust to an environmental organization and split the remainder between her mother and any surviving children of Pally. So, the trust would be split two ways, or so one would think," the judge said, looking for Rick's reaction.

"Something tells me you're about to say the trust has a little more to it," Rick said, withholding his knowledge of Delaney's half brother.

"So do you know what that is?" the Judge said.

"Depends. Isn't that the classic law school response?" Rick said.

"Pally had an illegitimate son," the judge confided without hesitation.

"Go on," Rick said.

"Well, that makes you and me, and Pally's lawyer the only ones who know and shouldn't be telling anyone. Or, at least that's what I'd like to think. That trust and Pally's son were supposed to be kept confidential 'til Delaney was 22. But Pally's estate lawyer might just have leaked out that information to some people who shouldn't know, like Barute," the judge said. "How old is Delaney now?"

"Twenty-one, Judge," Rick said.

"Sounds like it's crunch time for Barute," the judge said.

"Judge, who was Pally's estate planner?" Rick asked.

"Well, I don't know if you're working for him anymore, but his name is Winston Skroggsdad," the judge said.

"But he's in Barute's camp," Rick said surprised.

"Don't forget, Rick. Skroggsdad used to pretend he was a Democrat. Hell, maybe he was. Either way, at the time Pally made his will out, Skroggsdad was fightin' on Pally's side of the fence. Now he's cross-dressin'." the judge said. Both the judge and Rick stared at each other for a moment. "Does Delaney know about her brother?" the judge asked, not revealing whether he knew the brother was Sam Chesterfield or whether he knew the color of his skin.

"I don't think so, Judge. At least, not that I know of," Rick said.

"Now that you've told me what's goin' on these past few days my good-southern breedin' tells me that Barute knows about the trust and may have known for some time now," the judge said.

"God damn," Rick said.

"God damn," the judge said back. "You put it all together and you'll see that Barute is afraid of Delaney gettin' a hold of that money and becoming an activist like her father," the judge paused. "You know how much money a vice-president of a big oil company makes, Rick?" the judge asked. Rick shook his head. "I had one as a divorce client back when I was practicin' law and fifteen years ago he was haulin' in four hundred fifty thousand dollars annually. Can't imagine what that is in today's dollars."

"So, you don't think Barute's in it just for free fill-ups at the local Chevron?" Rick said dryly.

"I don't think so, Rick," The judge said. "In fact, the Mrs. and I got an invitation to the Capitol Building tonight for some GOP fund raiser. It's sponsored by Copperhead Oil. I'm sure you'll find a lot of your friends there."

"Without a doubt, Judge," Rick said.

"I'd be careful, son. Are you going to the police?" the judge asked.

"No, Judge. I may have been born at night, but I wasn't born last night," Rick said. "They're investigating the car bomb by now, and probably think I'm a dead man. If not, they'd certainly want to question me. Besides my current theory ain't gonna get anybody arrested. It's too thin," Rick said.

"Smart boy," the judge said. "Don't forget, son, you're holding a trump card."

"What do you mean?" Rick asked.

"You said it yourself. You're a dead man," the judge said. "Anyone know about this but you and me?"

"Not yet. But I've got to tell Delaney I'm okay. She'll be a wreck if she thinks I'm dead," Rick said.

"Son, do what you must to protect her," the judge said. "But keep it quiet. With you out of the picture, at least they might think Delaney will hang low and not get in the way," the judge paused while Rick nodded his head. "You need some wheels?" the judge asked.

"I do, of course," Rick said.

"Come on out to the barn with me," the judge said. "You want another one?"

"Sure," Rick replied. The judge made a couple more drinks and the two men headed for the barn in the back of the judge's property. The barn was dilapidated and leaning to one side as if ready to be pushed to the ground by a gentle breeze. Inside, the two men walked up to a tarp covered automobile. The judge pulled the tarp off to reveal a 1979 orange Nova.

"Three on the tree," the judge said, describing the standard three-gear transmission. "It was my daddy's before he died."

"Three on the tree, Judge?" Rick asked, amused.

"Three gears, all on the steering column. Can you drive a stick shift?" the judge said.

"My dad taught me when I was sixteen, Judge. No problem," Rick said.

"I start it once a month just for fun," the judge said. "You can borrow it as long as it doesn't end up full of plastic explosives," the judge tried to laugh, but couldn't. He looked at Rick earnestly, and with an avuncular affection, the judge put his hand on Rick's shoulder.

"Thank you, Judge. I'll be careful with it," Rick said.

"Be careful with yourself, son," the judge said. Rick and the judge embraced briefly, shook hands and Rick started up the orange Nova and left Monticello around eleven o'clock in the morning.

Rick knew Sam would be shucking oysters for the lunch crowd at Posey's by now. He wanted to see Delaney first to tell her about everything that had happened but he thought it better come from Sam. At that moment, Rick realized that Delaney's own life could be in danger. "Fuck!" Rick said out loud as he reached into his duffel bag for his cell phone. He dialed Delaney's number at home. The phone rang twelve times before the cellular call cut off. Rick tried Captano's after getting the number from directory assistance. Delaney wasn't expected in until 3:30 that afternoon.

Rick got the number for Posey's and called, hoping Sam would answer. The manager on duty said that Sam was picking up oysters at Apalachicola and should return within the half hour. Rick pressed down hard on the accelerator.

On his way toward St. Mark's, Rick, not wanting to be recognized, searched the judge's car for a pair of sunglasses. When he opened the glove box in front of the passenger's front seat, Rick found some crumpled maps, kleenex, old chewing tobacco, and a snub-nosed Smith & Wesson thirty-eight caliber handgun that had to be over a quarter century old. "Holy shit," Rick said softly to himself.

Ostensibly the judge kept the hand gun in the car for protection. Rick recalled the judge telling him years ago that he always kept a hand gun under his bench in court. "How else ya gonna keep order?" the judge had remarked. Rick smiled at his memory of the judge and thought seriously about the legal consequences of carrying a hand gun in an automobile without a license or permit. Rick checked the hand gun for bullets and found the chamber empty. He put the gun back in the glove box after finding a pair of sunglasses under the driver's seat.

Rick made his way to Posey's and arrived an hour after leaving Judge Tilly's house. Sam was alone in the restaurant behind the oyster bar. Rick walked in and smiled.

"Hey, Rick," Sam said. "What 'cha doin down here so early?"

"I need a beer and your ear," Rick said.

"I got a beer and two ears. Have a seat," Sam said.

Rick explained the events of the last 48 hours leaving out the part about Sam and Delaney being offspring of the same father. Unlike the judge, Sam listened with amazement and constantly interjected Rick's recount of the events with "Shit" and "You're fucking kidding me!" Sam believed Rick, but he just couldn't believe Rick at the same time.

"Sam, you and Delaney could be in trouble. I'm so sorry I've got you into this," Rick said.

"Shit, man," Sam said, feigning bravado. "I was into it long before you were. That fucking bastard Barute and the stuttering mother fucker can go to hell," Sam said. "What do you want me to do? I want to get even with those bastards."

"You've got to protect Delaney and yourself, Sam," Rick said. "I need you to wait for Delaney to get to Captano's at 3:30. She's probably at school now and she usually goes directly from school to there. You two need to stay at your mother's house for a couple of days. I don't know exactly what's happening here, Sam, but you've got to keep Delaney away from her house. I've got to nail one of these guys to get the others to fall. Right now, all I have is a blown-up car and a dead FBI man who everybody thinks is me. Just give me a couple of days," Rick explained.

"I understand. I'll do it," Sam said.

"And, Sam, don't forget, I'm a dead man. Don't tell anyone you've seen me," Rick said, "except Delaney."

"Don't worry. I'll act all sad and shit," Sam said.

"Don't be so dramatic," Rick said. Rick left the bar warning Sam to get to Delaney as soon as possible and out to Havana Chesterfield's for safe housing. Rick was only hopeful that Delaney would understand and that this nightmare would somehow end without anyone else he cared about being hurt.

PART THREE
- Cure -

26

It was nearly twelve thirty in the afternoon when Rick arrived back in Tallahassee. He checked into the Marriott Courtyard in downtown Tallahassee under the assumed name of John Burroughs. Exiting the car, Rick grabbed Judge Tilly's hand gun and packed it in his duffel bag.

In his room, Rick dialed directory assistance for Atlanta and found the judge's son, Willy Tilly's, work number. He called Willy to explain his predicament and ask for help. Rick introduced himself to Willy's secretary and was connected back to Willy.

"Will Tilly," the familiar voice of his friend said on the other end of the phone. "Is this the old man Rick I knew from college?"

"Hi, Willy. It's me. Your secretary doesn't screen very well. I'm down in your back yard right now looking at the Capitol Building and having a cocktail in your honor," Rick said.

"How the hell you been?" Willy asked. "What's it been, two, three years?"

"Yea, at least that. I'm sorry. I'm a shit for a friend," Rick said. "Hey Willy, I've been down here for a little while and a lot has happened to me. I need your help."

"Sure. Glad to help ya. What do you need, tickets to the FSU -

Florida game? Those will be hard to come by, but I can do it only if you'll take me along," Willy said.

"Tell you what, get me through this ordeal and I'll buy your ticket, food and drinks and take you to a game in a white limo like you were Deion Sanders," Rick said.

"Ah, the good old days," Willy said. "So what's up?"

Rick explained his chance meeting with Delaney Chase. Willy didn't know her but had remembered his dad talking about Pally's death. Rick went on discussing the conversation he'd had with Judge Tilly at the dog track, the events surrounding Sam and the fake KKK members, Billy Barute and his followers, the night with Ned Carson, and the car explosion. Rick didn't mention that the car explosion had killed Rick's best friend. He asked Willy to come to Tallahassee.

"Shit, old man. That's one helluva story. Are you sure you're not on drugs?" Willy kidded Rick. "I've love to come down and help, but I'm swamped at work," Willy paused. "What do you need me for? Can't you get some help from the law?"

"You know better than that, Willy. I haven't a pot to piss in yet," Rick said. "I just need you to help me get a statement from one of these guys. It won't take but one day and, I mean it, I'll take care of you with the Florida game," Rick said.

"I'd really like to, man," Willy said. "Seriously. But I'm just swamped. How about next week?"

Rick was dejected by Willy's response. He had to explain more. "Willy. Look. What I'm asking you to do is not a very friend-like request if I gave a damn about your safety," Rick explained. "I do give a damn, but you're the only one I know who can help." Rick paused. "You know that FBI man? Well, he was Red Wilhelm. My best friend from Chicago. He got killed because of me," Rick was shaken. "I've got to do something, Willy. This is too big. Too awesome for me. Please. . .I need your help and I'll protect you the best I can. I know what I'm asking is insane, but . . .I just need you," He finished.

"I'm not a very brave man, Rick," Willy said sarcastically. "I can tell you're shaken up by this," Willy paused. "Okay. How's tomorrow around noon?"

"Ah, thank you Willy," Rick said. "The sooner the better."

"So what do I need to do exactly?" Willy said.

"We're gonna shake down a slimy bastard named Ned Carson. Nobody will know you're involved either," Rick said. "By the way, we're probably going to fracture a few laws."

"Oh, really?" Willy said. "Then I guess it'll be like old times."

"Thanks, buddy," Rick said. "I'm at the Courtyard on Apalachee Parkway. Room 121. See you tomorrow." Rick hung-up the phone and clutched his pillow, staring silently into the empty room. He had no plan for the next day until burying his head in the soft white pillow. With a sick revelation of vengeance, Rick shucked the pillow case from its fluffy coil, grabbed a pocket knife from his duffel bag and began to cut eye holes in the fabric.

Rick tried to fall asleep over the next few hours, but accomplished only a few minutes of sleep. After nearly four hours of restlessness, he turned on the television to see if the news was covering the car bomb. It was five o'clock in the afternoon when the ticker sound of the Channel 3 news came over the television.

"Car bomb explodes this morning in Tallahassee," the female

newscaster said. "One man dead and police are looking for suspects. We'll be back with the full story after this message."

"This'll be interesting," Rick said to himself. He got up and made a pot of coffee while the commercial break completed.

"A car bomb exploded this morning in downtown Tallahassee in the Radisson Hotel parking lot," the broadcaster began. "Police Chief Charles Ham confirmed this afternoon that one man is dead after the apparent murder took place around 8 a.m. Included in the police recovery of the victim was a fireproof steel-lined briefcase located in the rear seat of the car which contained over $100,000 street value worth of cocaine. The police have not released the identity of the man in the car but said they received information from the rental car plate as to the man's identity. Chief Ham did comment that the victim was an Illinois attorney who was staying at the Radisson. Police suspect it is a drug deal gone bad but will await further investigation," the newswoman concluded.

Rick's throat swelled and anger ran through his blood. He felt violated and wondered how many people he knew would eventually get word of his shameful demise. He hoped Delaney and Sam would not believe the drugs were actually his. He knew he had to act fast. He called his parents and sister first thinking that the police were trying to contact them before releasing his name to the public. His mother wasn't home and Rick left a short message for her not to talk to the Tallahassee police until she talked with her first. He explained that he wasn't in trouble and she shouldn't be alarmed. He knew she would worry, but also that she would talk with him first.

His father was frightened after Rick explained his last forty-eight hours. Rick's father agreed not to comment if contacted by the police.

He told his father not to worry and that he had to get going. He felt
terrible putting his parents through this. Rick finished talking with his
father around seven o'clock. He had decided he would tell the police
later about Red. At this point, Rick thought, the police would only
question him about the murder and the cocaine in the car, without interest
in the political set-up now feared by Rick.

Minutes after talking with his father, Rick heard a knock at the
door. He sprang to his feet and recovered Judge Tilly's gun from the
duffel bag. Turning off the lights and the television, Rick drew the hotel
room curtains closed. Slowly, Rick moved in the darkened room toward
the door. His heart was beating into his head so hard that he found his
vision going in and out of blurriness. Rick leaned into the eye hole of the
door to see outside his room. He recognized immediately the face of his
college roommate. Rick opened the door.

"Hey, old man," Willy Tilly said confidently. He looked down
and then back up at Rick. "Nice gun."

Rick was relieved to see his old friend so early, as he wasn't sure
he could have lasted until the morning for his friend to arrive. "Wow.
How'd you manage to. . .," he was cut off by Willy entering the room, still
talking.

"Looks like my over-confident friend has lost a little moxie. A
gun? Really, Rick," Willy said. "Couldn't handle hearing you were in
trouble, so I left work right after we got off the phone. You were about
to ask me how I managed to get here so early weren't you?" Willy said.
They shook hands.

"Nice to see you, Willy," Rick said.

"Let's go screw with some heads," Willy said. "I called my dad on the way down here. You must have started him off good, he was drunk as hell, man! So, in between slurred consonants and syllables I managed to learn about your problem. My old man. He's a real cocksure bravado when he's drinking."

"What'd he say?" Rick asked.

"Ya'll boys go and get those bastards. Ya'll can kick some ass and avenge the death of a good man," Willy said, imitating his father. "Hell, I think you convinced him that Barute is capable of anything dastardly."

"Well, we'll find out pretty soon," Rick said. "Since you're here so early, let's go meet a friend of mine for a late night snack."

"Shouldn't we have a drink first," Willy asked.

"I'll make you a roadie. We've got to get going," Rick said. "Let me get a couple of things and I'll explain on the way. Incidentally, can we take your car? Your old man's orange nova kinda puts a bad light on my plan," Rick said.

"You mean it cramps your style, don't you?" Willy said.

"Typically, you'd be right, but not this time," Rick said. "What are you driving anyway?"

"Ford Expedition," Willy said.

"What color?" Rick asked.

"Black. Why?" Willy asked.

"Perfect for a G-Man," Rick said. "Let's go, I'll tell you the rest on the way to Ned Carson's hotel room. He's staying at the Fairmont Inn off Capital Circle," Rick said as the two left for Willy's car.

27

On the way to see Carson, Rick explained that Willy would be posing as an FBI man by using Red's I.D. "You got strawberry blond hair, Willy, just don't let him look at the picture long," Rick said. "He's probably had a few cocktails anyhow. All I need you to do is get him out to your car and in the back seat. Drive us all to the airport. I'll take it from there," Rick explained his plan to strong-arm Carson and even threaten him with his life, if need be, in order to get Carson to capitulate and tell the truth.

The black Expedition pulled into the Fairmont Inn parking area and Willy headed to the bar equipped with a description of Ned and a head full of confidence.

Carson wasn't in the bar, but the bartender said he had just left ten minutes earlier. Willy went to the front desk clerk and flashed his badge.

"Jeff Wilhelm, ma'am. Federal Bureau of Investigation. I'd like you to escort me to Mr. Ned Carson's room," Willy said.

The young male front desk clerk was impressed with the badge, but was obdurate. "I'm sorry Sir, but I'm not allowed to give out a person's room number," the clerk said.

"That's fine," Willy said. "I don't need his room number. I'm here for him and you're going to walk me to his room by yourself or with a security guard. It doesn't matter to me."

The clerk struggled for a reaction.   He relented for fear of becoming too involved.   "He's in 114.   And your name again is?" the clerk said.

"FBI, Sir," Willy said and walked away.

Willy knocked on Carson's door and Carson opened it almost immediately. Carson was brushing his teeth when he opened the door. "Yes. W-w-what is it?" Carson said through toothpaste and saliva.

Willy flashed his badge and stuck it right in Carson's face, too close for Carson to focus soon enough. "FBI, Mr. Carson. I need you to come to our headquarters and have a conversation regarding a drug dealer who was killed by a car bomb earlier today.   Witnesses said you may have known this man and who he might be dealing drugs to," Willy said.

"L-l-let me spit this out," Carson said. Carson walked to the sink and spit out the toothpaste and dried his mouth. "Hell, I d-d-don't know no drug d-d-dealers," Carson said.

"We don't doubt that Sir, but the department just requires that we ask a few simple questions. You'll be nestled here in your bed within the next hour," Willy said. "Come on, I have a car waiting."

The two men walked out of the hotel without talking. Willy opened the back seat door and Carson got in. Willy made his way around to the driver's side, got in, and started the car. Without saying a word, Willy drove the two men out of the hotel parking lot and toward Route 319 South and Tallahassee's airport.   Just as Carson began to ask where they were going, Rick came out from the cargo area behind the back seat and cocked Judge Tilly's unloaded hand gun into the back of Carson's neck.

"Don't turn around. Just keep looking forward," Rick said in a low, mono-toned voice. Rick was wearing the imitation Klan hood in the form of the white pillow case he cut up at his hotel room.

"W-w-what's this all ab-b-bout?" Carson said in a panic.

"Just hold still." Rick climbed into the back seat and sat next to Carson, still pointing the empty hand gun at Carson. "You hate niggers as much as I do?" Rick asked Carson through the eye slits of his make-shift Klan hood.

"What kind of FB-B-B I are you supposed to b-b-be?" Carson asked.

"The kind that have been following your every movement for the past six months," Rick said. "We know about the car bomb, Mr. Carson," Rick said. "You'll find your dead man down at Tallahassee Community General Hospital in the morgue. And you know what else you'll find? You'll find that the dead man was investigating you and Barute and the Senator and all you fucking clowns for the last two years. And you know what else sucks about being you? That man doing the investigation was a member of the Federal Bureau of Investigation who was specifically appointed by the Director of the FBI to look into you dumb fucks for illegal use of political funds, illegal fund raising, misappropriation of local tax dollars and conspiracy to commit murder." Rick was lying now, but it came easy when emotion was behind it. He was believable. He paused.

After a long silence, Carson began to speak. "L-l-listen. This is off the, the, the record. I've got a f-f-family to support and a livelihood to protect," He continued, "I had n-n-nothing to do with the car bomb,

I swear."

"You want to protect yourself, then give it to us off the record or we'll burn your ass on the record," Willy said while driving, taking an enjoyable part in the charade.

"They'll k-k-kill me too," Carson said.

"Who will?" Rick asked.

"I-I-I can't say," Carson responded, weakly.

"Well, let me help you say," Rick said. "We'll play Russian Roulette. For every word you say, starting now, that is not a proper name of someone involved in the car bomb I'll click this gun's trigger until a bullet finally goes off. Okay, ready, set, go."

"I c-c-c-c-can't," Ned said. Rick pulled the trigger twice.

"You're lucky he don't count stutters, or you'd be a dead man for sure," Willy said, enjoying the suspense.

"Please! Don't!" Ned begged. Another two trigger pulls from Rick.

"You've got a fifty-fifty chance of living past your next syllable," Rick said. "What will it be? Real gamblers would put it all on the table, but you don't look like a real gambler, Ned. Tell you what, don't place your bet, I'll just pull the trigger and we'll see what would have happened if you didn't say a name next," Rick said as he started to pull the hammer back.

"It was Billy!" Carson exclaimed. "Billy!"

"And the Senator?" Rick asked.

"And the Senator," Carson confided. "But please, please, if they ever find out how you know, I'll be killed."

"Oh, they'll know, Ned." Rick removed the fake Klan sheet from his head. "I've got it all on tape." Rick pulled a dictaphone out of his pocket and held it up. Ned stared in silence, completely terrified.

"What's your story, Ned?" Rick asked. Ned made no response. "You're already nailed, Ned. You've got my word that the FBI will give you protection and consider what you're about to tell us in deciding what we'll do with your sorry ass. Don't leave a thing out or we'll leave you to dry in the wind," Rick said, remembering fondly his fleeting childhood ambition of becoming a real-life FBI man.

"I just get information, Rick. I swear," Carson said. "This is b-bigger than you, you must know that."

"What do you mean?" Rick demanded.

"B-Billy's just working for the oil company," Ned said.

"What oil company?" Rick said.

"Copperhead," Ned admitted. "They're the m-m-money behind this. Billy's not really in charge. He's just doin' what they tell him."

"Like killin' Pally Chase and Coatie Gillen on the shrimp boat?" Rick said, pushing the revolver into Ned's neck.

"He t-t-told me he didn't mean for them both to d-d-die!" Ned said exasperated.

"Just Pally?" Rick said.

Ned paused and looked straight ahead into the night. He lowered his head and acquiesced. "Just Pally."

"Let me guess, Barute arranged to have a fuel line cut so a spark from the electric panel would ignite the boat on fire from the hull, causing the boat to smolder in flames and force its occupants to breathe the emissions of carbon monoxide. But, wonder of wonders, the tropical storm became a hurricane and Barute didn't even need a mechanical accident for the murder, mother nature caused one of her own," Rick said.

"As far as I know, that's s-s-something of w-what happened," Ned assented.

"Did Barute ever tell you this?" Rick said.

"No," Ned said.

"Then how do you know?" Rick asked.

"Billy told a hooker," Ned admitted.

Remembering Ned's girlfriend from Barker's Tavern, Rick asked, "And you were with the same woman?"

"Yes," Ned admitted. "She t-t-told me I've got a perverted f-f-friend and wondered if B-Billy was serious because we were all pretty drunk that night he told her. We were in D.C. for George Bush's inaugural in January of '89. I g-guess I didn't want to believe it then, but I thought it c-could be true."

"Ned, do you by any chance know who this call girl is?" Rick asked.

Ned hesitated. "I-I-I don't want her to get into trouble," Ned said.

"She won't, Ned. She didn't do anything," Rick said.

"Well, you remember that girl I was with at Barker's the other night?" Ned said.

"She travels with you guys?!" Rick asked. "Jodi Eastbrook?"

"B-Billy pays her well," Ned tried to rationalize.

"You're a couple of sick bastards, Ned," Rick said, shaking his head. "So why hit Pally?" he asked.

"Pally was about to b-b-beat Copperhead's successful bid to get legislative p-p-permission to drill off Panacea.   Billy had an in with Copperhead.   He was asked to do what he could, what was necessary, and his reward would be more than he could ever earn as a l-l-lobbyist," Ned said.   "Th-th-that's when he got Coroner Amato involved to cover up the autopsy findings.   Amato was c-c-corrupt anyhow so it wasn't hard to do."

"And now he's a Senator, God bless him," Rick said.   Rick considered Ned's remarks briefly.   "Just stay away from Barute and Senator Amato and we'll protect you. You helped us out Ned. You can believe me, I don't think you're capable of being as involved as they are," Rick said.   "We're going to Barute now to play your statement.   I'd advise you to stay away from them. Maybe catch a plane."   Rick looked outside the window and paused, "Oh, what do you know? We're at the airport. Let's go see if they take people flying on such short notice," Rick said.

"I d-d-don't know what to do," Carson said.   "How will I ever work again?"

"That's your problem, Ned," Rick said.   "If you're just a go-between, then the government might treat you lightly.   I'll promise you this.   I'm after Barute, not you." Rick paused. "So tell me Ned, where is Barute right now?"

"I don't know," Carson said.

"Ned, I'm through with you. Let's not play games.   One way or another, he'll know you talked.   The only question is whether he beats you, or both me and my friend in the FBI beat you. How many beatings are you interested in, Ned?" Rick said.

"He's at a f-f-fund raiser at the Capitol. It's a b-b-black tie thing.

A thousand dollars a ticket," Carson said.

"Why aren't you there?" Rick asked.

"Remember that g-g-girl you met sitting with me at the b-b-bar?" Carson asked.

"Okay, I get it," Rick said. "Tell your wife and kids I said hello, too."

Willy drove the Expedition into the Tallahassee International Airport and they walked Carson to the Delta Airlines counter. Rick paid for a ticket in Carson's name for Atlanta with a connection to Washington, D.C. They escorted Carson to the terminal and watched him check in. The next flight wasn't scheduled for another half hour. Rick and Willy waited until Carson boarded the plane at 8:40 p.m.

28

"Hey, old man. That was fun and everything, but we don't have a thousand bucks or a tuxedo," Willy said. "Think we should wait for Barute 'til he leaves the party?" he asked.

"No thanks, Willy. Barute thinks I'm a dead man. I want to see his face when I walk in. Him and all of his overstuffed buddies," Rick said. "Besides, chances are he'll be mingling with a group close to him and they might know what he's been up to. In particular, Senator D.D. Amato," he concluded.

The two men drove twenty-five minutes to the Capitol Building in downtown Tallahassee. With the FSU-Florida football rivalry being played that weekend, the traffic was busy and slow. The Capitol Building was brightly lit with arrays of rotating ground search lights lighting up the skies around the capitol rotunda. It looked more like Disneyland than a government building. People were everywhere, including news media equipment trucks and curious spectators who couldn't pay the price of admission. The event was a political gala centered on the guest of honor, Senator D.D. Amato, and sponsored by several corporations including the Copperhead Oil Manufacturing and Refining Company. Willy drove past the valet parking and parked the Expedition on College Avenue two blocks from the Capitol at 9 p.m.

"Can I use your cell phone?" Rick asked Willy.

"Go ahead. Don't cost me nothin.' Company phone," Willy said.

"Your dad said you were a parsimonious s.o.b," Rick said, and smiled.

"I'm not cheap. Just a smart money manager," Willy said.

"Whatever," Rick said. Rick dialed directory assistance for the Tallahassee Police Department.

"What are you calling them for?" Willy asked.

"Back-up. Haven't you ever seen that in the movies?" Rick asked. "It's always the maverick cops who don't ask for back-up getting killed in the end."

"Oh, so we're gonna get killed now?" Willy said, sarcastically, but appearing somewhat nervous. "Hell, we're not even cops."

"No. I just said I'm calling for back-up," Rick said, as he spoke into the phone. "No, ma'am. This isn't an emergency. I'm requesting some officers come to the Capitol Building to remove some undesirables who are disturbing tonight's fund raiser." Rick paused, listening to the dispatcher. "Ma'am, this is a fund raiser hosted by Senator D.D. Amato, I'm Duncan Spivey, his assistant chief of staff. Two men just came in without invitations or the thousand dollar admission fee and they're disturbing the whole event. Goddamned liberals is what they are. Protesting and everything. I'm afraid they may have more coming, so send a few cars, would you?" Rick paused again. "Thank you ma'am. Just tell them to walk on in." Rick ended the call.

Leaving the vehicle, Rick left his hand gun in the glove box of Willy's car and the two walked to the main entrance of the Capitol.

"How the hell you expect us to get in?" Willy asked.

"Willy, we've spent years together sneaking into bars and football games in this town when the lines were too long or we didn't have tickets," Rick said. "This is just another bar, my friend. And what do bars have at their front entrance?" Rick asked, not giving Willy time to answer. "Bouncers. And do bouncers have any equity interest in the establishment they're supposed to represent? Hell, no. So, I'm sure the front people here are paid flunkies at minimum wage, or worse, doing it for nothing. Just smile and act natural," Rick said.

The two men walked toward the Capitol Building traversing the picturesque alameda which was bordered with palm trees. They approached the entrance door where two young college girls were taking the thousand dollar tickets. Rick spoke before the girls had a chance.

"Oh my, is this Sloppy Joe's Bar? Damn, ya'll have a pretty strict dress code. Are the beers any colder here if you wear a tuxedo?" Rick asked.

One of the girls who was holding the programs for the event replied as if she believed Rick. "No, Sloppy Joe's is across the street," she said. "We're having a political event here; this is the Capitol Building."

"No shit," Rick thought to himself, but he only smiled and said, "Well, we have no preference. Don't tell me you girls are in the Young Republicans club at Florida State," Rick said.

"How'd you know?" the first girl said.

"Oh, my dad told me he'd have some beautiful Young Republicans working the door tonight," Rick said.

"Oh, who's your dad?" the girl asked.

"D.D. Amato. He tells me he's a senator or something. Is that true?" Rick asked, amusing the girls.

"He is not your dad!" the girl said, excited to be rubbing elbows with a senator's son.

"He is. Unless he keeps hanging around that fat bastard Billy Barute. If he does, I'll disown him," Rick said. The girls laughed together and stared back at Rick for his next words.

"I'll bet Barute has tried to charm you two by now," Rick said. "Don't let him fool you, he's really fat," Rick said. The girls laughed again. "Anyhow, I've got to let my dad know where I parked his car and give him the keys. Would you two mind if we just skipped in real quick. You can keep my driver's license for security if you'd like," Rick said. "We'll just be a minute and we promise not to eat any of the food."

The girls looked at each other and stated simultaneously, "Go ahead."

"Thank you," Rick said. "We'll be right back. By the way, this is Barute's son," Rick said, gesturing to Willy.

"Very funny," Willy said, red faced, as he looked at the girls.

"Don't be embarrassed, you'll never be as fat as your old man," Rick said to Willy and then looked at the girls and winked. "We'll see you in a minute. Come on, Junior."

The two men passed into the Capitol and made their way to the Rotunda near the center of the building. Men in black tuxedos and women bedizened tastelessly in fine costume jewelry and beaded dresses were everywhere. Over two hundred people were present and acting very grand ballroom like; they were smiling, laughing at everything, and looking around to see who was watching them have the time of their lives. Rick didn't see Barute immediately, but noticed the food table and walked toward the boiled crawdaddies obviously prepared New Orleans style. Rick grabbed a couple from the extra large serving bowl and ate them without the benefit of a napkin or a plate. Willy watched Rick and nervously looked around the room. Rick's confidence, or lack of nervousness, disturbed Willy.

"Rick, what are you doing? Let's take care of this thing," Willy said, as many of the guests began staring at the two men who looked completely out-of-place.

"I love crawdaddies," Rick said. "Anyhow, don't worry, I've just lost my appetite looking at that big fat guy standing over there in the corner with those two men," Rick said as he stared at Barute who was holding his own court telling some kind of ribald story to two admirers. "Here we go," Rick said. Rick and Willy walked over toward Barute who had yet to notice them. Just before they got to Barute a security guard stopped them.

"Hold it, boys. I don't think you belong here. Let's go," the guard said.

Rick looked at Willy. "Didn't this happen a few times to us in less expensive bars?" Rick said. Willy smiled nervously.

"This way, boys," the guard said.

"Hold on, Sir," Rick said. "We're here with that big guy there. Hey, Billy!" Rick said. Barute glanced over and saw the ghost he thought had been executed. Barute only looked perplexed and he tried to smile. Rick pulled the dictaphone out of his pocket and waved it for Barute's benefit. "Billy, this guard wants us to leave, but I told him you'd like to spend some time with us seeing as how Ned couldn't be here," Rick said to Barute.

Barute gave his best pose of feigned confidence. Fittingly, he even seemed to stutter when he said. "Th-that's right, Sir, they are friends of mine. You can let them be," Barute said to the guard. The guard let go of Willy and Rick and walked away. The three men standing with Barute only stared at Rick and Willy and waited for Barute's response to allowing the two intruders to stay.

"Boo!" Rick said. Barute only stared with angry bewilderment. "Would you like to step into a side office?" Rick said. "Incidentally, this could get a little embarrassing. You may want to ask your claque to remain out here," Rick gestured to the confused men who were standing next to Barute.

Barute ushered away the two men who had been standing with him, saying, "Let me take care of these guys and I'll be right back with you."

"Shall we?" Rick said.

"Follow me," Barute said, leading them down a corridor into the law library of the Capitol. The library was a large room filled with bookshelves full of law books and cases from the early nineteen hundreds. Its practical use now was one of a study with no recent books having been circulated there in a couple of decades. There were several oak study tables neatly arranged throughout the room. Barute leaned up against one of them and studied the floor pensively. Of the three men in the room, Rick took the lead in conversation.

"How does it feel to know everything you've worked for is heading right down the toilet?" Rick asked.

"I don't know what you're talking about," Barute said, without any confidence.

"Would you believe Ned Carson knows what he's talking about?" Rick asked. "Because Ned seems to have some details about you that I'm sure would spin your head around."

"Oh, really," Barute said. "Ned Carson's word ain't worth dick. He's been tryin' to get me into trouble since the day I met him."

"Well, he's succeeded. Right now he's in the custody and care of the Federal Bureau of Investigation signing a statement implicating you in the death of Pally Chase and myself. Only I'm not dead." Rick didn't hear the door of the library open behind him where Senator D.D. Amato walked in to hear the end of Rick's statement.

"Don't you mean, not dead yet?" Amato said. Rick and Willy turned around to meet Amato's glance. "Got a disturbing phone call from an airphone in a Delta Jet leaving Tallahassee International for Washington, D.C., Billy," Amato said. "Seems that Ned was worried about getting into some kind of trouble with the law. Thought you and I ought to know about it."

Amato pulled a handgun from inside his coat and stepped deeper into the room.

"Nice bluff, lawyer boy. Senator, I do believe you know the blond haired gentleman from Illinois," Barute said, now brimming with confidence, but looking hatefully toward Rick. "But I don't think we've had the pleasure of meeting the man who wished he was really in the FBI." He turned toward Willy.

"Let me see your identification," Barute said, walking toward Willy. Willy, now frightened, reached for his back pocket and his wallet. "Hold it, son. I'll do you the honor," Barute said, as he pulled Willy's identification from his wallet. "William Briar Tilly," Barute announced, still thumbing through Willy's wallet. "Oh, looks like he's a lawyer and all. Working at Basin & Powers in Atlanta." Barute stared coldly at Rick. "What a shame to have to kill two lawyers. I don't think the world could ever thank me enough."

Rick glowered at Barute. "I'm not a lawyer anymore," Rick said. "And you've already killed an agent of the federal government. The world may not give a damn, but I'll bet the feds will."

"I ain't killed nobody, yet, son. You should've left when you had the opportunity," Barute said to Rick. "Give me that dictaphone." Reluctantly, Rick handed the recording device over, and Barute pressed the play button. "Oooh, wee! Ned is a talker!" Barute said. Too bad he'll be the one to go down for all this. Poor son-of-a-bitch."

"I've got a car out front, Billy. Let's take care of these guys away from all this crowd," Senator Amato said. "I can't believe what you've gotten me into, Billy." Amato was nervous, but still pointing the gun. The four men could hear a commotion from the crowd outside the library. Rick hoped Tallahassee's finest had arrived.

"If you haven't killed yet, Senator, you're not gonna kill anyone," Rick said. "We don't need a black limo. Thank you anyhow. I think the police can escort us just fine."

"Your poker face faded a long time ago, son," Barute said to Rick.

"I'm not playin' cards here, Billy. It's obvious you're working without a full deck and the senator's is loaded," Rick said. "You're not such a good bluffer yourself, either," Rick said to Barute. "Ned told me you couldn't do your own dirty work," Rick said as he walked toward Barute, meeting him face-to-face."

"Stop right there," Amato said as he pointed the gun at Rick.

Rick turned toward Amato. "Senator. I don't know how much you're involved in trying to kill me earlier, but I do know you're not dumb enough to shoot a gun without a silencer in the middle of the Capitol. Even if you did cover up Pally Chase's death, you didn't kill him. So, don't go making it worse for yourself." Rick paused. "Shoot me if you like, but let me just tell Mr. Barute how much I've appreciated getting to know him," Rick said and cocked his arm back, releasing a fist full of indignation into the lobbyist's face. Barute fell to the floor as Amato looked on, stunned. Rick turned and spoke to Amato as he walked past him toward the door to the hallway. "So, if you're not gonna shoot me,"

Rick continued past the senator and stepped outside the door of the library and noticed six Tallahassee Policemen standing twenty-five feet away.

"Officers, the problem's in here," Rick summoned the officers.

"What the hell are you doing?" Amato said, hiding his gun back in his coat.

"I told the police everything already. I just thought they should hear it from you guys." Rick lied. Four of the officers walked into the library with their sergeant. The sixth officer remained outside the library.

"What's seems to be the trouble, men?" the police sergeant asked.

Reading the sergeant's badge, Rick introduced Amato and Barute, who was still lying on the floor, now bleeding profusely from the nose. "Sergeant McCray, this is William Barute," Rick said gesturing to the floor. "He's the 'damndest lobbyist this side of the Mason-Dixon line'," Rick said, quoting how Barute introduced himself in their first encounter. "And this man here is Senator Amato," Rick gestured to the senator. "He's carrying a hand gun in a government building without proper authority."

"Sergeant, this man has no idea what he's talking about," Barute said, anxiously getting to his feet. "Ned Carson is a lying son-of-a-bitch, and I'll prove it in court. He's the man you want, not me." Barute's statement could not belie his obvious worry in the presence of the police.

"What do you mean? You're not who he says you are?" Sergeant McCray stated.

"No, I mean. . .," Barute stopped himself, realizing the police weren't called to come after him and that Rick hadn't told them anything yet.

"We were called to investigate a disturbance," Sergeant McCray said. "What are you talking about?"

Barute stared in silence, then turned to Rick. "You lyin' bastard," he said.

"You fat bastard," Rick said to Barute.

"Sergeant, in the senator's armpit you'll find a handgun that is probably loaded," Rick said as two of the officers immediately drew down on all of them, pointing their guns separately at each man to ward off sudden movement by either. "And in Mr. Barute's hand is a full confession on tape from a Mister Ned Carson implicating Mr. Barute and the senator here in the car bombing we had here this morning, among other things," Rick said.

In desperation, Barute took the tape from the dictaphone and bolted for the bathroom in the back of the library, tearing the tape from the cassette as he ran.

"Hold it, Sir!" Sergeant McCray yelled.

Barute continued his best attempt at running, and the sergeant followed him. Rick heard the toilet flush and Barute emerged from the bathroom under the escort of Sergeant McCray, who was now holding the gun and the remains of the micro-cassette tape. "The tape is damaged, but we can still get the audio from it. I think this desperate act and his previous statement are enough to detain these gentlemen for questioning," McCray said. "Sir, I'd like you and your friend to come along too, please," McCray said to Rick.

"Sergeant, I can't. I'm afraid that I've got to go see if a couple other friends of mine are okay," Rick said. "They could be in danger. I'm the one who called you here in the first place under the name Duncan Spivey."

"We got the call from a Duncan Spivey, but who is that? You?" the Sergeant asked.

"Nobody, just a name I used to use in idle conversation with boring debutantes," Rick said.

Just then, Amato broke in. "Tell him, Billy. It might not be too late!" Amato said to Barute.

"Too late for what?" Rick demanded.

"Nothing. Shut the hell up, D.D." Barute said. "Just shut the hell up."

"Too late for What?! Rick demanded.

No response came from Barute or the Senator. Rick grabbed Willy by the arm. "Come on, Will, we've got to go!" Rick broke through the officers shielding the exit from the library and the two men raced through the crowd to leave the Capitol and get to Willy's Expedition.

"What's going on?!" Willy yelled as the two men ran down

College Avenue.

"I don't know. We've got to get to Delaney and Sam!" Rick exclaimed. "There staying at Sam's mom's house"

"Where is that?" Willy said.

"Sopchoppy. Give me your keys," Rick yelled as Willy handed him the keys to the Expedition. Rick hit the unlock button as the two approached the vehicle and they were barely in the car when Rick put it in gear and floored the gas pedal. Rick raced the Ford Expedition down Highway 319 to Sopchoppy. He was traveling 95 miles an hour on the two-lane highway followed by two squad cars. The officers chased the Expedition into Sopchoppy with the squad car sirens screaming and blue and red lights flashing.

"Why don't you call them?" Willy asked as they sped down the highway.

"Ms. Chesterfield doesn't have a phone. Never has," Rick said.

All of the vehicles arrived at the home of Havana Chesterfield nearly simultaneously. As Rick put the Expedition into park and started to exit the vehicle, a red and purple explosion erupted from under Havana Chesterfield's front porch.

"Delaney!" Rick screamed. "No!" He burst from the Expedition as burning parts of wood from the house were hitting him and the vehicle. He shielded his face from the heat and debris of the explosion. The house was consumed instantly by the fire and Rick, fleetingly, thought he could make it in and out of there alive. Grief overcame him as he began to recognize that nobody inside, however, was coming out alive. Rick slowly made his way toward the burning home enduring as much of the heat as possible. The flames caused the wood frame of the home to crackle as loud as hail falling violently on a tin roof. Rick could distinguish no other sound save that of the fireburst which was now surrounding him. As Rick approached closer to the house, he thought he heard the faint cry or scream of a female voice.

"Delaney?!" "Sam?!" "Havana?!" he yelled. No response came as Rick continued toward the inferno. When he reached the front porch he heard a car horn blaring a steady monotone. Rick turned back toward Willy and the suburban. By now, five pairs of vehicle lights were pointing high beams toward Ms. Chesterfield's home. Rick squinted to try to make out the figures of those behind the lights. He was blinded by the bright white beams and took a step away from the house, closer to Willy and the other vehicles.

Rick looked into the blinding headlights and yelled. "Willy! Willy!" He shielded his face and turned around. As Rick turned back toward the house he tried to find movement on the inside. Any sign of life at all. He started back toward the front porch when an arm landed on his shoulder from behind. Startled, Rick turned to meet the tear-filled eyes of Delaney.

"Rick!" Delaney yelled over the noise from the flames.

Rick said nothing as he stared at what must have been a hallucination or a ghost. Slowly, he reached toward her face with his left hand. Skin on skin disproved Rick's thought that he was dreaming. His other hand came up to Delaney's face as he focused in on her. Erupting from emotion, Delaney plunged into Rick's chest and he embraced her. Delaney was crying after the short embrace and she kissed Rick softly.

"Come back from the fire, Rick. It's okay. Everybody's okay," she said in a soft voice. Rick embraced her again and grabbed her hand as the couple withdrew from the flaming home toward the others standing near Willy's Expedition.

Walking back, Rick was greeted by a crying Havana Chesterfield who ran to meet Rick and embrace him. "It's okay, baby," Ms. Chesterfield said, trying to smile, but crying. She touched Rick's face with her hand. "It's okay."

Sam followed his mother to Rick. "Your friend here says you've exposed the assholes who did this. Thank God, Delaney has a smart dog," Sam said.

"What happened?" Rick asked Sam.

"We found Southpaw barking like crazy under the porch, and Delaney thought he trapped an animal or something like he does at home. He's always chasing the squirrels there. When we checked it out, we saw the bomb. I didn't see no timer or nothing but we sure didn't think we had any time left. Needless to say, we made fast tracks for the neighbor's Chevy Van over there and hid behind it just as the bomb went off," Sam said.

"And Southpaw?" Rick asked.

"He's in here," Willy said, pointing to his Expedition.

"We wouldn't leave without him, Rick," Sam said, looking to Rick for a smile of assurance.

Rick smiled at Delaney and he exhaled for what he thought was the first time in ten minutes. Rick, Sam, Havana, and Delaney embraced together.

"Mr. Morrissey, Sir, I'm special agent Don Chimara." Mr. Chimara stepped out from a crowd of six men in dark suits. "I'm from the Federal Bureau of Investigation. We need to take you with us to the

Tallahassee Police Department. Mr. Barute is in protective custody with Senator Amato. We need your statement, Sir," Chimara said.

Rick looked at the special agent. "I know. Do you know about Jeff Wilhelm?" Rick asked.

"Yes, Sir, we do," Agent Chimara said. "We know all about it." Chimara paused. "I'm sorry, Sir."

"What's he talking about?" Delaney asked.

"Sir, we really have to get going," Agent Chimara said, insisting. "We'll take care of your friends. They'll be fine."

"I'll have to explain later. I'll call you at home," Rick said to Delaney. Rick thanked Willy and said goodbye to his friends, and Delaney. He climbed into Agent Chimara's black Yukon and was driven away with police escort.

29

From one o'clock in the morning until three, Rick answered questions posed by the FBI and the local police at the Tallahassee Police Department. Rick explained the events leading up to the bombing of his car, Red's contribution to exposing Barute, Amato, and Carson, and Rick's relationship with Delaney Chase.

Rick learned from Agent Chimara that Delaney, Sam, and Ms. Chesterfield would be under government protection for the next several days because of an investigation the fed had launched into Copperhead Oil. Rick's thoughts were weighing on his friends from Panacea and he wondered where Sam, Havana, and Delaney would be spending the night, wishing he could be with them. Heavier still was the ache in his heart over the loss of his friend, Red. Rick thought about Red's life and the sad fact that he had no family. In an odd sense, it was nearly comforting to Rick that Red's parents did not have to see their son perish before they had. Though Red never married nor had children, Rick thought about what a great father he would have been. Rick considered that he was the closest thing to next-of-kin that Red had. Though they never admitted it to one another, Red and Rick not only behaved as best friends, but they had a respect and love for one another like brothers. Rick asked for and was given permission to accompany Red's remains back to Chicago.

| PANACEA |

Agent Chimara explained that Ned Carson was apprehended in Washington, D.C., and was on his way back to Tallahassee in the same government jet that Rick would be escorting the remains of his friend, "Red" Wilhelm, back to in Chicago. By 3:15 in the morning Rick was given a police escort to Tallahassee International Airport with the hearse carrying Red's remains going before him. As the motorcade carrying Rick made its way across the tarmac at the airport, Rick noticed Ned Carson being led away from the lear jet in shackles. The two men made eye contact and Ned Carson appeared to be crying. Rick felt like crying too, but for different reasons. Staring at the man who nearly got Willy Tilly and him shot, Rick stopped in his tracks and watched Ned until the FBI positioned him in the back of a squad car.

Rick boarded the jet and took a seat next to the window. He was sitting alone with the closest member of the FBI being three rows away. It was Rick's first time in a luxury lear jet complete with its leather seating and richly carpeted and decorated cabin, but Rick failed to be impressed. He only hoped that he would be undisturbed during the three hour flight to Chicago. A gentle rain began to bounce off the wings and windows of the plane as the pilot closed the cabin door to prepare for take off.

Within minutes, the plane taxied and defied gravity off runway nine. Rick stared out the window, never once looking away from the skies outside. Rick observed the rain disappear as the plane flew above the clouds. It was painfully ironic to Rick that just as the skies quit providing the moisture in his vision, Rick's own eyes filled with tears and he wept silently.

The lear jet landed at Midway International in Chicago and Rick

met the county coroner who would take Red's remains to the crematorium
at Holland's Funeral Home in downtown Chicago. Rick rode with the
coroner and met with the funeral home director, Gabriel Holland. Rick
explained Red's demise and how to get in touch with the few relatives
Red had in Wisconsin.

Red and Rick had both agreed earlier in their lives that, when
death finally came, they wanted to give all their organs away and then be
cremated. They both enjoyed the philosophy that people come from the
earth, return to the earth, and, in between, they garden. Taking up any
more space after death than they did before they were born was thought
of as a selfish act, though neither disagreed with those people who wanted
to be buried. Rick was disappointed by the fact that nobody would
benefit from Red's well-intended gift of organ donation. The one
scenario the two men had never imagined was that one of them might be
cremated while still alive, leaving all organs worthless.

It was ten o'clock in the morning by the time Rick finished
arranging Red's funeral service and scheduling his formal cremation the
next afternoon. Having been awake for over twenty-four hours and
physically and emotionally punished during most of that time, Rick knew
he needed to sleep, though he was afraid he wouldn't be able to. Rick
hailed a taxi from Holland's Funeral Home and instructed the driver to
take him to the Westin Hotel on Michigan Avenue. Fearing he wouldn't
be able to sleep, Rick stopped the driver at a liquor store one block short
of the hotel. Rick intended to buy a bottle of bourbon and drink himself
to sleep if exhaustion alone wouldn't do it. He tipped the driver and left
the cab.

Rick checked into the Westin just before noon and undressed in his room before realizing that he hadn't any other clothes to wear. He poured a glass of bourbon without ice or water and sat down on the edge of the bed. Rick stared at the drink he'd made as it sat on the bedside table. For fifteen minutes Rick looked that the full glass as his mind raced. He tried to think of nothing and eventually did. Without drinking a drop of bourbon, Rick fell asleep sitting up and then collapsed onto the bed. He slept for eight hours.

By eight o'clock Rick arose and dressed. His agenda for the evening was twofold. He needed to eat something and then buy some clothes for the next day. When he returned from supper and obtaining a wardrobe for the next day, Rick remembered his own family and called his parents. Both his mom and dad were saddened by the news of Red's death and they were frightened by the attempt on Rick's life. He was beseeched by his parents to return home for a while to get away from whatever dangers may still exist in Panacea and to mourn his friend's death in peace. Rick declined his parent's invitation and explained to them his need to get back and make sure Delaney and the Chesterfields were okay. Rick explained his affection for Delaney in greater detail to his mother. His mother was surprised to learn of her son's dedication to Delaney and remarked that it was the first time she'd ever heard Rick so enamored with someone. He wanted to tell his mother how much he was in love but he feared Delaney and he might not end up together and he didn't want to set himself up for a fall. After Rick spoke with his parents, he left the phone off the hook and tried, unsuccessfully, to sleep through the night.

The next morning Rick changed into his new clothes and checked out of the hotel, leaving the rest of his clothes from the night before behind. He went to breakfast and dined with a protestant minister, Jack Shelby, who would be officiating at Red's memorial service that afternoon. Rick explained Red's life to the minister and gave him a few insights into Red's sense of humor so the eulogy wouldn't be completely flat and serious.   After breakfast, Rick took a taxi to Holland's Funeral Home where he watched over the cremation of Red's remains. None of Red's relatives or friends were present for the cremation service but Rick learned that there would be about ten to twelve people attending the memorial service that would be held on a coast guard ship anchored at Navy Pier at three o'clock.

Rick rode with the funeral director and Red's ashes to Navy Pier. Already on board the Coast Guard cutter were a few of Red's cousins and friends from Calida, along with some coworkers from the FBI whom Rick had never met before. Rick was both disappointed and relieved that nobody from Vince Planet's bar attended the service. Though he didn't want to see anyone from the life he left behind, he was disappointed for Red that, perhaps, some of Red's Chicago friends may not have heard of his death yet.   Rick shook hands and embraced those who came to pay tribute to Red's life and the cutter left the harbor for the service to be held and Red's ashes to be strewn out in Lake Michigan.

When the privately chartered cutter was nearly five miles off the coastline, the service began with Reverend Shelby's delivering a touching, yet humorous eulogy.   At the close of the eulogy, Reverend Shelby stepped from the podium and picked up the velvet sack that held Red's ashes. Shelby stepped to the boat's stern and held the sack upside down while reciting "Ashes to ashes, dust to dust. So we come from the earth, and we return to the earth."

"And in between, we garden," Rick said softly to himself as he watched the ashes drift into the wind and into the icy cold November waters of Lake Michigan. Rick approached the stern and gently laid a wreath of red carnations on the water and watched it float away with the ashes. The last of Red's ashes reached the water and the cutter turned back in for the pier. During the thirty minute trip back to the shore, the mood turned from solemn to reflective and conversational. It seemed to Rick that most of the people were trying to console Rick more than one another. Rick was appreciative and welcomed the kind remarks.

When the boat finally docked, Rick said goodbye to Red's relatives, friends, and coworkers. He then thanked Reverend Shelby and walked back to the bow of the cutter to look out over the lake one last time in honor of his friend. Rick was by himself for only three minutes when Mr. Holland approached him and placed a hand on Rick's shoulder. "Are you riding back with me to the funeral home?" Holland said. "Or can I give you a lift somewhere?"

Rick turned to thank Mr. Holland. "Oh, thanks for waiting for me," Rick said. "I'll be getting a taxi back to O'Hare. I'm heading back to Florida."

"Are you sure I can't take you to O'Hare?" Holland said.

"Thank you. I really appreciate all you've done for Red and me. I'll be fine. I'm grateful though," Rick said.

"Okay, Rick," Holland said. "There's one more thing."

"Yes," Rick said.

"Well, usually when someone is cremated the next of kin receives a small urn with the loved one's ashes," Holland said. "I have this for your friend's next of kin." Holland held out the dark glassed urn. "Since his parents are deceased and he wasn't married, I believe it should go to you, if you want it. You two must've been very close."

Rick stared at the urn-and looked up at Mr. Holland with tears in his eyes. "Thank you," Rick said.

"You're welcome," Holland said, who then turned away and walked off the cutter. Rick watched as Holland left and then he thanked the boat captain before leaving himself.

Rick paid a visit to the FBI before going to the airport. The FBI informed Rick of the charges of Conspiracy to Commit Murder and Murder which Barute, Carson, and Amato would face. Executives at Copperhead Oil were now being targeted. Rick knew from past experience in the legal system that the investigation and formal charges would not conclude for many months. He was too grief stricken to call on Delaney and, instead, hoped earnestly that he would be accepted upon his return to Panacea. Rick wasn't too sure if his presence in Panacea would be appreciated or regretted, whether he was an apotheosis in friendship or a pariah. He hoped he would land somewhere in between. He didn't even know in his own heart whether it was all worth it on a personal basis. All he could think about was Delaney as the taxi took him through the downtown streets of Chicago to O'Hare International. On the way, Rick noticed a vacation billboard promoting the Caribbean that read, "Have a fling with your life." They were words Rick had spoken to Delaney on their sailboat journey weeks before, only Rick accidentally substituted the word "life" with "wife." Rick smiled and wished Delaney fit that description.

After arranging travel through Delta Airlines to Tallahassee, Rick walked to the duty free shop in the international terminal at O'Hare. He immediately noticed a jewelry counter and approached the clerk. "Do you have any gold pocket watches?" Rick asked.

The female Asian clerk smiled and responded in perfect English, "Yes, Sir, we have several of them. Let me take them out for you." The clerk displayed five gold pocket watches in front of Rick. Only one of them had a gold plate covering the face that had to be opened to tell the time. Assuming the pocket watch Pally Chase had given Ms. Chesterfield burned up with her home, Rick hoped Havana would appreciate the gift.

"Do you do engravings, ma'am?" Rick asked.

"Yes, but the man who does it doesn't come in until later today," the clerk responded.

"Can you try?" Rick asked. "I'll pay extra. It would really mean a lot," Rick pleaded.

The clerk smiled. "Well, I'm not supposed to, but, since we're not busy, well sure. There'll be no extra charge, though. I'll be back in a few minutes." Rick wrote down the inscription he wanted and the clerk went into a back room where Rick could hear the engraving pen cutting through the gold. She emerged, placed the watch in a gift box, and rang up the sale.

Rick gave the woman three one hundred dollar bills for the two hundred fifty dollar sale and told her to keep the change for her trouble. "Thank you. Really," Rick said. "Please take the extra money and spend it foolishly on someone." The clerk smiled and tried to respond, but Rick just smiled back and walked away.

Rick walked to his terminal gate and waited in silence for the plane to begin boarding. Rick was the last one to board the 727 which had just flown in from Tallahassee, via Atlanta, earlier that afternoon.

Resting upon Rick's seat in the twelfth row was that morning's edition of the Tallahassee newspaper left behind by the previous passenger. Rick glanced at the paper before removing it to sit down. His eyes widened as he read the headline which glared, "Senator Suspected in Murder Scandal!"

Rick grabbed the paper immediately and sat down in earnest to read the story. His eyes were moving to the next word in each sentence before his brain could understand what it was contemplating. The story read, "An emergency panel of the grand jury was commissioned yesterday to hear evidence of a conspiracy between Florida State Senator D.D. Amato, lobbyists William Barute, Ned Carson, and vice-president of Copperhead Oil, Carl Pagan, to commit murder. After just four hours, the grand jury returned a true bill of indictment against all four men for various charges, including murder of an agent with the Federal Bureau of Investigation, Jeff Wilhelm, and the attempted murder of Illinois Attorney, Rick Morrissey." Rick read on after overcoming the initial shock of reading his own name in the story.

"Additional charges of attempted murder and arson have been brought against William Barute, a lobbyist for Copperhead Oil, for arranging the bombing of an area residence which has not yet been disclosed. According to newspaper sources, William Barute is now the chief suspect in a murder plot that took the lives of two local men in 1988, including among the two murdered, Pally Chase, from Panacea. Chase had been an active environmentalist who opposed drilling off the Emerald Coast when he met his demise in the arms of Hurricane Gilbert. Until recent evidence had been revealed at the grand jury and through an investigation by the FBI, Chase's death, and that of another man on the doomed boat, Coatie Gillen, had been deemed accidental.   Both men had been presumed dead by drowning after the Hurricane overturned their boat. However, documents discovered from a search warrant served on local attorney and lobbyist, Winston Skroggsdad, and from the widow of Pally Chase, revealed that the two men died of carbon monoxide poisoning from a gas line that was channeled into the galley of the boat the two men were operating. Senator Amato, who was county coroner at the time, is being investigated for forging and tampering with official government documents from the time of Pally Chase's autopsy, which Amato had conducted.   Amato is not suspected in the death of either men.

"William Barute had been a former employee of Chase's, working for the Chase commercial fishing company until beginning work as a lobbyist in 1980. Ned Carruthers, a fellow lobbyist who worked mostly for Barute is expected to testify against his boss under an immunity deal proposed by the District Attorney. The investigation continues, according to the FBI."

Rick reread the story three times and then stared out the window, astonished over the course of events that he had initiated, if not orchestrated.   After connecting flights in Atlanta, Rick landed in Tallahassee at midnight.

30

Rick returned to the Marriott Courtyard hotel room he had left behind two days earlier. It was just after midnight when he walked into the main entrance. The attractive young woman operating the front desk took notice of Rick immediately and smiled at him.

"Checking in?" she said, flirting with Rick.

Typically, an invitation to flirt back with a beautiful girl was Rick's forté and consummate interest. Now, though, Rick didn't see her as an attractive woman who thought he was attractive. In fact, Rick barely noticed she was even of the opposite sex.

"Already have, ma'am," Rick responded without a smile. He made his way to the stairs and to his room to collect his remaining belongings. He called Delaney's number with the hopes of finding her at home and no longer in need of protection from the government. There was no answer at Delaney's and Rick, frustrated, tried again every half hour until falling asleep at 3 a.m.

When he woke at 8:30 the next morning, Rick called a taxi from his room and asked for a ride to Panacea to find Sam and, hopefully, to see Delaney. Rick didn't flinch when the taxi company dispatcher told him the fare would be $60 for the one-way, thirty minute ride to Panacea. He headed out the door of the Marriott Courtyard and waited on the cab.

| PANACEA |

On his way to Panacea, Rick wondered silently about the past several weeks and stared out the cab window over the Panhandle landscape that he had come to love as a boy in his formative years and now as an individual on the brink of manhood - a stage of his life that should have come years ago for Rick, had he not denied it and fought it so often in his superficial ambitions to defy maturity and time.   Rick felt alone because of Red's absence and yet complete because of his dedication to help the people he'd come to respect and love in Panacea.   The trip had its worth in development of the human soul, but it had come at such a price to others.

Rick had the driver go past Delaney's home but there was no sign of Delaney.   He instructed the driver to go to Posey's where Rick hoped to find Sam preparing for the lunch crowd.   When the taxi arrived at Posey's, Rick gave the driver a hundred dollar bill and exited the car. The tip was exorbitant but, being driven by guilt most of his life, Rick thought any kindness he could show to others would help assuage the pain of having ever done somebody wrong.   He walked into an empty oyster bar and asked for Sam.

The bartender smiled widely at Rick from behind the bar. "Sam doesn't start for another hour.   Would you like a beer?"

"No beer, thanks. Do you have any iced tea?" Rick replied.   The bartender poured from a homemade vat of sweet tea and gave Rick an enormous glassful.

"Could you please let Sam know that I'm sitting out on the dock?" Rick said. "My name is. . .," Rick was interrupted.

"Rick Morrissey. I know. Everybody knows.   You're a good man, Mr. Rick," the bartender said with a smile.

"Thank you," Rick said, somewhat confused by the compliment. Rick nodded at the bartender with only half a smile and went out on the dock to embrace the panhandle sunshine over the Gulf waters. Rick watched as a playful manatee floated by under Rick's swinging feet. He thought about Delaney.

Rick heard the sound of flip-flop sandals reach the wooden dock and begin coming toward him. He turned to see Sam with two draft beers in his hands and a reassuring, but gentle smile on his face. Rick gave a weak smile back and said hello.

"Brought you a cold one and today's newspaper. You're a hero, Rick. I thought yesterday's headlines were good. Hell, you've really cracked some nuts opens. Says here Copperhead Oil is linked to some pretty shady characters with long histories of being arrested for some pretty serious shit. They're pulling out all drilling initiatives in the panhandle pending the investigation. Hell, they're going out of business, buddy. Have a beer."

"No thanks, Sam. Iced tea is perfect right now."

Sam pulled out two cigarettes, lit one for himself and offered the other to Rick.

"No, I'm good on smoking for a while," Rick said. "I just wanted to stop and say hello," Rick said, avoiding the subject of Delaney and his hopes for their future. "Is everything okay?"

"We're all fine," Sam said. "Are you staying long?" he asked.

"You mean today or in the future," Rick replied.

"I mean, what are you going to do now?" Sam asked.

"I don't know, Sam. I've thought about trying to make it down here and then I've thought about going home," Rick said.

"Home?" Sam said. "This ain't good enough for you? Where the hell you think you're going?"

"That I don't really know," Rick said. Rick reached into his pocket and retrieved the gold pocket watch he bought in Chicago. "I almost forgot about this," Rick said.

"What is it?" Sam asked. Rick opened the gift box exposing the watch to Sam. "Nice," Sam said, smiling.

"It's for your mom, Sam. Just in case I don't get a chance to give it to her, would you mind?" Rick asked.

"Shit, you'll have your chance," Sam said, taking the watch out of the box. Sam opened the face and read the inscription out loud. "In a hundred years from now, all of it *will* matter." Sam paused and looked at Rick. "What's that supposed to mean?" he asked.

"It's just something your mom and I talked about. She'll understand what it means. You're too young to know," Rick said, kidding Sam.

"Shit, too young my ass. Well, if she doesn't tell me, Mr. Secret Man, you'd better," Sam smiled back at Rick.

"Okay. That's fair enough," Rick said.

"So you going back into law practicin'?" Sam asked.

"I doubt it. But I don't know," Rick said.

"What will you do if you stay here?" Sam asked.

"I'm not sure. I'd like to find something not law-related," Rick said.

"Boy, everything in the world is law-related," Sam replied with a chuckle.

"You know what I mean," Rick said.

"Why don't you go into fishin'?" Sam asked. "Your latest fishin' expedition landed a couple of big ones in the tank of life."

Rick smiled at the compliment. "Fishing for fish though?" Rick looked at Sam surprised. "I don't know much about fishing as a career," Rick said.

"You want a partner?" Sam said. "You can use all the help you can get."

Rick looked at Sam with childlike wonder, genuinely touched by his remark. "Sam, that's a nice gesture. Really. That means a lot to me," Rick said. "But you've got other dreams ahead of you. You're gonna finish college and have a career of your own. Sam, you're gonna be somebody," Rick concluded.

"Stop gushing. I'm not talking about me," Sam said. "I'm talking about my baby sister." Rick looked curiously at Sam. Sam turned to look inland toward the bar. Rick's glance followed, in turn.

Just then Southpaw emerged onto the dock and he ran up excitedly and licked Rick on the face. Rick and Sam laughed as Southpaw nearly knocked Rick off the dock trying to get too close to him.

Smiling and holding Southpaw, Rick asked, "So she knows?"

"She just found out," Sam said. Sam looked at Delaney as she entered the dock area smiling. "Never a finer partner, Rick. Never a finer partner."

"I've always thought that myself," Rick said. They both smiled at Delaney in silence as she approached.

"I hope you don't hate me, Rick, after all I've put you through," Delaney said with a caring smile as she walked closer toward the two men.

Rick stood up. "I don't, Delaney."

"Do you still love her?" Sam asked. Delaney blushed.

Rick paused. "No, I guess I don't," he said, smiling.

"No?! " Sam said, incredulous. "What the hell do you mean, 'no'?"

"I don't just love her," Rick said, continuing while looking at Delaney, "I am *in* love with her."

Delaney walked closer to Rick.

"You're her panacea, man," Sam said. "You know that?"

Rick looked at Sam. "You know what, buddy?   I've got seven years of college behind me, four of them living right next to this town with that namesake, yet I have no idea what that word means," Rick said.

"Panacea.   It's a Greek word that means a cure-all or universal remedy," Sam said. "Panacea is a cure for all ills. You're it."

"I don't know, Sam," Rick replied softly, smiling at Delaney, "I'd say I'm the one who's been cured."

EPILOGUE

Pally-Red Fishing Charters opened for business six months after the felony indictments were handed down to politico Ned Carson, Senator D.D. Amato, Copperhead Oil Company's three vice-presidents, and lobbyist William Barute. Catering to locals and tourists alike, Pally-Red Charters planned to play host to individuals and groups seeking the thrill of fishing the open waters of the Gulf of Mexico for dolphin fish, grouper, and amberjack, as well as hunting for Florida lobster. Rick and Delaney invested an equal amount of capital into the business and purchased a forty foot and a thirty-six foot cruiser which they docked off Apalachicola harbor in Panacea one mile from the same location as Chase Commercial Fishing operated over a decade before. The couple's plan was to have Rick operate the weekday business while Delaney pursued her degree. On the weekends, Sam would take out the smaller rig with another part-time employee while Rick and Delaney would share time on the larger boat. Within the year, they planned to expand the business to St. George Island and, later, to initiate a sailing cruise charter from St. George Island to Key West during the summer and early fall months.

On the first day of business, Meredith Chase was the guest of honor to christen the forty- foot cruiser, *Southpaw II*. Though Ms. Chase had done her share of boat launching in her younger days, invariably by breaking a bottle of Dom Perignon over the bow, Rick persuaded her to launch *Southpaw II* with a limited reserve bottle of Maker's Mark Bourbon. In a touching and cogent poem, Meredith dedicated the boat to her late husband, her daughter and Rick, and to the people of the

| PANACEA |

Florida panhandle.

For this first excursion, Pally-Red limited its passenger list to residents of Panacea only. A crowd of thirty-five Panaceans joined the co-captains, Delaney and Rick, on May 12 for the maiden voyage of the *Southpaw II*. After an afternoon of successful fishing, Delaney and Rick dropped off the passengers and returned to the oyster flats of Apalachee Bay for a purview of the end of season oysters and a collection of their last bushel before the waters became too warm in the summer for harvesting oysters.

Rick's idea to snorkel from the boat was greeted enthusiastically by Delaney and they each jumped into the Gulf with their swimsuit, mask, and snorkel. Rick dived down first through the salt water ten feet until he reached the continental shelf and the Gulf floor which was partly sandy and partly grown over with mostly live oysters along with some empty oyster shells. The water was crystal clear with a visibility of twenty-five feet and the remaining sun in the sky gave the underwater world a bonfire-type glow. Rick found the area of oysters he was seeking and surfaced to bring Delaney back down with him.

The two then submerged to the bottom ten feet below and began to examine the oyster bed. While Delaney was gathering part of a bushel, Rick reached into the back pocket of his swim trunks to retrieve the two empty oyster half shells he had placed in his pocket on his previous dive.

He got Delaney's attention and displayed the shell from the palm of his hand. As she reached for the crustacean, Rick opened the top half shell to reveal a platinum ring with a traditional cut diamond embedded on top. Delaney's eyes widened as she looked at Rick in ebullient wonder. She took off her mask and swam into his arms. Rick took off his mask and they kissed as they began to float up to the surface.   Breaching the waters, and exhaling for the first time, their embrace intensified as the kiss that began below the surface grew more passionate. The warm sun was setting over the western Gulf horizon as they pulled away, looking into one another's eyes.

And she said yes.

ISBN 1553695526